Praise for
BETH SHERMAN
and *DEAD MAN'S FLOAT*

"A tight, funny mystery . . .
Everything that Sherman writes is right on target."
Asbury Park Press

"A nifty character angle."
Publishers Weekly

"Alive with intrigue, Beth Sherman creates a fine
mystery novel, which like the ocean itself takes you on
a frantic thrill ride of unexpected directions."
Atlanticville

"Cleverly entertaining and skillfully written."
The Courier-Post (Cherry Hill, NJ)

"A straightforward, no-frills, engrossing mystery . . .
story-telling on a high level."
Staten Island Sunday Advance

"*Dead Man's Float* can really make a
good summer day better."
The Press of Atlantic City

"Breathtaking action keeps the reader
riveted to the page . . . dialogue shimmers . . .
Sherman's sense of humor lends a light touch."
Mystery Time

Other Jersey Shore Mysteries by
Beth Sherman

DEAD MAN'S FLOAT

DEATH AT HIGH TIDE

A JERSEY SHORE MYSTERY

BETH SHERMAN

AVON

TWILIGHT

This is a work of fiction. Names, characters, places, and incidents either are the product of the author's imagination or are used fictitiously. Any resemblance to actual events, locales, organizations, or persons, living or dead, is entirely coincidental and beyond the intent of either the author or the publisher.

AVON BOOKS, INC.
1350 Avenue of the Americas
New York, New York 10019

Copyright © 1999 by Beth Sherman
Published by arrangement with the author
Library of Congress Catalog Card Number: 98-91019
ISBN: 0-380-73108-8
www.avonbooks.com/twilight

First Avon Twilight Printing: June 1999

AVON TWILIGHT TRADEMARK REG. U.S. PAT. OFF. AND IN OTHER COUN-
TRIES, MARCA REGISTRADA, HECHO EN U.S.A.

Printed in the U.S.A.

WCD   10 9 8 7 6 5 4 3 2

For Jessie Rose,
with love

Acknowledgments

I'd like to thank the following people for their help, expertise, and advice: my excellent agent, Dominick Abel; my wonderful editor at Avon Books, Trish Lande Grader; celebrity makeup artist Bruce Wayne Fisher; Johanna Keller, a first-rate teacher; Doug Turner, at Miramax; Steve Pullan, trichologist at the Philip Kingsley hair salon in New York City; my husband, Andy Edelstein, for his continued support and encouragement; and finally, all my friends in Ocean Grove, New Jersey, and especially Diane and Pete Herr at the Ocean Vista, for helping me fall in love.

Chapter 1

*Beauty isn't just skin
deep. You need great
lipstick, blush, and
mascara, too.*

Mallory Loving, *Loving You*

The trailers rumbled down Ocean Avenue, one
after another, like a herd of elephants stamped-
ing a watering hole. They were massive and silver and ugly; the ground seemed to shake as they hurtled
down the street. At the north end of the beach they
stopped, taking the parking spaces normally reserved for
residents of the town. When the doors of the trailers
opened, the crew tumbled out, lugging equipment: cameras, lights, generators, large scrims, thick coils of
snakelike cables. The movie people wore headphones
and spoke to each other through walkie-talkies, even
when they were no more than ten feet apart. They
dragged the equipment over the wooden planks of the
boardwalk until they reached the steps that led down to
the beach. There they stopped, surveying the bleached
sand, the dazzlingly blue water that glinted in the morn-

ing sunlight. One of the men lugged a camera down the steps and onto a piece of cardboard. But the cardboard wouldn't glide over the sand; the camera appeared to be stuck. There was a flurry of activity on the boardwalk as people ran back and forth to the trailers, followed by frantic shouts and curses.

"Did you ever see anything like it in your life?" Helen Passelbessy said to Anne Hardaway. "Reminds me of itty bitty ants who can't climb a hill."

They were sitting on Anne's front porch overlooking the ocean, eating a breakfast of jelly donuts and iced tea. Though the film crew was three blocks away, the two friends had a bird's eye view of the scene.

"Do they even have a permit to block off the beach?" Helen asked. She sounded annoyed. There were two things Anne's best friend couldn't tolerate: pretentious people and wasting time. As far as Helen was concerned, the movie people were guilty on both counts. "It's a gorgeous day," Helen said. "What are we supposed to do? Swim in the bathtub?"

Anne smiled. Leave it to Helen to nail the problem. Ever since the *Dark Horizon* cavalcade had arrived ten days ago, it was as if the sleepy town of Oceanside Heights had been under siege. There was no place you could walk, no place you could eat, no place you could shop, without tripping over an actor or a cameraman or one of those pesky production assistants who delighted in stopping traffic for no apparent reason. The Heights was only one square mile wide. There wasn't room to shoot a movie.

"Why couldn't they have picked another spot on the Jersey shore?" Helen lamented. "Like Avalon. Or Seaside Heights."

"The quaint quotient's not as high," Anne said, gesturing at the houses on either side of her own pale yellow Victorian cottage. Like most places in the historic town, the homes had been built at the turn of the century and featured a potpourri of architectural delights—sloping gables, graceful mansard roofs, lacy gingerbread fretwork, picturesque widow's walks.

"So?" Helen said. "How hard could it be to take one of these beauties and recreate it on a Hollywood back lot? Hell, I'd give 'em the blueprint for my house, if they wanted."

"Did you hear they're using Hannah's place?" Anne hooked her thumb toward the house next door, a lavender Queen Anne with projecting bay windows, three balconies, and a majestic gray turret.

"How much is she getting?"

Anne sighed. "You don't want to know."

"What about chez Hardaway? God, Annie, wouldn't it be a hoot? This old place in a movie."

Anne examined her house with a critical eye. Yellow paint was flaking off the front. The grass needed cutting. The roof leaked. The cornice was a wreck. A couple of spindles had come loose from the upstairs balcony. And the stained glass panel over the front window was cracked.

She tried to imagine the house plastered on a big screen in a darkened movie theater and burst out laughing. Helen joined in. Down the street, the crew were moving pieces of equipment around, like large chess pieces on a board. A row of silver Porta-Pottys gleamed in the morning sun. Beyond them stretched the ocean, serene and still under a cloudless August sky—entirely off-limits.

"It's hot as Hades, and I've got the day off," Helen announced, stretching her arms above her head. She was tall and athletic and didn't like sitting still for more than three minutes at a time. "You want to skip chaos central and go to a *real* movie at the mall?"

"Can't," Anne said, sweeping her long red hair out of her eyes. "I have to work."

Helen clapped one hand over her mouth, like a child feigning embarrassment. An outspoken woman, she never hesitated to say exactly what was on her mind.

"Oops. Here I am going on about how much trouble these Hollywood types are and I totally ignore the fact that you have to deal with them." She bit into a jelly donut, brushing powder off her T-shirt. "Spill," she said playfully. "What's Mallory Loving really like?"

Anne paused. Her green eyes took on a serious cast. What was Mallory like? Troubled. Self-centered. But who wouldn't be after the life Mallory had led? Abused by a mother who beat her with clothes hangers. A drug addiction problem that nearly tanked her career. Two failed marriages. Three suicide attempts. What was Mallory Loving like? A twister whirling out of control. *Dark Horizon* was Mallory's last chance at a big screen comeback. If she was a little testy, a little edgy most of the time, who could blame her?

Besides, there were worse assignments than ghostwriting Mallory's autobiography. Phil had promised that when *Loving You* was published next year, the book would make tons of money. Not to mention the foreign rights, the film option, the film itself (starring who else? Mallory Loving), the audio deal, and if the stars were really in alignment, maybe a sequel.

"We're talking solid gold here," Phil had told Anne, when he'd handed her the assignment. "A real money-maker. And the kicker is she's coming straight to you. They're making the movie in Oceanside Heights."

"You're kidding," Anne had replied. "No free trip to L.A.?"

"Maybe next time, kiddo. Hey, it's perfect when you think about it. Hometown girl leaves Jersey to become an actress. Makes it in La La Land. Sleeps with half of Hollywood on her way to the top. Gets hooked on drugs and booze. Then orchestrates a major league comeback. Perfect for a tell-all. Just perfect. Not to mention all the beauty and exercise tips you're gonna throw in."

"Uh, Phil," Anne had interjected. "The Heights isn't Mallory's hometown. She grew up next door, in Landsdown."

"So what?" Phil had said. "It's still the Jersey shore. Think about all the girls in all the shore towns who'd love to trade places with Mallory Loving."

Anne had twirled the phone cord between her fingers, listening to Phil talk about how much moolah *Loving You* was going to make for Triple Star Publishing.

That was the actual word he'd used: *moolah*. Anne had pictured him sitting at his rickety wooden desk in Nowheresville, North Carolina, in an office overlooking a furniture wholesaler and a store that sold used electronics. Phil probably had his feet propped up on the desk and was running the numbers on his pocket calculator. A tell-all, huh? Spending quality time with a washed-up actress on the comeback trail. It definitely had potential, a change from the stuff Anne usually wrote about—how to trim your thighs in sixty days, how to prevent your marriage from self-destructing, how to clean no-wax floors and burned saucepans. At least this book wouldn't contain the words *how to* in the title. Still, she couldn't resist needling Phil a little.

"Hey, boss," she'd said. "Did you see the article in the *Times* magazine section a few weeks ago? The one about ghostwriters?"

"Nope."

Anne knew he was lying. Phil got the *Times* delivered to his office every day. He disdained the local paper, calling it a "boring rag."

"There was a whole article about how ghostwriting is big business. It's practically a cottage industry in the publishing world."

"That so?"

"It said that ghosts are getting six-figure advances. The people who wrote autobiographies of Lee Iacocca, Colin Powell, Tanya Tucker, O.J., they pulled in some pretty big numbers. Now they're called co-authors with their names on the cover of the book. Some of them even appeared on *Oprah*."

Phil Smedley had coughed into the phone. "Look,

Annie,'' he'd rasped. ''We're not talking O.J. here. Mallory Loving could be big again. Or this movie could flop and nobody'll give a rat's ass about a two-bit actress fresh out of rehab. I like to look on the bright side is all.''

''Assuming you're right,'' Anne had said. ''Couldn't we up my royalties a little? For God's sake, Phil. I'm getting the exact same amount for *Loving You* that I got for Mary Lou Popper's household hints.''

Phil had groaned. ''I have to pay royalties to Mallory, too, you know. I could go as high as four percent.''

''Five.''

''Anne, you're killing me here.''

''I've read about Mallory Loving. She sounds like a first-class prima donna.''

''So? Mary Lou wasn't?''

No, Mary Lou was. They all were—the assorted shrinks, diet doctors, religious leaders, and minor TV personalities Anne had dealt with over the last five years. She was thirty-seven years old and she'd ghosted over a dozen books. Sometimes extracting information from the ''experts'' was about as pleasant as having a periodontist work on your gums.

''Five percent,'' Anne had said firmly. ''Or you can turn this over to somebody else. Somebody who'd love to spend a few weeks in scenic Oceanside Heights; go down the shore for a while. It shouldn't be hard to find a writer, Phil. The beach is lovely this time of year.''

''All right. Twist my arm, why don't ya? Five it is. I'll type out a new contract today.''

''Great,'' Anne had said cheerily. It would have cost Phil money to put a writer up at one of the inns in town. Factor in meals and a car allowance and you didn't need a calculator to figure out that getting her to ghost the book was a cheaper proposition. She lived in the Heights year round, cooked her own meals. And now here she was, interviewing La Loving and finding out more than she'd ever wanted to learn about Benzedrine cocktails, studio casting couches, and the fine art of making pornographic movies, which was how Mallory had gotten her start.

Anne turned to Helen and rolled her eyes. "Mallory is trouble," she said. "Pure and simple."

"Yeah? I heard the movie's in trouble. Every day something else goes wrong."

Anne nodded her head. "It's strange," she said, taking a sip of iced tea. "There are all these 'accidents' on the set. Equipment was stolen. Camera lenses mysteriously got broken. Film's been overexposed. Yesterday the cable on the generator was cut. Caused a small electrical fire. I heard one of the cameramen say it had been tampered with."

"Then I'm not the only one who'd like the cast and crew of *Dark Horizon* to take a hike."

"Apparently not." Anne looked over to where the crew was setting up. "The delays are costing the studio millions of dollars."

Helen grimaced. She was a loan officer at the Central Bank of New Jersey, and understood profit and loss better than most people Anne knew.

"How about we go see what's going on," said Anne, standing up. "I've got another interview with Mallory in half an hour."

"Fine by me. My nephew's been dying to get her autograph. Could you do me a favor?" Helen rummaged through her pocketbook and pulled out a disposable camera. "Can you take a few pictures of Mallory for Stevie? He's thirteen. It's a terrible age. All he thinks about are movie stars and cars." She handed Anne the camera. "I'd do it myself, but I'd look like an overage groupie."

Anne took the camera. "No problem. Knowing Mallory, she'll be happy to pose."

The two women walked down the street toward where the film crew was setting up. Already the humidity was climbing. It was a perfect beach day. The sand stretched out invitingly, like a tawny carpet. Waves lapped the shoreline, breaking with a gentle shushing sound. Normally the beach would be packed on Saturday morning, thick with blankets and umbrellas and tourists slathering on suntan lotion. But now, thanks to the movie people, it was deserted, save for a few brown pelicans scavenging for food at the water's edge. The shore looked as pristine and photogenic as a postcard.

Actually, Anne thought, the whole town appeared to be waiting for its proverbial close-up. The Heights was nothing if not pretty, the perfect backdrop for a movie. On one side of Ocean Avenue stood the grand Victorian homes, painted beguiling shades of cotton-candy pink, seafoam green, and sky blue. With their shutters, shingles, and ornamental trim, the houses were reminders of a more genteel age. On the oceanfront side of the street, wooden piers jutted into the water, towering above moss-covered rocks. Farther down the street, at the corner of Trinity Lane, was a large white church with brilliant stained glass windows and a steeple that soared toward the clouds.

In some ways, Anne loved the familiarity of the place, the sense that while the world frantically changed gears, the Heights remained a bastion of calm, as placid as the lakes flanking the town. From time to time she longed for the anonymity of a big city, to be lost among the company of strangers. But she knew she wouldn't be happy for long. She loved the ocean, the way light spilled onto the waves at dusk, the cry of the gulls outside her window, the smell of salt and sea grass.

They really should be shooting a period romance, she mused. A film where actresses wore long pastel dresses with bustles and carried frilly parasols to shield their complexions from the sun, where men courted women in the backseats of horse-drawn carriages, and love letters were composed with quill pens, dipped in ink. Not a techno-thriller called *Dark Horizon*, with computers and spies and enough special effects to make your head spin.

She and Helen were nearly opposite the film crew when they spotted a knot of people gathered on the porch of the Sail Away Inn, overlooking the boardwalk. Anne recognized a few of her neighbors and several merchants whose stores were located on Main Street. The last time so many locals had gathered to stare at the beach was during the fall of '92, when a nasty storm ripped through the area, causing $1.2 million worth of damages. Anne imagined this was how people must look when they think they've spotted alien life forms—their eyes slightly glassy, their mouths agape. Of course, it wasn't far off, when you thought about it. The presence of the movie folks was as close to an alien invasion as the Heights was going to get. Up ahead, two members of the crew were unloading what looked like a small black crane. One of the men was plastered with tattoos, giving his skin a greenish tinge. The other one had a shaved head and earrings piercing his lip and eyebrows. As they dragged the crane across the boardwalk, it made a screeching sound, like a wounded bird.

"Freaks," muttered Nathan Kurnetsky, the owner of Moby's Hardware store. "Belong in a circus. The whole lot of 'em."

"The wages of sin are never cheap," added Lucille Klemperer, a sharp-tongued woman in her early sixties who lived to serve Jesus. Lucille was what Anne called a "church biddy." She went to services twice a day, three times on Sunday, and could recite bits of Scripture to fit any occasion.

"So what have we missed?" Helen asked, crossing her arms over her chest. "Are you guys hanging around because you want to be cast as extras?"

"I wouldn't dream of it." Nathan sniffed.

Anne chuckled. Helen had moved to the Heights only seven years ago. She was still considered an "outsider" by those born and bred in town.

"Why don't you ask your friend here what's going on?" said Eleanor Granville, another gray-haired church biddy. "After all, Anne's thick as thieves with these show biz folks."

"Hey," Anne said with a shrug. "It's a tough job. But somebody's got to do it."

"I supposed you should be used to . . . disturbances," Eleanor said, coughing into her palm.

Anne felt herself flush. Eleanor was making a veiled reference to Anne's mother, Evelyn, who'd developed Alzheimer's disease in the mid-1970s, before anyone realized it was a physical ailment. The townspeople had thought Evelyn Hardaway was just plain nuts—wearing three sweaters and a ski parka on the hottest day of the year, forgetting her husband's first name, losing her way en route to a neighbor's home, nearly setting the house on fire. *Like mother, like daughter.* It was a refrain Anne had heard since grammar school. That was the problem with living in a small town; you could never shake free of the past. Evelyn Hardaway had died years ago. But the stigma remained. Anne was considered odd by some people in the Heights because she wasn't married with three children, because she didn't garden or do charity work, because she spent hours holed up in the library researching her books, and because she never, ever went to church.

"They're only making a movie," Anne said to Eleanor Granville. "Not communing with the devil."

"Hah!" exclaimed Lucille. "You know what those show folk were doing last night? Swimming in the ocean without a stitch of clothing on. I saw them with my own two eyes."

"Oh, my," Helen exclaimed in mock horror. "Stop the presses. Somebody call the *National Enquirer.* Besides," she scolded gently, "you shouldn't have been watching."

"Joke all you want, Helen Passelbessy," said Eleanor. "But it's no laughing matter. You see how much flesh some of these ladies are exposing? You smell the drugs at night? It's wicked, I tell you.''

"Apparently not everybody minds," Anne said. She pointed down the block to where a dozen of her neighbors were perched on lawn chairs, as if mesmerized, watching the crew set up. "And there's another fringe benefit. It's not every day the church gets oodles of money."

"We haven't accepted that money yet," Nathan Kurnetsky reminded her. "A sizable portion of the congregation does not want the Church by the Sea to be filmed. Under any circumstances."

"Those barbarians will not set one foot inside the Lord's house," Lucille pronounced solemnly. "Not while I'm alive to stop them."

"Gee, Lucille. How much are they offering now?" Helen said, grinning. "Eight thousand? Ten thousand? That's an awful lot of book sales, don't you think?"

Anne couldn't help chiming in. "It's going to cost at least that much to electrify the cross again. But don't say yes too soon. If you hold out, I bet they'll double their offer."

Helen burst into laughter. "Maybe even triple it," she joked. "Come on, Annie. Let's see what's cooking in Sodom and Gomorrah."

As they crossed the street to the boardwalk, a woman emerged from one of the trailers. Catching sight of them, the woman waved. "Anne, over here," Mallory Loving called out, pushing a strand of her golden hair away from her face. It was a beautiful face, Mallory's ticket to movie stardom. Blue eyes, flecked with just a hint of gray. Porcelain skin. Full pouty lips. She was in her early thirties and had on white cotton shorts and a tight pink midriff top that showed off her voluptuous figure. After her first film, the tabloids had nicknamed Mallory "Luscious Loving." It was old-fashioned, but then Mallory possessed old-style glamour.

Each time Anne was with Mallory she felt practically

invisible. Especially around men. When Mallory walked into a room, the actress seemed to send out invisible messages to the male species: *Want me. Love me. Look at me.* And they did, in a heartbeat. It filled Anne with exasperation, not to mention envy. Beautiful people got away with more. They didn't have to make nice or work especially hard to get noticed. They just had to show up. Ironic, when you considered that a fair amount of *Loving You* would be filled with Mallory's beauty tips. Mallory could scrub her face with dirt each morning instead of soap. She'd still be a knockout.

"Anne, I'm so, so sorry. But I can't do our interview," Mallory said breathlessly, grabbing hold of Anne's arm and pulling her closer, like a schoolgirl with a secret. Mallory flashed her most beguiling smile and fixed her sapphire blue eyes on Anne. When Mallory turned on the charm, she was hard to resist. She had a way of drawing you in, making you feel lucky to be part of her inner circle, basking in her reflected glow. "I would love to chat," Mallory said, sounding so sincere Anne almost believed her. "But I have to run an errand in town."

"When will you have some time?" Anne said, after she'd introduced Helen, who was studying Mallory as if the actress were a gilt-edged portrait in the Newark Museum. "We still have a lot of ground to cover." Despite Mallory's contrite manner, she felt a flicker of annoyance. Of the eight interviews she'd managed to set up, Mallory had canceled four. Instead of answering Anne's questions directly, Mallory preferred talking randomly into a tape recorder when she was alone. It took Anne hours to wade through the stream-of-consciousness tapes, and she still hadn't been able to put all the information in order. At this rate, the book would never be finished on time. She only had another two months left.

"You know the scenes we shot yesterday?" Mallory said. Her tone was conspiratorial, as if Anne were a fellow actress on the back lot at MGM. "The light meter was busted. Sixty-seven takes down the drain. Of course, if Howard didn't insist on all those long angled shots, we would have been done sooner. My face is starting to look like a jigsaw puzzle on screen.''

Anne suppressed a grin. Howard Koppelman, the director, had suggested that Mallory refrain from watching the dailies because she complained so much—not enough close-ups, too many profile shots, the camera wasn't capturing her better side. It was a suggestion she elected to ignore.

Just then, the director walked up to them, trailing a cloud of production assistants. He was in his mid-forties, with a lean, rangy build and hair the color of Greek olives. His face was lined and leathery, his eyes hidden behind mirrored silver sunglasses. He wore jeans, a black T-shirt, and a black baseball cap. On the shirt and cap were the words *Dark Horizon*, written in red script.

''Hey, gorgeous,'' he said to Mallory. ''You were due in wardrobe two hours ago.''

''What's the difference?'' Mallory replied breezily. ''I cannot do those scenes again. No how, no way.''

''Of course you can,'' Koppelman said, arranging his features into a smile. ''But if you veto one more outfit, you may be making this movie in the buff.'' He laughed heartily. Mallory didn't. ''I know it's rough to reshoot the scenes,'' he said, draping an arm over Mallory's shoulder. ''But it happens sometimes. You're the consummate professional. Everyone knows that. I bet you're giving Anne the lowdown on acting, right?''

''Just telling her the truth: Acting is murder.'' Mallory stepped away from Howard and straightened her shoulders. She had great posture, holding her body erect so she appeared taller than she was. ''Don't worry about the book,'' she said jauntily to Anne. She reached into her black vinyl Prada bag and pulled out a sheet of loose-leaf paper. ''Here are some beauty tips. Dynamite stuff. And I made a list of topics we've barely covered. Starting with my first husband. I've got some really juicy stuff on him.'' Mallory winked. ''He was even worse than Howard, if you can believe it. Not that Howard didn't have his share of secrets. Remind me to tell you about *Torrid Tori*.'' With that, she turned and stalked off, toward her rented black Lexus. There was an awkward silence.

Mallory's mood swings were the stuff of legend. If she liked you, if you were useful to her, she could be highly engaging, turning the full force of her personality, her dazzling charisma, in your direction. But if she sensed you were beneath her or if she decided you'd done her wrong, she'd cut you dead in no time flat. Howard Koppelman fell into the latter group. Mallory made no effort to hide the fact that she despised him, for three reasons: He'd been the one who'd led her into pornographic movies in the late 1980s. He'd introduced her to drugs. He'd ditched her and their marriage for another woman. Any one of the above would have been a serious offense. Taken together, all three were unpardonable and had earned Howard the place of honor on Mallory's shit list.

''I'm going down to the water for a minute,'' Helen said, shuffling her feet uncomfortably. ''Be right back.''

Howard Koppelman waited until both Helen and Mallory were out of earshot. Then he said, ''How's the book coming?''

''So far, so good.'' When a project was stuck in neutral, Anne had learned not to advertise it.

''When do you think it'll be out?'' His expression was pleasant, but Anne detected a note of uneasiness in his voice. Why was that?

''Next summer. To coincide with the movie.''

''Well, if you're interested in being an extra, just let me know. Did Mallory tell you about my deep dark past?''

So that was it. Mallory had something on him.

''A little. Who's *Torrid Tori*?''

His expression was hard to read. He looked slightly

embarrassed. But underneath his discomfort, Anne sensed a faint current of anger. "It's a flick Mal and I made back when we were first married." He gazed at the shoreline, where Helen was arguing with a production assistant about the right to cool her tootsies. Anne noticed his voice had dropped a couple of notches. "Pretty boring stuff, actually. Unless you appreciate the genre. I've come a long way since then. 'Former porn director makes it in Hollywood.' Maybe you should be writing *my* story."

"Well, you were a big part of Mallory's life."

Howard smiled broadly this time, showing off his neatly capped teeth. "If you're interested in ancient history."

For the umpteenth time, Anne wondered why Howard had cast Mallory in *Dark Horizon*. He struggled to please her at every turn, but Anne got the feeling he was merely pretending, forcing himself to coddle her.

"How do you feel about working with her again?"

"Mallory's a pro. She's got a proven track record, and the talent and drive to be box office gold." He sounded like he'd memorized the pitch, practicing until he got the sincerity part just right.

"But . . . ?" she coaxed.

"But there's one thing you should probably know."

"What's that?"

The morning sun played across Howard's face. He leaned forward, his sunglasses bobbing like silver fish. "She's been acting high strung lately. If she's about to crash and burn, make sure she doesn't take you with her."

Chapter 2

Forget the Atkins diet,
the Pritikin diet and the
Beverly Hills diet.
There's only one way to
lose weight: Eat less,
exercise more.

Oceanside Heights was unlike most other towns on the Jersey shore. Founded in 1896 by a Methodist minister, it was originally known for the fervent camp meetings held by the ocean. Back then, ten dingy tents were erected on a sand drift, and men and women knelt in prayer, their eyes riveted to the glassy waves and the bright, sun-dappled horizon. The faithful built a church in a grove of hickory trees, surmounted by a cupola with a bronze bell. It eventually proved too small to accommodate worshippers, and a second church went up, with tree boughs as a roof, providing shade but leaking water on the congregation each Sunday it rained. A few years later, a larger building was constructed, the Church by the Sea, nearly the size of a football field, seating ten thousand worshippers in relative comfort.

Gradually a little town sprang up around the church, dotted with picturesque Victorian houses, rambling inns, and quaint shops. Bordered by freshwater lakes to the north and south, and the ocean to the east, the town was dubbed "God's own acre" by the locals.

Tourists always oohed and ahhed about how precious the Heights was—"retro" someone had called it—as if the whole place had been constructed by Disney, complete with split wooden fences and curved wrought-iron streetlights that cast a soft, steady glow at night. The religious element only added to the mystique, creating a sense of community, of solidarity, that made this corner of New Jersey even more insular.

Enter Into the Kingdom of Heaven on Earth proclaimed the sign at the entrance to the town. But whose heaven was it? Anne wondered. The heaven depicted by the ministers preaching in the Church by the Sea? The heaven sought by people around the country, who gathered each summer to live in the hundred and fourteen tents surrounding the church, tents equipped with bathrooms, mini-kitchens, and electricity, allowing the faithful a way to commune with the Lord while enjoying all the modern conveniences? Or the heaven on earth that was part of the unspoiled Heights landscape—crabs scuttling by the water's edge, honeysuckle growing wild on the cliffs above the beach, the way the sky turned the color of ripe watermelon before fading into night?

Over the years, the towns surrounding the Heights had changed. Some became wild vacation spots for high school and college kids who got drunk or high on the boardwalk and were periodically arrested for minor violations. Other towns decayed, their faded motels and amusement parks lapsing into unintentional kitsch. But the Heights remained a "Christian seaside paradise," which meant that many of the townspeople were dismayed that Mallory Loving was making a movie on its fair shores. The naysayers considered the movie people a decadent lot, who showed a distinct lack of respect for

God and country. Of course, not everyone agreed. Restaurateurs and innkeepers, who were making money off the cast and crew, thought the film was the best thing to hit the Heights since sliced bread. For years Oceanside Heights had been in the shadow of Cape May, its sister Victorian town on the southern tip of the Jersey shore. Cape May was brilliant at promoting itself. Each summer there were guided trolley tours, afternoon tea served at half a dozen inns, a music festival, a whale-watching boat, and "living history" shows, where actors dressed up as nineteenth-century landowners. The Heights simply couldn't compete. The best it could do in the marketing department was the annual summer house tour, an occasional flea market on Pilgrim Pathway, and the Founders' Day Parade.

Dark Horizon was going to change all that, and finally put Oceanside Heights on the map. The plot was simple: Jersey shore housewife surfs the Internet and accidentally stumbles on a terrorist plot to destroy the entire Eastern seaboard. Or, as one studio executive put it, *Black Sunday* meets *The Net*. Atmospheric exteriors were being filmed in the Heights; the interiors would be shot later, on a Hollywood studio lot, and the computer-generated special effects would be tacked on at the end. So far, the film had been a financial boon for the Heights; many of the locals were being used as extras or handed envelopes stuffed with cash for permission to use their turn-of-the-century Victorian porches and flower-strewn yards as backdrops.

From what Anne could see, however, moviemaking was about as exciting as basting a turkey. It wasn't unusual for the actors to arrive on the set at 6:30 A.M., and then sit around for hours on end, playing cards, reading, getting their makeup done and their hair styled, talking on their cell phones, blocking out scenes, until finally, after many retakes, they got to emote.

This afternoon several of the actors had gathered under a white canvas tent on the beach, to escape the heat.

Throngs of onlookers were kept at bay by production assistants, who had cordoned off more of the beach, along with a sizable stretch of Ocean Avenue. Under the tent was a table laden with mineral water, diet sodas, bagels, corn chips, fat-free muffins, sandwiches, fruit salad, three pies, and five different kinds of biscotti. One thing about the movie biz, Anne thought. You never went hungry. No matter what time of day it was, there was always tons of food on the set. A movable smorgasbord.

When Mallory arrived with her entourage—she traveled with a hairstylist, a makeup artist, a personal trainer, a masseuse, a personal assistant, and a publicist, whose main job seemed to be trying to coax a reporter from *Entertainment Weekly* to come to the Jersey shore and write a piece about her return to the screen—Nick Fabien, Mallory's personal trainer, hustled her over to his makeshift mini-gym. He'd set up a Nordic Track, a Stair Climber, two blue vinyl exercise mats, and several free weights in one corner of the tent. After Mallory had spent forty minutes on the track and the stairs, Nick put her through what he called his "Body Blaster routine"— leg lifts, hip raises, toe touches, butt lifts, pelvic tilts, and reverse crunches. Anne had to shoehorn her questions in between situps, which was definitely a pain in the butt. Mallory had enough trouble sticking to one subject when she was standing still.

"Inhale . . . exhale . . . inhale . . . exhale," Nick chanted. He held Mallory's feet firmly in place, exhorting her to touch her toes with her fingertips as she lifted her chest off the mat. With his burly physique, bulging muscles, and red trunks, Nick looked more like a lifeguard than a personal trainer. The only part of his body that wasn't tan was his thumb, which was wrapped in gauze and taped with a splint to his index finger. His hair was black and puffy in front, like he'd spent an hour in front of the mirror with a blow dryer and a tube of mousse.

"What happened to the ice cream parlor?" Mallory said. She was breathing heavily. Beads of perspiration had formed on her forehead, mascara pooled under her eyelids. "I went to get a yogurt, and it's gone. There's a coffee place there now."

"Right," Anne said. She got up and started snapping pictures of Mallory with Helen's disposable camera. Might as well make herself useful doing something, since Mallory didn't seem to want to talk about the book. "The Strange Brew. Nagle's moved to Crescent Avenue, behind the Mini-Mart."

"I loved this one flavor they had. Vanilla yogurt with M&Ms."

"Brand X? They still make it."

Mallory struggled to reach her toes. "Wasn't that the best ever?"

Did she ever actually eat? There wasn't one ounce of fat on her entire body. Anne found it hard to believe Mallory had once been Marcia Lovitz of Landsdown Park, a high school dropout on the fast track to nowhere. Growing up across the lake in Landsdown, Mallory had seemed to fixate on the Heights as an oasis, coming there on weekends to soak in the scenery, like a child with her nose pressed against a bakery window. Mallory was constantly trying to retrieve pieces of her vanished youth. Did the lady who owned the Dress Connection, where everyone shopped for prom gowns, still give you a linen handkerchief when you bought a dress? (Yes.) Were there still antique cars in the Founders' Day Parade? (Yes.) On Sundays, did they still ban people from the beach until after twelve noon? (Yes, you were supposed to be in church till then.)

"Actually," Anne said, finishing the roll of film, "when you get right down to it, not much has changed. A cherry Coke at the pharmacy still costs a quarter. And they still make ice cream the old-fashioned way at Nagle's, churning the cream and sugar in a wooden barrel."

"God, Brand X was delicious. My absolute fave flavor." Mallory panted, struggling to catch her breath. She was sweating, throwing her upper body forward in spastic jerks.

Was this what "no pain, no gain" meant?

"Let's talk about your first husband," Anne said, hoping to shift the conversation away from dairy products.

"He was . . . lousy in . . . bed." Mallory gasped, trying to catch her breath. "Did I mention that?"

Only about half a dozen times. Anne had been a senior at Oceanside High School when Gerald Finch was a freshman. He lived and worked in the Heights. She was kind of sorry to hear about his failings in the bedroom. But it went with the territory. Good ghostwriters eventually learned everything about their subjects and the people around them, from their bathroom habits to what kind of cereal they ate for breakfast.

"You and Gerald lived in L.A. when you first got married," Anne said. "What was that like?"

But Mallory wasn't listening. Her cheeks had darkened to crimson. Her breathing was labored. Nick placed a large hand behind Mallory's head, as if to help raise it higher. "Last ten," he urged.

Mallory grunted. Her stomach was washboard flat. Anne couldn't remember the last time she'd done a sit-up. Junior high gym class?

"Hey, Nick." One of the perky production assistants materialized at his side. "Your cousin's here to see you. Says it's important."

"Thanks. We're done," he announced. Mallory lay on her back, panting. "Tomorrow we'll work your upper body," he said, getting up. With a backward wave he jogged in the direction of the boardwalk, toward where a beefy-looking man was standing.

"About the time you spent in L.A." Anne began.

"Not now."

Great. Another day shot to hell.

"When's a good time?" Anne persisted. This was one of Mallory's problems. She wasn't exactly reliable.

"Tomorrow afternoon. In the meantime, I made you another tape. Jill has it." Terrific, Anne thought. More of Mallory's ramblings to wade through.

Mallory rolled onto her side, propped one hand under her chin, and struck a cheesecake pose for an invisible photographer. "Think I could do an exercise spread for *Cosmo*?" she asked. "Get *Cosmo* on the phone, Jill."

"Yes, Miss Loving," said Jill Bentley, Mallory's super-efficient, twenty-something assistant, who was sitting on a metal folding chair, typing on her laptop.

Dressed in a lime green pants suit and matching heels, Jill looked like she'd rather be behind a desk in an air-conditioned office. Hers was the type of "glamour" job that was usually anything but. Lousy pay, long hours, being bossed around. In Anne's experience, these sorts of job usually went to young women with Ivy League educations and generous trust funds. Jill had neither. There was something cheap about her, from her "Joizy" accent to her flashy costume jewelry and two-inch-long fake nails. Petite and pale, with a long, horsy face and short brown hair, she played nursemaid to Mallory's tempestuous Juliet.

Now Jill picked up her cell phone and started dialing. With her other hand she continued to type. Neat trick, Anne thought. But can she balance a pencil on her nose?

"Hair . . . makeup," Mallory called out. A scared-looking young man clutching brushes and a tray speckled with colored powders materialized at Mallory's side, followed by a heavyset woman munching on a Ring Ding.

"Betty, my ends are starting to split again," Mallory said to the hairstylist.

"Not to worry. I've got a great clarifying conditioner we can try," Betty said cheerfully, giving Anne a quick wink.

"With SPF?"

"Absolutely. You can't be in the sun unless you're wearing sunscreen."

Anne smiled. Thank God for Betty Flugelhorn. Without her, Anne wouldn't be privy to Mallory's ever-changing schedule, not to mention the gossip Betty feasted on along with Hostess Snack Cakes.

Betty knelt beside Mallory, pulled out a large comb, and started rearranging the actress's hair. "Are you thinking up-do for this afternoon or tousled twist?" Betty asked, sweeping Mallory's blond locks into a top-knot.

"What about the thing you did the other day? With the pigtails?"

"Double loops?" Betty said, sticking a bobby pin between her teeth. "Great look for you. Cool and sleek in the heat."

Just then, Howard Koppelman entered the tent and clapped his hands. "All right, people. Time's a wasting. Let's do some blocking. Mallory, you're up."

Mallory waved Betty away and scrambled to her feet. "Not now, Howard. I have a migraine."

"This won't take long, hon. I promise."

"Then use a stand-in," Mallory snapped. "I'm getting a deep tissue massage." Before Howard could reply, she stalked off down the beach, followed by Betty and the makeup guy.

The director started to go after her, then appeared to think better of it. He beckoned to one of the other actresses who was about the same height as Mallory. As the camera trailed her, the woman walked ten paces down the beach, stopped at an X mark on the sand, and wheeled around.

"That work for you, Joe?" Howard said to one of the cameramen.

The man shook his head no.

"Then let's try it again."

The scene was two minutes long: Bored young Jersey shore housewife picnics with her kids on the beach, just a few feet away from the boardwalk where two terrorists watch her every move. The terrorists were sweating. They wore dark suits and slouchy hats with wide brims that made them look like the Blues Brothers.

"Whose bright idea was it to put us in suits?" groused Mallory's husband, Dakota, mopping his face with the back of his tie. His shoulder length brown hair was pulled back in a ponytail. Already his suit was looking wrinkled. The script called for him, as the head terrorist, to kidnap Mallory's character, then fall madly in love with her. Anne had read in *Variety* that the studio was hoping to create on-screen sparks from their off-screen marriage.

Before the film crew had arrived in the Heights, Anne had gone to the library and pored over old newspaper clippings, doing background checks on all the people in Mallory's life. Dakota's real name was Lenny Kunkle. He had been born in Rapid City, South Dakota, and claimed to be part Native American. On the cover of his latest CD, he was made up to look like an Indian chief, his high cheekbones decorated with war paint, his tall, lanky frame draped in a buckskin outfit made especially for him by Ralph Lauren. Anne learned that Dakota had headed East when he was seventeen, working his way across the country by playing guitar in roadhouses and back room bars.

By the time he reached New York, he had put together a band, singing about gritty blue-collar cities and working-class Joes who lost their factory jobs and sat around the house drinking Schlitz. During the day he drove a cab. At night he played in obscure, smoky clubs in the East Village, periodically sending out fliers to record company executives at every label listed in the Manhattan phone book. It took five years for a rep from EMI Records to sign Dakota to a contract. He became an overnight sensation, with three hit singles, a huge following in Japan, and a thirty-two-city nationwide tour. But the band broke up, the economy rebounded, and at the age of twenty-five, Dakota was on the verge of becoming a has-been. His last CD featured songs about Native American life: alcohol-impaired young men, poverty-stricken women, fifth-graders who dropped out of school and turned to prostitution. A group of Native American politicians and businessmen had held a news conference to register a formal protest. The album was misleading and insulting, they said. And to top it off, the closest tie anyone could make between Dakota and the Indian Nation was that his mother had once sold T-shirts and baby carrier "papooses" to tourists visiting a Sioux reservation. Desperate to rev up his flagging career, Dakota headed to California in hopes of becoming an actor. He'd already gotten a small role on the sitcom *Life's Work* and a shaving cream commercial when he met Mallory Loving at a party. They'd been married seven months.

"I want to know why we're wearing suits," Dakota griped. "Aren't we going to be a little conspicuous?"

"Have you read the entire script?" Koppelman countered. Dakota looked blank. "I didn't think so. Your character is coming from a CIA party. You don't have time to dash into a phone booth and change into your bathing trunks."

Before Dakota could respond, a woman in a low-cut black swimsuit rushed up to Howard Koppelman. "Do I look all right?" she asked, tugging at the fabric and pirouetting in a circle. "It's not too tight?"

"You look fine, Caitlin," Howard said. "But we're not ready for dress rehearsal yet. Why don't you relax awhile? We start filming again after lunch."

Caitlin Grey played Mallory's younger sister, another bored New Jersey housewife, accompanying Mallory's character to the beach. Anne wondered why Hollywood screenwriters thought women in New Jersey were so bored all the time.

"Hi," Caitlin said, walking over to Anne. "Do you have a minute?"

"Sure." Betty had told her about the dissension on the set—the catfights, the name-calling, the stormy off-camera scenes between Mallory and Caitlin. She wondered what Caitlin wanted from her.

"We can talk in my trailer. It's air-conditioned," Caitlin said.

She looked like a slimmer, younger version of Mallory—same blond hair, full lips, blue eyes. But where Mallory projected a hard-edged glamour, Caitlin was all dewy innocence, like a college cheerleader ready to perform a pom-pom routine at the big game.

The tourists penned behind the barricades grew boisterous as Caitlin approached. Cameras clicked wildly and people shoved one another, jostling for position. Brandishing T-shirts, postcards, restaurant menus, and kites, they clamored for Caitlin's autograph. She waved and blew a kiss before disappearing into the trailer she shared with two other actresses. It was long and narrow, barely accommodating three cots, two dressing tables, a rack of clothes, and a small kitchenette. Programs from regional theater companies were taped to the walls, along with black-and-white head shots of Caitlin.

"So," Caitlin said, seating herself on a cot and throwing a white terry-cloth robe over her bathing suit. "You're writing a book about Mallory."

Her smile was meant to be ingratiating, but Anne found it off-putting. Caitlin reminded her of a game show hostess. They looked like they were rooting for the contestants. But Anne suspected they secretly hoped the male host would take a powder so they could read the questions, instead of posing with the cars.

Anne sat down opposite her. "Actually, it's supposed to be Mallory's book about Mallory. I'm the ghost-writer."

"Well, I think she's wonderful. Better than Meg Ryan, even."

"Uh huhn." So this little tête-à-tête was actually a fishing expedition.

"I really admire Mallory," Caitlin continued. "She's someone I can learn a lot from. And I was just wondering . . ." Caitlin ran her tongue lightly across her lips. "Well, I was wondering if she's said anything about me, if I'm going to be mentioned in the book."

You better believe it, toots. Mallory had a lot to say on the subject of Caitlin Grey. She'd called Caitlin a "no-talent conniving cow who'd sleep with anyone to get to the top." And that was just for starters.

"She's spoken about you," Anne said aloud.

"Because, I mean, you always find personality—" Caitlin stopped, searching for the right word. "Personality . . . conflicts in film."

"I heard about the mud pie incident."

"Oh, that." Caitlin rolled her eyes. "Much ado about nothing."

"Could I get your version, for the record?"

"Why not?" She leaned forward, flashing a hundred-watt smile. Anne wondered if her gums ached from showing so many teeth. "We were filming a beach scene. It was real sunny, and Howard . . . Mr. Koppelman, had to bring in special reflectors so it wouldn't be too bright, and we were all sitting around waiting. I detest delays. It ruins my concentration. So I started making mud pies. It had rained during the night, and the sand was kind of wet. I'd made about three of them, when Mallory came over and started saying what a dope I was, getting all dirty when we were just about to start shooting. She probably didn't mean anything by it. We were all kind of on edge because the shoot is running so late. Anyway, I got up, and I lost my balance a little. Like I said, it was wet underfoot. The pie slipped and landed on Mallory. It was an accident."

Betty told Anne it had taken over an hour to get the mud out of Mallory's hair. The publicist was hopeful that the incident would draw reporters from major magazines and newspapers. Negative press was better than no press at all.

Anne decided to switch gears. "What's your take on Mallory's marriage?" she asked Caitlin.

"Dream couple, crazy in love." She sounded sincere, but her smile wasn't quite as shiny, as though an invisible hand had lowered the dimmer switch.

"Really?" Anne said, raising an eyebrow. "I hear some of the crew is taking bets on whether they'll last till Labor Day."

Caitlin primly folded her hands in her lap. "My mother taught me if you don't have anything nice to say, don't say anything. Speaking of which, if Mallory slanders me in that book, I'll sue the both of you."

"Is that right?" Actually, Mallory had named six directors and four producers that Caitlin had slept with to land jobs on soap operas, TV mini-series, and films. The mildest name Mallory had called Caitlin was a "cretinous whore." It had gotten progressively worse from there. "Let's just say she doesn't think much of your work."

Caitlin's nostrils flared. She looked like a thoroughbred lining up at the starting gate. "My work?" Caitlin repeated. "What does that porn queen know about acting? She couldn't act her way out of a paper bag."

"It must be difficult for you to stay focused in your scenes together," Anne said, trying to score some sympathy points. If Mallory continued to be elusive, it might be a good idea to chat up the people around her.

"Know what I do?" Caitlin said, eagerly taking the bait. "I give my character a whole back story with Mallory's character that isn't in the script: Mom favoring me when we were growing up, sibling rivalry, her pathologically insane jealousy, the fact that my kids are much smarter than hers and my husband is more successful. Helps me connect with my character."

There was a knock on the door of the trailer. "Come in," Caitlin chirped.

The door swung open and Nick Fabien poked his head

in. "Lunchtime," he announced. "Chicken sandwiches, mineral water, lemon meringue pie."

Caitlin made a face. "Those sandwiches have been sitting out in the heat for hours. We're all going to get salmonella or something."

"How about we bag it and head over to Quilters?" Nick said. "I'll round up Dakota."

"Is Mallory going?" Caitlin asked.

Nick rolled his eyes. "La Loving is scheduled for an herbal wrap. The coast is clear."

"Then count me in."

Nick said, "What about you, Anne? Want to join us?"

"Sure."

"Maybe we could get through an entire meal without mentioning the Dramatic Diva," Caitlin said. "Wouldn't that be lovely?"

Chapter 3

*If you use a lip pencil,
fill your entire lips by
blending in from the
edges, using a color that's
one shade darker than
your lipstick. To help keep
your lipstick on, take a
tissue, separate it, place
it over your mouth,
and brush face powder on
your lips. This helps
"set" your lipstick.*

Quilters was located on the ground floor of the Quilting Bee Inn, a pale green three-story Victorian building on Main Street. As its name suggested, the restaurant was decorated with dozens of antique quilts, mounted on the walls: patchwork crazy quilts, geometric Amish quilts, embroidered album quilts, white Double Wedding Ring quilts and symmetrical Log Cabin quilts. In the center of the room was a giant quilt showing the history of Oceanside Heights, and incorporating images of the beach, the boardwalk, the Church by the Sea, the pastel-colored Victorian cottages, the marina, even Moby's Hardware store, which had commissioned five elderly ladies to sew the quilt and piece it together.

Food was served cafeteria-style, piled high on turquoise Fiesta ware plates. Quilters prided itself on hearty fare like creamed ham on toast and meat loaf with mashed potatoes. Each day there was a different flavored pudding. Anne grabbed a plate of macaroni and cheese and a tall glass of lemonade—a Heights bargain at $3.55.

Caitlin had loaded her tray with corn bread, tomato soup, tuna casserole, creamed spinach, a deviled egg, chocolate milk, and coconut custard pie. Where did Caitlin put the calories? Anne wondered. She had no hips at all.

"Is salad a dirty word in this town?" Nick asked as he ushered the group to a white Formica table for four. He'd slipped on a tank top, which accentuated his broad chest and massive forearms. On his tray was an anemic looking grapefruit and a roast beef sandwich slathered in gravy.

"Oh, hush," Caitlin teased, taking the seat opposite him. "The food's fine. Reminds me of Indiana. There was the sweetest little diner in the town I lived in. With the best French fries I ever tasted."

Dakota grimaced. "Midwestern diners are the pits. Used to work in one of 'em. Grease on a griddle."

"As long as I'm clogging my arteries," said Nick, pointing to his roast beef, "I could use a beer."

"The way you down a six-pack, you'll need more than one," said Dakota. All three of them laughed. Without Mallory around, they acted like kids at recess, more relaxed, less self-conscious.

"Sorry. No beer," Anne interjected. "The Heights is a dry town."

"A what?" Nick said, leaning forward. Anne could smell his cologne, a pepperminty scent blended with citrus notes.

"A dry town. None of the stores or restaurants sell liquor."

"You mean like Prohibition?" Caitlin giggled.

"Kind of," Anne said. "The Methodist ministers who founded the Heights prohibited drinking. And the rule stuck."

"I get it," Dakota commented. "No Jell-O shots. No wet T-shirt concerts. No rock-'n'-roll beach parties." He sounded wistful, as if he missed them.

"We're more of a family-friendly place," Anne said. "If you want a taste of the real Jersey shore, you have to go further south, to Wildwood or Seaside Heights."

"No drinking," Nick said. "Bummer."

You don't know the half of it, Anne thought. When she was growing up, there were all sorts of rules she had to follow, especially on Sundays. No ball playing. No roller skating. No bike riding. No swimming. And it wasn't only kids who had to adhere to the regulations. Her parents weren't allowed to drive on Sundays. In fact, they had to park the Buick Electra in a lot in Neptune before midnight on Saturday nights and pick it up again early Monday morning. Her mother couldn't hang clothes out to dry. Her father couldn't work in the yard or do minor repair projects around the house. The Sabbath was the Lord's day, the day of rest.

She scanned the restaurant. Quilters was usually bustling at lunchtime. But the noise level had dropped dramatically, and it wasn't hard to guess why. Although the foursome occupied a corner table, they were clearly the focus of attention. People seemed fixated on Dakota and Caitlin, ignoring their food to stare.

"Do they bite?" Nick said to Anne.

"Pardon?"

"The way everyone's staring, like it's feeding time at

the zoo.'' Anne noticed Dakota and Caitlin didn't seem to mind.

"We don't get movie stars in the Heights every day.'' Anne chuckled. "It's a big deal.''

"Have you lived here all your life?'' Caitlin asked, spooning soup into her mouth.

Anne nodded. "Born and raised. My house is right on the beach.''

"Which one?'' Caitlin said.

"The yellow Victorian cottage, on the corner of Ocean and Seaside Avenues.''

"With the geraniums out front? Oh, it's darling. Just darling.''

"Thanks,'' Anne said, with a grin. If Caitlin was trying to score brownie points, she'd picked the wrong thing to focus on. Anne didn't exactly have a green thumb. The potted geraniums and scraggly-looking petunias were a quick substitute for time spent planting a real garden.

When her mother was alive, there'd been a glorious garden out front, brimming with marigolds and hollyhocks and tall, slender sunflowers. But when Anne was eleven, Evelyn Hardaway began doing curious things—watering the flowers without a skirt or panties on, digging up all the tulips and serving them for dinner in a "stew,'' snipping the heads off her prized roses and pelting them at stray cats, seagulls, and, once, the minister's wife, who was so taken aback she had to miss Vespers and lie down in a darkened room with a cool cloth over her eyes. The neighbors reacted with concern at first, which gradually shifted to horror. As Evelyn became more "crazy,'' their friends drifted away. Anne found herself becoming increasingly disenchanted with the church. Her faith in God, miracles, and salvation disappeared like footprints erased by the tide. Her parents divorced, her father moved away, the seasons changed—and still Evelyn showed no signs of getting better. Anne felt herself turning inward, filling journals with her private hopes and fears. Years later she realized the only positive thing to come out of that dismal period was her love of writing. Words became her outlet. Finding out about people, recording their thoughts, their histories, their very lives, became a way to connect with others, without revealing much about herself.

"How's the book coming?" Dakota asked, interrupting her reverie. He sounded disinterested, just making conversation. But Anne saw his eyes were alert, as if the answer mattered.

"So far, so good," she said slowly. "It's a lot less hectic than the movie biz."

"Tell me about it," Caitlin complained. "We're weeks behind. Every other day something breaks or disappears, like we're jinxed or something."

"You worried the big boys are going to pull the plug?" Nick asked, taking the last bite of his gravy-soaked sandwich.

"Considering how far over budget we are, it could happen," Caitlin said, in an undertone. "We're supposed to come in at $80 million—$40 million for production, and another $40 mill for marketing. You know what I read in *Variety*? Production costs are already up to $60 million, and we might even break a hundred." Looking around warily, she flashed a perky smile at an adjoining table of middle-aged women in flowered pastel dresses. When she spoke again, her voice was hushed. "People in the industry are calling the film *Doomed Horizon*, this year's *Water World*. But, the last thing we need are a bunch of negative rumors."

"Who the hell cares?" Dakota said angrily, spearing a mound of green Jell-O with his fork. "I mean, what's the point?"

"You okay, cowboy?" Nick said to Dakota. "You look a little down."

"I should have stuck with music," Dakota said bitterly. "This acting stuff is bullshit."

"But you're marvelous," Caitlin protested. "You make the part come alive."

"Mallory doesn't think so."

Nick looked at his watch. "I knew it," he crowed. "We only lasted twenty minutes before somebody mentioned Mal."

"It's a little hard to forget she's around," Caitlin said ruefully. "Can I have your pickle, if you're not going to eat it?"

"Sure." Nick picked it up awkwardly and passed it across the table.

Caitlin looked at his taped fingers. "By the way, how'd you hurt your thumb?"

"Lifting weights. But the doc said it'll heal quick, get fixed right up."

"I wish this picture could be fixed," Dakota said, sinking his fork into a tower of mashed potatoes. "Koppelman's a loser. The script sucks. I should be touring Australia with my band."

"Wouldn't that be hard on you and Mallory?" Anne said. "The separation, I mean." It was tough asking dumb questions and sounding sincere at the same time.

"Uh huh," Dakota said. With his knife, he flicked a couple of peas into a puddle of creamed corn.

Wow, Anne thought. How informative. Can I quote you on that?

"Speaking of Mallory," Caitlin cut in, "I heard she's back on drugs."

Everybody at the table turned to stare at her. Anne prayed it wasn't true. She tried to gauge the others' reactions. Dakota seemed surprised. Caitlin was triumphant. Nick's eyes were trained on his empty plate. She couldn't tell what he was thinking.

"Where'd you hear that?" Anne asked Caitlin.

"It's all over the set." Anne noticed Caitlin wasn't bothering to keep her voice down now. "Explains a lot, don't you think?"

"Geez, I hope to God it's not true," Nick said. "But

she's exercising different. She's become kinda manic, like she's on speed. And she gets awful tired.''

There was a faint but unmistakable smirk on Caitlin's face.

Dakota pushed his tray away and leaned back in his chair. "It figures," he said wearily. "The husband's always the last to know.''

After ten days of listening to Mallory reminisce on tape, this is what Anne knew: Marcia Lovitz's life hadn't been easy. Deadbeat father who abandoned the family when Marcia and her twin sister, Sheila, were three. Alcoholic mother who beat up her kids and squandered her welfare checks on gin and cigarettes. A ramshackle two-bedroom house in a crime-scarred neighborhood in Landsdown Park, where drugs were as easy to get hold of as Milky Way bars, and the random sound of gunfire punctured the night. Molested at age seven by one of her mother's boyfriends, Marcia learned early on that the world was a violent, scary place. The only way she'd survive was by reinventing herself.

Her first break came in high school. While her friends were getting high behind the football bleachers, Marcia wandered into the school auditorium and auditioned for a play called *Time Out for Ginger*. She didn't get cast, not even a small part. But the algebra teacher who was moonlighting as a director said she could help out by painting scenery. Two nights later she showed up at his apartment in a raincoat, with a bottle of cheap Chablis. Before he could ask her to leave, she slipped inside and opened the coat, revealing her nubile, naked fifteen-year-old body. The next day she was playing Ginger.

Acting was like nothing Marcia had experienced before. Better than drugs, better than sex, it gave her a rush, an emotional high that left her drained, craving more. After her triumph as Ginger, she starred in five other high school productions, including the title role in *Gypsy* and Ado Annie in *Oklahoma*. It hardly mattered that she couldn't sing. By then, she'd learned how to apply makeup so it accentuated her natural good looks. She spent hours in front of the mirror, experimenting with blush and eyeliner, using the free testers at Stern's makeup counter. Each time, she created a whole new look with a different color palette—soft pinks, tawny oranges, golden flesh tones, lush reds. She dressed in clothes a size too small, practicing how to wiggle her hips when she walked, how to light a cigarette, how to be sexy. It was the ultimate makeover; the last thing to go was her name. She chose Mallory because it was different, unusual, the complete opposite of drab, boring Marcia. Loving was obvious. The word represented how men would treat her, how powerful she would become. At night, in bed, she whispered her new name to herself; the words tripped off her tongue, smooth and polished as pearls.

At sixteen she was ready to make her escape. She stopped going to school, gathered her savings—$53.75, which she kept in a drawstring purse around her neck. One morning she packed a bag and left the house. Her mother trailed after her. "You think you can walk out on me?" her mother had screamed. She threw a bottle that grazed the back of Marcia's head. Twenty-four hours later, Marcia was back in Landsdown Park. Mother had called the cops to report the disappearance of a minor. They'd intercepted the Greyhound bus bound for California.

"Loser. Slut. Bitch," her mother had taunted the minute Marcia walked in the door. Marcia had run to the bathroom and locked herself in, sobbing. She couldn't stand it. Two more years of this drab, dirty town—the drug dealers whistling at her when she walked down the street, the endless batches of greasy fries she'd have to cook at the Burger Barn, her mother's boyfriends, groping her in the hall, trying to get into her pants. There must be some way she could get out. And suddenly, there was.

His name was Gerald Finch. He was eighteen years old, and he lived in the next town, Oceanside Heights. There was nothing particularly remarkable about Gerald. Average build, dark hair, brown eyes. But two things about him appealed to Marcia: He'd won a scholarship to UCLA, and he wanted to marry her. As Mrs. Gerald Finch, she could live in California, cast off her old life, let her twin sister, Sheila, be the one to hold down after-school jobs and finance her mother's drinking. Marcia was getting out.

Anne paused at the keyboard and reviewed what she'd just written. Not bad, considering she had had to wade through hours of Mallory holding forth on sandals, thigh cream, Percosets, fad diets, rehab, and hair extensions to get it. Her notes were still a jumble of dates, events, places. But what was on the screen captured the salient points of Mallory's childhood, the pain and despair, the feeling of being trapped, the way Mallory used people to get what she wanted. It was simple, really. Mallory wanted to be loved. "Universal theme," Anne typed in parentheses. "Wants to feel she belongs, to find a man who makes her feel needed." Of course, there were still things that had to be fleshed out. Mallory's relationship with her sister, for instance. That could be interesting. Not to mention her marital problems with Dakota. By the time the book was published, they'd probably be divorced.

This was the way Anne worked when she ghosted an autobiography: First, write the facts down from beginning to end, then change the voice to the first person, to Mallory's voice, as though Mallory were the one telling the story. Ghostwriting was tricky. You had to get your facts straight, to cut through the subject's posturing and defenses, without being too intrusive. Writing someone else's autobiography was like trying to cup a firefly in your hands. From a distance the facts were shiny, tangible objects. But under close scrutiny, they dissolved into a messy stew of wishes, lies, and dreams. Memory wasn't only subjective, it was downright unreliable. Anne had found that most people viewed their own lives through a filter—assigning meaning, shuffling emotions, rearranging the nuances of each day, each year, to suit their liking.

There was ultimately something satisfying in getting to the truth. For a couple of months, Anne became a human diary, soaking up all sorts of information, piecing it together. Then it was adios and on to the next assignment.

She typed out snippets of Mallory's latest tape, adding them to the file of notes she'd already transcribed. Over the weekend, she'd go through all the notes again and put them in chronological order. She reached into a plastic file box and pulled out a red floppy disk labeled *Loving You.* Popping it into the computer, she saved the latest entry onto the disk.

Loving You. It was kind of catchy. They could subtitle it *The Rise and Fall and Rise of Mallory Loving.* Or *How Anne Hardaway Spent Her Summer Vacation.* Today was August 26. The first draft was due November 1. She should make the deadline easily, as long as Mallory agreed to do more face-to-face interviews. Anne figured it was a control issue: Mallory didn't want to have to answer specific questions. She'd rather set her own agenda. Period.

Anne glanced at the clock. Four P.M. Ten at night on the Italian Riviera, where Jack Mills was spending two glorious weeks, overseeing the building of a luxury hotel. Jack was an architect who lived and worked in New York City. Tragedy had brought them together last summer when Jack's brother, Tigger, was killed. Tigger's body had washed up on the beach, and she and Jack had figured out who killed him. But that was another story.

Ever since they'd first met, she and Jack had gotten together mainly on weekends, about twice a month. Anne supposed they were "dating," a word that brought to mind superficialities—dinners out, small talk, game playing. That wasn't what they were doing. But she didn't quite have a handle on the relationship, either. She couldn't tell whether she was in love with Jack. She only knew she missed him more than she wanted to.

"You'll love Portofino," he'd told her before he left. "It's the most romantic place on earth." If it weren't for Mallory Loving, Anne could be sipping a Bellini at a café overlooking the Mediterranean right about now, staring into Jack's cornflower blue eyes. What if Jack ran into Mallory on the Riviera? Not Mallory, exactly, but a Mallory type. A gorgeous blond with legs that wouldn't quit. Would he be smitten and fall into bed with her? She considered calling his hotel, then vetoed the plan. He'd probably be at dinner, anyway—not seated across the table from a beautiful Italian bombshell, she hoped.

Grabbing a soda from the refrigerator, Anne headed out to the porch, armed with Mallory's latest beauty tips and a copy of *Variety*. She'd gotten into the habit of reading *Variety* every day. It shocked her how much money some actors made. More than baseball players or the President or heads of major corporations. Millions of dollars, for three, four weeks of filming. Nice work, if you could get it. Anne skimmed through the beauty tips Mallory had given her earlier: *Always apply a light moisturizer under your foundation. The key ingredient in an herbal bath is dried lavender. To make your hair even shinier, add ¼ cup of lemon juice to ½ cup of water after you shampoo. If you haven't got an eyelash brush, apply the round part of the spoon to your lash line and push up.*

Fascinating, simply fascinating. It had as much meaning in Anne's life as quantum physics. Altogether, there were about two dozen tips. Makeup. For Mallory, the jars of colored powders and cream held out the hope of transformation. Well, it worked, didn't it? Marcia Lovitz had become Mallory Loving, a butterfly whose wings

were painted with lip gloss and mascara. Anne folded
up the paper and stuck it back in her pocket. Maybe she
should begin each chapter with a different tip. Or change
the title of the book: *Loving Your Face. The Skinny on
Skin. Mallory's Guide to a Marvelous You.* She sighed
audibly. She'd been spending way too much time talking
to Phil.

On the beach, it looked like the movie people hadn't
made much progress: crew members standing around,
tourists penned behind a dozen blue sawhorses. Same
old stuff. The big white tent flapped in the breeze. From
her chaise lounge, Anne could see Dakota arguing with
Mallory by the water's edge. Dakota looked like he was
trying to talk her into something. He gesticulated wildly
with his hands, making pictures in the air. Mallory stood
there impassively. After about a minute, she turned and
walked away. He ran alongside her, still trying to make
his point. But she acted like she didn't hear. Suddenly
the tent flew up in the air, like a great white balloon. It
stayed airborne a few seconds, then veered toward the
ocean where it hovered a moment, floated, and sank beneath the waves. "Hurrah for Hollywood," Anne whis-
tled under her breath.

Chapter 4

*To strengthen your hair,
mix an egg into your
regular shampoo. To
thicken your hair, add a
tablespoon of powdered
gelatin to your shampoo.
To repair damaged hair,
combine 1 tablespoon
of castor oil with
2 tablespoons of your
conditioner. Massage your
entire head and scalp.
Leave on for twenty
minutes, with a warm
towel wrapped around
your head. Then rinse.*

The party was ostensibly to celebrate Mallory's twenty-eighth birthday. Anne had read somewhere that Mallory's birthday was August 27, not 26, and knew that she was actually thirty-two years old. But who could quibble if the actress wanted to shave a few years off her age?

When Anne pulled up to the house Mallory was renting, the place was decked out in tiny white lights. It was a large, asymmetrical Queen Anne–style house on a narrow plot of land, on Beechwood Avenue. Painted a cheery shade of apricot, with sky blue trim, the house had a turret, two balconies, a wraparound porch, and a projecting bay window. The clapboard facade, massive stone chimney, and carpenter's lace trim on the underside of the gables gave the house a frilly, storybook air. She'd heard Mallory was paying $5,000 a week to live in the five-bedroom Victorian, which was patently ridiculous. For that amount, you could rent a house in the Heights for practically the whole summer. But the studio people didn't mind being ripped off. Fact is, they acted like they expected it.

Anne walked up the stone steps, past the wraparound porch decorated with white wicker furniture. The front door was open. In the living room, about two dozen people were nibbling hors d'oeuvres and sipping white wine. Pink streamers and balloons hung from the ceiling. Donna Summer's "Love to Love You Baby" blared from the stereo.

"Hi there," Mallory called out, blowing an air kiss in Anne's direction.

Anne walked over. She had on a white linen dress with silver buttons down the front. But now she wished she'd selected something else, something more sophisticated. Mallory wore a tight black slip dress, which exposed her curves beneath the fabric. Her skin was healthy, flawless. Her hair bounced when she moved. *I really should take better care of myself,* Anne thought. *Spring for a manicure. Use a moisturizing mask.*

"Hey, you look great," Mallory said, emphasizing the *great* so it fairly sang.

A backhanded compliment. The tone implied Anne usually looked less than spectacular. After murmuring a

tepid thanks, she examined Mallory closely, searching
for signs that the actress was back on drugs. The only
hint of it were her eyes, which were slightly red and
watery. In one hand she held a tall glass containing a
fizzy clear liquid with a wedge of lime bobbing just beneath the surface. Seltzer? Vodka tonic?

"Mallory, we need to set up a time for our next interview," Anne said firmly. "And no more tapes, okay?
We have to talk face to face."

"Don't worry so much. I'll come over tomorrow afternoon around five-thirty. With great stuff for the book.
I promise." Mallory flashed a warm smile and touched
Anne's arm, as if to reassure her. This was the high-
voltage, you're-my-best-friend Mallory, but Anne
wasn't buying.

"You've been saying that for over a week now."

"Have I? Okay. I can see you need a preview." Mallory linked arms with Anne and led her into a small
study adjoining the living room, closing the door behind
them. "You want hot? You got it." She sat down on a
chintz-colored sofa and crossed her legs. Her lips were
blood-red. "How's this?" She paused, for effect. "My
darling husband's voice is shot. On his last album, he
lip-synched the words. Paid some kid to sing the lyrics,
and they fixed things in the recording studio so nobody'd
know."

"Are you sure?" Anne said, incredulous. The muffled
sounds of the party floated into the room. Music and
tinkling glasses and the low roar of talk. She wondered
why Mallory would want to destroy Dakota's career.

"Sure I'm sure. I'm married to him, aren't I?" Mallory's fingertips tapped against the glass. "I know all
his secrets. And I'll lay out every one of them in my
book."

"Do you know the name of the stand-in singer? The
sound engineers? Or anyone else involved in the cover
up? We'll need careful documentation." Yes, this qual-
ified as first-rate gossip. But she could almost hear Phil

Smedley whispering one word in her ear: *libel.*

"Of course I'll name names," Mallory said impatiently. "Geez, I thought you'd be more excited."

She got up and studied herself in the mirror, appraising her reflection.

"I'm just curious why you'd want to ruin him," Anne said.

Mallory spun around. "Because the marriage is fini." She tilted her head back and took a long slow sip of her drink. "We're splitting up, just as soon as we wrap this picture."

Was it seltzer? Something stronger? "I'm sorry."

"Don't be," Mallory snapped. "I'm better off without him. Tomorrow I'll tell you some real juicy details about my two other exes. Plus a few Hollywood scandals I happen to know about." Her eyes glittered. "It's payback time. This book is going to knock the stuffing out of a whole lot of people."

The door to the study opened, and Jill Bentley poked her head in. "Oh, there you are, Mal," said Jill. "It's almost time to open your presents."

"Tomorrow. Five-thirty sharp," Mallory said to Anne. She checked her reflection in the mirror again, then walked to the door, her heels clicking against the hardwood floor.

Well, Anne thought, as she drifted back to the living room, now we're finally getting somewhere. She'd have Phil's contacts in New York check out Dakota. If it turned out to be true, should she position the news up front, in chapter one? Or more toward the middle of the book, so it came as a revelation? She could just imagine the press release Phil would send out: *Dakota Is Over* or *Rock-'n'-Roll Ruin.* Sometimes she thought Phil would have had a splendid career as a tabloid journalist. Out of the corner of her eye, she noticed someone waving to her. Betty Flugelhorn. Anne made her way over.

"Hey," Betty said excitedly. She was perched on a

couch, digging into a plate of vegetable dumplings. "Love your face."

"Thanks. I just spent two hours at Stern's. Cost me $109.95."

Betty's expression was disapproving. "You should have come to me," she scolded. "I'd have given you stuff for free."

Anne sighed. "And miss the makeover? Heaven forbid. You know what the woman behind the counter said to me: 'Hon, you'd be pretty with the right makeup.' "

It had been a nerve-wracking session, and when the makeup lady was finished, Anne hardly recognized herself in the mirror. Her face looked smoother, her eyes stood out more. So she'd spent over a hundred bucks on a handful of eye shadow, blush, and lip gloss. She'd wanted to get all dolled up for Mallory's party. Now she was starting to wonder why.

"Did you hear about the tent?" Betty said excitedly.

"Yeah, I happened to see it."

"Someone must have loosened the fabric from the poles," Betty said, keeping her voice low. "More mischief afoot." Betty was a hairstylist from San Ysidro, California, whose job was to insure that Mallory's hair was fluffed and cut to big-screen perfection. Her unofficial job was to give Anne the lowdown on *Dark Horizon*. Not that Anne had recruited Betty to be her eyes and ears. But Betty loved to dish, and in Anne, she'd found a receptive audience.

"That's not all," Betty said excitedly. "When I got back to my trailer, I found all this stuff missing. Lipsticks, eye shadows, wigs, face powder."

"Do you know who took them?"

"Not yet. But I'll find out, believe you me. Meantime, I have to order more supplies from New York. And who knows how long they'll take to get here."

A teenage boy carrying a tray of stuffed mushrooms walked by. "I'll try one of those," Betty said, grabbing three off the silver tray. She was plump, with fleshy arms and broad hips. Large white teeth protruded from her mouth in a prominent overbite. Her own hair was frizzy, shoulder-length, the color of dried marigolds.

They'd met the first day of filming when Betty introduced herself and admired Anne's hair. "It's real, isn't it?" Betty had said. "The color, I mean."

"Last time I checked."

"I knew it," Betty had crowed. "Freckles. Fair skin. You're a natural redhead."

"This surprises you?" Anne had said, chuckling.

Betty had rolled her eyes. "Ninety percent of the redheads in this world are fakes. You should see the roots! My God. Most of them have such dark hair, the dye doesn't take. They end up with this ugly copper color. Looks like rust on a lead pipe."

"Sounds pretty ghastly."

"Like Halloween fright masks." Betty had looked Anne up and down. "Let me guess. You're . . . thirty-five?"

"Thirty-seven."

"Size eight?"

"Correct."

"Virgo?"

"Sagittarius."

"I can tell a lot about people from their hair. You're the athletic type, right?"

"I run sometimes. That's about it."

"And you work with your hands. Am I right or am I right?"

"Positively psychic. I'm a writer."

"Thank God I met you," Betty had said. "I'm dying to get away from all these neurotic actors."

The memory of that first meeting with Betty still amused Anne. Betty reminded her of that battery-operated bunny on the TV commercials. Once she got started, she could talk for hours nonstop. About dye jobs or liposuction or anything else that flew into her head.

"So," Anne said to Betty, as the hairstylist plucked

several pigs in a blanket from a passing tray. "Did you guys get anything done today?"

"Not a thing," Betty said with a grin. "Another washout, more money down the drain. I think Koppelman's going to blow a gasket. Know what else? He's upped his offer to light the cross. Twenty-five grand, if he can film inside the church, that is."

Anne looked over at Howard Koppelman, who was standing beside a table stacked with gaily wrapped packages. He had on an expensive-looking blazer over faded blue jeans. He looked uncomfortable, out of his element. Unlike on the set, nobody seemed to be paying much attention to him.

"Shoot," Anne said. "I forgot to bring Mallory's gift."

"You mean you actually bought her something? Nobody else did. Jill went into town this morning and got a mess of stuff. She signed people's names to the cards. By the way, do you like Mallory's hair tonight?"

Anne glanced at Mallory. Her hair did look especially pretty. It framed her face nicely, accentuating the brightness of her eyes.

"I did it special," Betty said proudly. "Hot rollers, cool curling iron. A little teasing on top. I think it suits her. Believe it or not, her ends get a little dry. So I add a tablespoon of honey to two tablespoons of her shampoo."

Jill Bentley clapped her hands together loudly. "Okay, everybody. It's time to open the presents."

Mallory sat down on the sofa. Her face had the greedy expression of a child about to devour a week's worth of ice cream and cake. The guests formed a semicircle around her.

Jill picked up a rectangular-shaped package, wrapped in floral print paper. "Happy B'day, Mal," Jill said, handing it over.

Mallory ripped off the paper. Underneath was a box of stationery decorated with miniature seashells. Anne recognized the box, from the Pirate's Cove gift shop in town. Jill picked up the card, which had slipped to the floor. "From Nick," Jill announced.

"That's news to me," Anne heard Nick Fabien mutter.

"Didn't anyone buy her a new personality?" muttered a female voice to Anne's left.

Anne whirled around. Caitlin Grey was leaning against the wall, holding a glass of white wine. Her expression was cheerful, almost pleased, like she was the one whose birthday they were about to celebrate.

"On to the next gift," Jill announced gaily.

She took a large box, adorned with a pink bow, from the pile. Mallory opened the box, peeling away layers of pink tissue paper, and pulled out a folded white paper. She studied it for a moment, growing paler. "Is this someone's idea of a sick joke?" she demanded. Her eyes scanned the crowded room. "Which one of you did this?"

"What are you talking about, Mal?" said Howard Koppelman. "What's wrong?"

"You'll appreciate this, Howard," she said, sounding angry and scared at the same time. "It's right up your alley." She began reading aloud:

"Dear Slut:

I seen all your trash movies. When I get you alone, I'm going to make you pay. I ache for you, sugar. I get crazy thinking about all the things I'm going to do to you."

Somebody giggled nervously. Then the room grew quiet.

"You been a bad girl. You need to be punished. I'm going to cut you till you bleed, till you're begging me to stop. I know you want me, baby. Say

*it. And I'll squeeze you till your body is limp and
your heart stops pumping . . .''*

As Mallory continued reading, the letter became more
pornographic, the content more violent and obscene.
Mallory had lapsed into a childish sing-song. She held
the paper stiffly in front of her, fidgeting with her hair,
as if she were a schoolgirl forced to recite in class.

After about a minute, Howard Koppelman interrupted,
snatching the letter from her hands. "That's enough."

Anne heard people whispering. The buzz in the room
was almost palpable, like a strong electric current. She
sensed shock, confusion, titillation. And something else,
something dangerous.

"I don't understand," Jill said, looking upset. "Who
left this here? I didn't . . .''

"Who did this?" Mallory said, glaring at the party
guests. "Who did this? Who's trying to scare me?" Her
voice sounded husky, as if her throat were dry. Her eyes
were shining. She stared at Dakota, then shifted her gaze
to Howard. "You think I don't know what this is
about?" Mallory said angrily, looking around the room.
"So I made a few porn flicks once upon a time. You
think you're better than me because I got paid for taking
my clothes off?" Her voice quavered. Her arms were
wrapped tightly around her chest.

Anne glanced around the room. Who could have written the letter? Everyone seemed uncomfortable, even
Caitlin, who was pretending to study the books lodged
in a pine corner cupboard. Anne tried to read their expressions. Puzzlement, certainly, and embarrassment.
But Anne sensed they were embarrassed *by* Mallory, not
for her.

"I'm a big star," Mallory was shouting, her voice
edging into hysteria. "None of you would be here if it
weren't for me."

She snatched the letter from Howard Koppelman and
began to read it again, from the beginning. *Dear Slut.*

All of a sudden, Anne wanted to leave. The room was hot and airless. And Mallory was just getting warmed up. "I'm out of here," she whispered to Betty, whose mouth was hanging open, too stunned to finish her plate of chicken fingers.

As Anne headed for the door, she heard Mallory's high-pitched laugh, brittle as glass. Outside, the night was still. Stars pricked the black velvet sky.

Chapter 5

To avoid getting lipstick on your teeth, stick your index finger in your mouth, close your lips around it, and pull your finger out. Any excess lipstick will be instantly removed. Dry matte lipstick is much less likely to get on your teeth than creamier glosses.

Oceanside Heights looked especially pretty at night. Many of the houses in town were lit from the outside, so that the shutters and brackets, the sloping gables and ornate gingerbread trim, the widow's walks and turrets, were clearly outlined. Lace curtains fluttered from bay windows. Stained glass panels took on a soft, welcoming glow. And people sat in rocking chairs on their front porches, sharing gardening tips and gossip with their neighbors. There was an air of romance about the Victorian homes. With their fish-scale shingles, arched doorways, and decorative moldings, the houses had propelled the Heights to its status as a designated historic landmark. After dark, they looked like fairy tale cottages.

Anne had rolled down the top of her red '68 Mustang. As she drove through town, she took several deep breaths, inhaling the salty air. It was cooler by the beach. The breeze tickled her face, rearranged her hair. Driving north on Ocean Avenue, she headed to Landsdown Park. When she reached Grassmere Lake, she turned left, skirting the water as the road circled toward Landsdown. Back when she was a child, goldfish and turtles swam in the lake; water lilies flecked the surface, sprouting yellow crocuses that magically folded up each night and blossomed again each morning. There were boats shaped like swans that you could ride around in. Anne had drifted in the swan boats for hours at a time, lying on her back, counting clouds. But now the lake was polluted, one sign of Landsdown's corruption and decay.

Landsdown was a city where statistics flourished: highest crime rate in the state of New Jersey, lowest median household income, worst public recreation facilities, most drug busts, highest dropout rate. But the numbers told only half the story. To get a true feel for Landsdown, you had to see it for yourself—the abandoned, boarded-up buildings, vacant storefronts, garbage rotting in the streets. Crime gripped the city. Even at midday, people were afraid to walk by themselves, wary of what lurked behind the next crumbling house, of the violence that could erupt without warning.

Anne stuck to the main thoroughfares, driving fast. The streets were practically deserted and not well lit. Occasionally she passed a group of teenagers, getting high under the yellow glow of a street lamp, the music on their boom boxes cranked up full blast. But then there would be nothing for blocks on end, except vacant lots and torn up buildings with their windows ripped out,

their skeletal frames exposed, like the carcasses of dead
animals. At the corner of Marcus and Pitt, she made a
right. She slowed the car, trying to spot the numbers on
the houses. A full moon blazed in the sky, throwing a
dab of light on the pitch black street. And suddenly there
it was, 311 Pitt Street, the old Lovitz place. A small,
ramshackle one-story bungalow that tilted ominously to
the side as if it might collapse any minute. Weeds clotted
the tiny yard. A broken shutter flapped against the side
of the house. Somewhere nearby, a dog howled mournfully, followed by the sound of breaking glass. Anne
shivered. The street was empty, dark. All the houses
looked deserted. She'd have to come back in the day-
time, try to see if she could get into the bungalow. It
could prove helpful when it came to depicting Mallory's
childhood, a touchstone in deciphering the actress's psy-
che.

Making a U-turn, Anne doubled back toward downtown Landsdown. Two new apartment complexes had
been erected during the last several years, the byproduct
of a mayoral candidate who announced plans to rehab
thirty-five vacant buildings and "take back" the town.
At the end of his term, only two of them were com-
pleted. Anne was looking for one called the Landsdown
Arms. It came into view suddenly, a plain red brick ten-
story building with narrow metal terraces tacked onto its
facade. She parked directly in front, where she could
keep an eye on the car.

Inside the small vestibule she scanned the names on
the wall. "Lovitz, S" lived in apartment 4B. Anne
punched the buzzer, waited. One of the lights in front
of the building was out. The street was half dark, empty.
Not the safest place in the world to be hanging out, Anne
thought. She pressed the buzzer hard just as the outer
door of the building swung open.

An elderly, stoop-shouldered woman entered the vestibule. Anne moved aside so the woman could unlock

the inner door leading to the lobby. But the old lady didn't move.

"What do ya want?" she said to Anne.

"I'm looking for Sheila Lovitz."

"Sheila's not home."

Was this some sort of good neighbor policy? The woman's face sagged. Her filmy gray eyes surveyed Anne with suspicion. "You selling something?"

"I'm a friend of her sister."

The woman examined Anne from top to bottom, apparently trying to decide whether she was secretly concealing a set of Ginsu knives.

"You best come back at ten, ten-thirty," she said, finally.

"Is Sheila out to dinner?"

"Nah. She's over in Bradley Beach. At the bingo."

"Thanks," Anne said, on her way out.

She'd been meaning to interview Mallory's twin sister for days now. Mallory had talked a lot about her childhood, how troubled it was, how violent and bleak. Anne wanted to make sure she had all the facts. Just in case Mallory was embellishing the truth a bit for her fans, in case there were any grounds for a lawsuit.

Returning to the car, she headed back toward home. Landsdown was just north of the Heights; Bradley Beach was the next town to the south. It was a typical shore town, with a boardwalk, a smattering of seafood restaurants, and a population that tripled during the summertime. The bingo parlor was across the street from the beach. In all the years Anne had lived in the Heights, she'd never gone there. Actually, none of her neighbors played bingo. Although it was a relatively mild form of gambling, the churchgoing, God-fearing people in the Heights didn't care for it. But it was popular in Landsdown. When she got to the bingo hall, she had to park two blocks away because of all the cars lining the streets.

The hall itself was a narrow smoky room, outfitted with gray metal folding chairs and plywood tables laid end to end in rows. The place was nearly full. Seated at the tables were roughly a hundred people—blue-collar types, factory workers, maids, bus drivers, retired folks with modest pensions and stained teeth from a lifetime of chain smoking—hunched over cardboard cards and small sheets of paper on which various numbers were printed. They had the lined, worn-out faces of the poor. Not your typical tourist crowd. Some people had as many as twenty cards spread out in front of them. Anne wondered how many of them blew their pensions or welfare checks in a single night.

Hanging from the back wall was a large electric board; half the numbers on the board were lit up. A teenager in a baseball cap stood in front of a glass container filled with dozens of Ping-Pong balls that leaped in the air like popcorn frying in a pan. The boy reached his hand into the container and pulled out a white ball. "I 22," he announced into a microphone. Six television monitors posted around the sides of the room showed a close-up of the ball. There was a soft rustling sound as people who had I 22 on their cards filled in the space with plastic chips.

"Wanna buy a card?" said an old lady with three white hairs sprouting from her chin.

"No, thanks," Anne replied. "I don't feel lucky tonight."

She scanned the room, searching for Sheila Lovitz, and spotted her in the back because of her resemblance to Mallory, a young woman in denim overalls and a white T-shirt. Spread out on the table in front of her were several cards, dotted with small purple chips.

"Sheila?" Anne said, sitting down next to her.

"That'd be me." said the woman, without looking up. Her brown hair was parted in the middle. It fell forward, half hiding her face.

"My name's Anne Hardaway. I'm writing Mallory's autobiography, and I was wondering if I could ask you a few questions."

At the mention of Mallory's name, Sheila's chin jerked upward. She fixed her clear blue eyes on Anne. The resemblance was uncanny. Same cheekbones, same pouty lips. The only difference was her hair. Where Mallory's was long and blond, Sheila's hung to her shoulders and was a mousy, undistinguished shade of brown. If Mallory was a cosmetics queen, Sheila had an earthy beauty, a natural-looking glow. Her face was entirely devoid of makeup, making her seem younger than Mallory, although of course they were the exact same age.

"I'm sorta busy right now."

"Could I talk to you another time then? When it's more convenient?"

"Nope. Not interested," Sheila said flatly.

"B 12," intoned the teenager, holding up a Ping-Pong ball for inspection, as if the crowd doubted his word.

"Bingo," someone shouted.

Sheila Lovitz picked up an odd-looking plastic tube from the table and swept her hand deftly across the cards. The plastic chips stuck to the tube. Within seconds she had collected every last one of them. After she'd finished, she turned and looked at Anne.

"If you want to know anything about Marcia, you better ask her yourself," Sheila said, smiling a little. She sat up straight in her chair, her shoulders back, as if there was an invisible string between her spine and the top of her head. "By the way, you've got lipstick on your teeth."

Anne pulled a small mirror from her handbag. On her left front tooth was a streak of Cinnamon Surprise gloss. *Damn.* She'd probably been walking around like this all night. She pulled out a tissue and wiped the tooth clean. This was the absolute last time she'd experiment with eye shadow and lip gloss. The last time.

"Your sister's got me thinking about makeup," Anne said, by way of an explanation. "I'd like to talk to you about growing up with Marcia, how your childhood was, stuff like that."

Sheila's eyes crinkled in merriment. "Our childhood sucked." She laughed. "We were raised by a woman who should have been locked up."

"On what charge?"

"Being an unfit mother, for starters. Physical abuse. Drugs. You name it. Didn't Marcia tell you that?"

"The next game's a fifty-fifty special," the teenager at the microphone said. "Winner gets half of tonight's receipts. A grand total of $667."

Sheila spread some paper cards out on the table. "This is my best event," she said excitedly.

"The first number," the boy said, "is O 61."

Sheila grabbed a yellow marker from a plastic bag filled with chips. Her hand flew over the papers, pausing briefly on each square to check if she had the number.

"What's the most you've ever won?" Anne asked.

"Twelve hundred dollars."

"Seems like you could shell out a lot of money each night on the cards."

"Absolutely," Sheila agreed. "Ten games a night. Say you spend about ten, fifteen dollars a game. It adds up."

"How many games are left?"

"Three: Double bingo. The letter T. And the full-card grand prize."

Anne raised her hand, signaling to the old woman who had been walking around the hall selling cards.

"I'll take a sheet of ten for the next game," Anne said.

"You feeling lucky after all?"

Anne glanced sideways at Sheila Lovitz. "Maybe."

The Blue Marlin restaurant on Route 35 in Bradley Beach served authentic Jamaican cuisine: jerk chicken, plantains, conch chowder. It was a friendly, low key place, with lackadaisical service and a tropical mural painted on the wall that substituted for miles of banana groves and the sun-bleached shores of Montego Bay.

Anne stirred her daiquiri idly. The more Sheila talked, the more it became clear how different she was from her sister. Sheila taught fourth grade at Landsdown Park Elementary School, where metal detectors didn't do much to deter kids from showing up with knives, box cutters, and the occasional gun. Sheila had been mugged twice in the parking lot. Now she carried a spray can of Mace and a set of car keys that sounded a screeching alarm at the press of a button. She lived in a one-bedroom rental apartment in the Landsdown Arms with a tortoise, six angel fish, and a one-eyed cat named Harry she'd rescued from the back of a car that had been stripped for parts and set on fire. She didn't date much, didn't get out much, in fact, except for bingo, which she played religiously, three nights a week. Her last relationship had been with a high school baseball coach who spoke hopefully of marriage and then left town abruptly, leaving no forwarding address. She talked so much and so openly that Anne wondered whether she had many friends to confide in.

"Men," Sheila complained, taking a sip of Red Stripe beer. "You can't live with 'em. And you can't pretend they don't get on your nerves."

"I guess your sister's had the same problem," Anne said, steering the conversation where she wanted it to go.

"Yeah. But the difference is Marcia never gets dumped. She always manages to land on her feet."

"How often do the two of you see each other?"

"Once every couple of years. We're not very close."

"Have you been on the set at all?" Anne asked. "I don't remember seeing you around."

"I've been meaning to drop by. But I haven't had time." Sheila cupped her chin in her hand and frowned. "Actually," she corrected herself. "That's a lie. I've had plenty of time. I just didn't want to."

Anne looked at her expectantly.

"Marcia . . . Mallory . . . is a little too much to take

sometimes. She puts on this whole movie star act. But she forgets I knew her when. I hate it when she lords it over me that she's a hotshot now, making gobs of money. Going to fancy Hollywood parties, like they show on *ET*. Ever watch that program? It's not bad, if you're into fluff.''

"You don't seem like you are."

Sheila threw her head back and laughed. "Hardly. It's a big deal for me if my kids can read at the first-grade level or if they make it through the year without getting shot. I drive a beat-up Chevy. Everything I own can just about fit in the trunk. You know where I go on vacation? Atlantic City. Big whoop, right? It's not exactly St. Bart's or Bali. But then, I'm not exactly the wild type. The last party I went to was in honor of our principal's retirement."

Anne signaled the waitress and ordered a slice of sweet potato pie and a second daiquiri. "Another beer?" she asked Sheila.

"Why not?"

When the waitress walked away, Anne said: "Teaching requires a lot of dedication. You must really like it."

"I hang in, do what I can to help. A couple of us started a scholarship program with a local bank. It's a special fund. The bank matches what we put in, to try to send some of these kids to college. I know it sounds corny, but if you can get to them early, I mean really get through to them, you can make a difference."

"Has Mallory contributed?"

Sheila gave a tired laugh. "Are you kidding? The only person Mallory looks out for is Mallory. When we were kids, she was the class bully. She'd pick fights with kids twice her size. Other girls were scared of her." Sheila stared intently at Anne. "Guess that's not going in your book."

Anne shrugged. "Why not? It's about Mallory's life, warts and all."

"Yeah? Then there's something you ought to know about my sister."

"What's that?"

"She doesn't take kindly to anything that shows her in an unflattering light. No criticism, no hint she's ever done anything bad."

"But she's told me all kinds of negative things about herself. There was her drug addiction, her suicide attempts, her failed marriages. She's hardly a poster child for perfection."

"I bet Mallory put her own special spin on her problems," Sheila said darkly. "How everyone done her wrong. Poor misunderstood Mallory, growing up in a dog-eat-dog world. Trust me. She's the dirtiest dog of them all."

Anne studied Sheila carefully. Mallory's twin sister appeared perfectly amiable, except for the vein of resentment she'd been mining for years. A while back, Anne had ghosted a book for a radio talk show psychologist called *My Sister, Myself* that was all about sibling rivalry. She'd learned identical twins often harbor intense feelings of jealousy toward each other, even when the two siblings share a close, loving relationship. When they didn't, hostilities escalated. "I get the feeling there's more you're not telling me," Anne said.

The corners of Sheila's mouth tightened, her blue eyes flashed like glazed porcelain. "Why dredge up ancient history?"

"Why not?" Anne countered lightly. "How often do you get the chance to rake your sister over the coals?"

Over the years, she'd found that given the chance, people would tell you the most personal, intimate things about themselves. Chalk it up to ego, loneliness, sheer stupidity. Why tell a perfect stranger your most private secrets? Right now, Anne had to admit she felt a little guilty pumping Sheila. But not guilty enough to stop. After all, she told herself, the facts were what mattered.

A few facts and a deadline equaled one best-selling autobiography.

Sheila appeared to think it over. "You're right," she said slowly. "Although it's not exactly hot gossip anymore. I couldn't sell it to *A Current Affair*, like those nudie pictures someone got hold of. Still . . ." She paused, as if imagining the possibilities. "Okay, here it is. Mallory stole my fiance. She married him. Then she up and dumped him, when he wasn't any use to her anymore."

"You mean . . ."

"His name was Gerald Finch. My high school sweetheart. The love of my life. I was supposed to go out to California with him. Have two kids, a dog, the whole enchilada. But then Mallory entered the picture. Before I knew what hit me, she'd convinced him he was really in love with *her*."

"And the one-way ticket out of Landsdown, that was hers, too."

"You got it. 'Course, the marriage didn't last long. Three years, four months, and one week, but who's counting?"

"I knew Gerald in high school," Anne said. "He seemed like a nice guy." Actually he was a nerd who'd blended into the background. But this was good stuff. She couldn't wait to hear Mallory's take on it.

"When Gerry moved back here, to the Heights," Sheila continued, "I tried to start things up again. We went out a couple of times, but I could tell he wasn't interested. He's still hung up on Mallory."

"Is that right?"

"Sure. He never married. I think he dates less than I do, if that's humanly possible. Once she'd managed to worm her way into his bloodstream, it was like slow-acting poison. The poor guy's still got it bad."

"Mallory never mentioned that," Anne mused.

"Does she even know you're talking to me right now?"

"Nope."

Sheila took a swig of beer. "Well, I wouldn't tell her if I were you."

"Because she'd turn on me next?"

"Bingo," Sheila said, with a grin.

Chapter 6

The sun streamed through Anne's bedroom window at 5:15 A.M., dappling the white coverlet with light. Her bedroom faced east, with a glorious view of the ocean. The beach was deserted at this hour. Pink streaks smudged the sky as dawn broke over the water, which changed from brackish green to an aquamarine hue that meant the start of another beautiful day.

Anne pulled the pillow over her head and considered going back to sleep. She and Sheila had stayed at the Blue Marlin until midnight, when the restaurant closed, and then had continued their discussion on the Bradley

Beach boardwalk, where Anne had taken out her tape player and asked if she could record the conversation. She'd felt conflicted about it, since Sheila was divulging all sorts of intimate information about herself, her past, and her famous sister. If you handed people enough rope, chances were they'd hang themselves. Which didn't mean she was thrilled to play hangman.

Anne found she liked Sheila, even felt a little sorry for her. It couldn't have been easy, growing up in Mallory's shadow, watching Mallory catch the breaks. After all these years, Sheila was still bitter about losing Gerald Finch. Bitter and angry. She couldn't seem to move on with her own life because Mallory had taken the most important thing in it.

By the time Anne had gotten home, it was after two. Although she was dog-tired now, the show outside drew her to the window. Orange and scarlet ribbons billowed across the horizon. The sky blushed pink as light flooded the beach, illuminating the sand, the piers, the waves licking the shore. She'd lived in the Heights for thirty-seven years, and sunrises still had the power to delight her, just as they did when she was a child. Settling on the window seat, she watched the sky blaze and ebb, the colors fading into a soft eggshell blue that spread like a wash applied to canvas.

Just as she was about to turn away, her eye fastened on a solitary figure. A little farther down the beach, large moss-covered rocks stretched from the water's edge to an orange buoy about fifty feet from shore. There was someone on the rocks. A woman from the looks of it, picking her way carefully over the jagged, slippery stones. Anne couldn't see the woman's face. But something in the way she carried herself made Anne think of the Lovitz sisters—a prideful way of walking, head up, shoulders back. The woman wore baggy jeans, sneakers, and a baggy green plaid shirt. Her hair was tucked under a baseball cap. Without warning, sea spray reared up and splashed her. She stumbled slightly, recovered her balance. Turning, she headed back toward shore, moving slowly as she struggled to establish her footing.

Anne opened the window higher and stuck her head out. "Hey," she called out. "Mallory? . . . Sheila?"

The woman didn't answer. She probably couldn't hear with the wind blowing hard off the ocean. By this time she'd made it back to shore and was walking quickly toward the north end of the beach.

Anne came away from the window. It probably wasn't either Lovitz. Mallory would never have dressed so shabbily, and it was unlikely Sheila would pay a visit to the Heights. Anne threw on a tank top, shorts, and sneakers. Grabbing her Walkman, she went outside and did some quick stretches on the front lawn. She went running three or four times a week, usually right before breakfast. Her favorite route was along the boardwalk, followed by a loop around Grassmere Lake. It was a scenic run, with the ocean on one side, and one mile of piquant Victoriana on the other. Today she had to take a detour down Embury Street, since the film crew was setting up around the lake. She briefly considered sprinting by the supercilious production assistant at the corner of Embury and Ocean Avenue, but thought better of it. No sense alienating the aliens. She ran more slowly than usual, perspiring in the heat. It was going to be another scorcher.

When she got home, she took a quick shower, then fixed herself scrambled eggs, a toasted English muffin, and a cup of coffee. After she'd eaten, she left a voice mail message for Phil Smedley, telling him what Mallory had said about Dakota's lip-synching. Then she sat down in front of the computer and rewound her tape recorder. In a few moments, Sheila Lovitz's voice filled the room.

". . . later on, she told me she never loved him. It was all a game to her," Sheila was saying. "A selfish little game."

Anne played it back, created a new file in the computer, and began to type.

It was late afternoon when a sharp knock sounded on her front door. She got up and opened it. Betty Flugelhorn was standing on the porch. Her eyes shone like two dark raisins in the pudgy folds of her face.

"Can you believe it?" Betty said breathlessly. "Have you heard?"

"Heard what?"

"Oh, God. You don't know. Where have you been all day?"

"Right here. Working on the book."

"Mallory's missing. She's disappeared."

Anne looked at Betty, stunned. She felt as though she'd been sucker punched. Ushering Betty inside, she closed the door and led the way to the living room. Betty plopped down on the faded chintz sofa. Her hair was messy, her hands fluttered in the air, like errant hummingbirds.

Anne sat down in an adjoining armchair. "What do you mean Mallory's *gone*? Did she leave a note?"

"Nope. Her bed hasn't been slept in. Her car's not here. Koppelman is beside himself. This'll set production back even further."

Anne couldn't believe it. If Mallory flaked, there'd be no book. Period. She glanced at her watch. Five-twenty. Mallory wouldn't be arriving for the promised interview. *Damn*.

To Betty, she said, "How do you know she's left for good? She might have gone for a drive or something."

"No one's seen her all day. She had a hair appointment with me at six this morning. She never showed."

Anne frowned. She thought back to the woman she'd seen on the rocks. Could it have been Mallory? It was possible. But why would the actress be wandering the beach at dawn dressed like that? "When's the last time you saw her?" Anne asked.

"Last night, at the party. I left about one, when it was breaking up."

"How did she seem?"

Betty paused, wrinkling her nose as if she smelled sour milk. "Imperious. Bitchy. Her queen of the manor routine."

"She didn't seem upset?"

"Oh, you mean about that horrible letter. What a gross thing to do." Betty opened her handbag and pulled out a package of Ring Dings. Ripping open the cellophane, she popped one in her mouth. "I sure hope they find the sicko who wrote it."

Anne thought back to last night. She remembered feeling a twinge of worry when Mallory had read it aloud. Worry and disgust. And something else. Something dangerous. "What's the buzz on the set?" she asked. "What are people saying?"

"Well, theory number one is that Mallory knows the picture is going to bomb and decided to bail early."

Anne shook her head. "Mallory has a lot riding on this movie. She wouldn't just walk away."

"Okay. That brings us to theory number two." Betty's eyes glinted with excitement. She simulated a drum roll on the oak coffee table. "The illicit affair." Anne watched Betty intently. The hairdresser had a self-satisfied I've-got-a-secret look. The one thing she loved more than food was gossip. "Mallory is cheating on Dakota," Betty announced triumphantly.

"How do you know?"

"A couple of times this week, I saw traces of dark hair dye under her French manicure, first thing in the morning. Dakota doesn't dye his hair."

"But Mallory does, right? She's not a natural blond."

Betty drew herself up stiffly. She looked as if she'd been slapped. "I'll have you know I use only the finest peroxides, not cheap store-bought stuff."

"Aren't there other reasons why she might have dye on her hands?"

Betty looked at Anne defiantly. "I can't name one. Besides," she said, munching on the second Ring Ding, "I've seen this kind of thing before. Forget lipstick on a hankie. Hair dye on the hands is twice as incriminating. Some of my clients have had their husbands followed because I tipped them off to the dye. It gets under the fingernails and it's wicked hard to get out."

"Okay. I'll bite. Who do we know that dyes their hair?"

"Koppelman, for one. He's got a lot of gray. And Nick Fabien. Nick's vain, but too cheap to spring for two-color processing." Betty thought a moment. "Oh, and that creepy guy who's always hanging around the set."

"Which creepy guy?"

"Mallory's first husband."

"Gerald Finch?"

"Yeah. He's still got a thing for her, if you ask me. He's always lurking around, making lovesick faces at Mallory, like a puppy who can't find his way home."

"Really? I've never seen Gerald on the set."

"Trust me. He's there. He comes around early in the morning, when Mallory's getting her face put on."

Interesting, Anne thought. She was gradually discovering a whole new side of Gerald Finch. If he was still hung up on Mallory, could he have something to do with her disappearance?

"Let's assume you're right," she said. "Even if Mallory's having an affair, I don't think she'd risk tanking her career to run off with a lover. Not when she could divorce Dakota and take up with whoever she wants."

Stuffing the remaining bits of cake in her mouth, Betty used a tissue to dab at the crumbs. "Which brings us to theory number three," she said briskly. "The kidnapping scenario."

"Go on," Anne said cautiously

Betty could barely contain her excitement. "The big boys at the studio took her," she said dramatically. "La

Loving was sinking the picture, causing more delays. So they decided it'd be best if she took a dive."

"You mean we're going to find her body in some swamp near the Meadowlands?" Anne said in disbelief.

"Hey, you've never been out to Hollywood. Some of those studio boys play pretty rough."

"You know what I think? I think Mallory probably went for a joy ride down the shore and lost track of time. Or she heard about a Prada sale at the Short Hills mall and couldn't resist."

Even as she spoke, she knew it didn't ring true. There was no way Mallory would miss a hair and makeup session voluntarily. Hair and makeup were her life. What if Mallory was hooked on drugs again? Was she off on a bender, popping uppers in some cheap dive?

Aloud, she said, "Let's head over to the set and see what's going on."

"Okay by me," Betty said, rising. "But could I get a beverage first? Chocolate makes me thirsty."

"Sure," Anne said. "I've just got to save something to disk." She waved her hand in the direction of the kitchen. "There's soda in the refrigerator."

Anne went into her office and walked over to the file box that held her floppy disks. She rifled through the contents, looking for the red one containing her notes on *Loving You*. The disk wasn't there. She perused the box twice, then bent down to search the shelf underneath her workstation. Everything was in its place—the tech support books on computers, the extra box of blank disks, the new printer cartridges, the stacks of copy paper. Don't panic, she told herself. It had to be here somewhere. She walked around the room, sifting through papers and books on her desk. From the kitchen, she heard the clatter of plates, the sound of Betty helping herself to leftovers. It had to be here somewhere. Only it wasn't.

On impulse, she sat down at the computer and called up her Mallory Loving file. She kept two copies of everything—one on the hard drive and one on disk, in case the computer crashed. Her files were gone. How could that be? She'd been transcribing her notes, along with the tapes Mallory had made, onto the computer since they'd first started working together a week and a half ago. Could the machine have screwed up and deleted her files? She looked in the computer's recycling bin, where all the purged files were sent, until another command zapped them from the screen permanently. Nothing, zilch. Anne's head began to pound. Her stomach felt queasy. Ten days of work erased. All she had left was the list of beauty tips Mallory had given her, only because she hadn't bothered to type them into the computer.

She ran over to her desk and opened the bottom drawer where she kept the Mallory audio tapes. They weren't there.

She took a deep breath and faced facts. There was no mistake. The files on *Loving You* were gone.

Howard Koppelman had exhausted his store of patience. Since *Dark Horizon* began filming, Anne had seen him coax performances from his cast under a host of trying conditions—thunderstorms, damaged equipment, sound problems, lighting snafus. He reminded Anne of the Little Dutch Boy. Only this time the dike had sprung an unpluggable leak. The director was pacing back and forth like a caged polar bear at the zoo, his hands clenched into fists. He looked like he was about to punch somebody out.

"Jesus Christ!" Koppelman shouted to his assistant, who was standing right beside him. "What the hell are we supposed to do?"

It was close to midnight, and still no sign of the missing actress. Some of the actors and crew had gathered on the lawn of the house Mallory was renting. The porch lights were on, illuminating sandwich wrappers and empty paper cups, traces of a hastily eaten supper. Crickets chirped mournfully in the tall grass; moths fluttered near the house, beating their wings against the glass. The night was sultry and still. Even the breeze felt hot and dry.

Caitlin Grey sidled up to the director and squeezed his arm sympathetically. "Mallory will be back, Mr. Koppelman," Caitlin said in a reassuring tone. "I mean, where would she go?"

Koppelman smiled tightly. "If I knew the answer to that, I wouldn't be standing here like an idiot."

Mallory's disappearance had cost the film another full-day delay. They'd tried to shoot around her absence, filming exterior locations, what Koppelman called "picturesque shit," and ended up wasting most of the morning and afternoon. Mallory was in nearly every scene. It was hard to pretend she didn't exist.

Spotting Jill Bentley, Koppelman crossed the lawn. "Where the hell is she?" he barked. "Are you covering for her?"

Jill's pants suit was wrinkled. Her face wore the distracted expression of a mother who discovers her child has wandered off. "I called everyone I could think of, everyplace Mal might have gone," she said wearily. "I don't know any more than you do."

"We could notify the police, report a missing person," Caitlin piped up.

"And announce to the world that this film is in trouble?" Howard said. "No thanks." He turned on his heel and walked over to where Anne and Betty were sitting on lawn chairs. "This is some publicity stunt you and Mallory dreamed up, isn't it?" he said to Anne. "A way to get some ink for that goddamn book."

His face appeared haggard and worn. Anne realized for the first time that he wasn't as young as he looked, probably pushing fifty. Why did he look so worried every time he mentioned the book?

"I can't work if Mallory's not here," Anne said. "How am I supposed to write it if she's missing?"

"Mal's a media whore," Howard countered. "She'd do anything to get her face in the papers."

Quite a change, Anne noted, from the usual party line. With Mallory missing, he didn't have to pretend she was so wonderful anymore.

"Still . . ." Jill cut in. "She would have told me if she'd been planning something. I'm in charge of her daily schedule."

"Have you considered that Mallory might have been abducted?" Betty interjected.

"Abducted?" Howard repeated. "What on earth for?"

Several crew members edged closer. It occurred to Anne that if Mallory were around, they wouldn't be there. She wasn't the type who socialized with the people hired to make her look good.

"That letter she received last night," Anne said. "It wasn't exactly a love note."

While she'd initially dismissed Betty's theory, she was starting to become concerned. Mallory had been missing for nearly twenty-four hours. And someone had broken in and stolen Anne's files. Were the two related? She'd asked her neighbors if they'd seen anyone lurking around her house. No one had. She'd also had the locks changed. But her uneasiness lingered. It gave her the creeps to think of somebody going through her desk, touching her things.

"You know, you might be right," Jill said. "Mallory's gotten several of these notes."

They all turned to stare at her.

"Oh, my God!" Betty exclaimed. "She's been kidnapped."

"The notes are upstairs," Jill said. "I'll go get them." She trotted toward the steps and disappeared inside the house. Even in the midst of a crisis, she retained her take-charge attitude.

"Do you mean to tell me that some kind of sex fiend kidnapped Mallory?" Howard said sarcastically. With a wave of his hand, he dismissed the suggestion as ludicrous. "It's probably the other way around. She's run off with some stud and they're humping like rabbits right this minute."

Betty glanced at Anne and raised an eyebrow, as if to say, "I told you so."

"Do you know if she's been seeing someone?" Anne said to Howard.

"You mean is she cheating on her husband? Who knows? Mallory's always looking for the new best thing. Best script. Best part. Best lay." He glared up at the moon and scowled. Swatting a mosquito away from his face, he continued his restless pacing. Anne could almost hear him tabulating the losses in his head. If they were so far over budget, would his salary be cut? Would he ultimately be held responsible?

When Jill finally reemerged from the house holding a packet of letters, Howard bounded over to her and grabbed them. As everybody stood around and watched, he read each one. It seemed to take a long time. After he'd finished, his expression was pained.

"Here," Howard said suddenly, thrusting the letters at Anne. "You're a writer. What do you make of these?"

Anne walked toward the porch light to have a better look. The letters were typed, single-spaced, and enclosed in standard white envelopes. All were dated, but unsigned.

She scanned them quickly, reading trite declarations of love. *I want you. I need you. I can't live without you.* The last one was different, more graphic, more violent. Phrases jumped out at her. Ugly phrases about Mallory's anatomy and what the letter writer would do to her when he got her alone.

Anne pictured Mallory trapped and helpless, cowering beneath a man, her clothes torn, her eyes riveted to the knife as it hovered in the air and slashed down, down, tearing at her skin.

"It's a joke, right?" Jill said hopefully.

"No," Anne said. "No. I don't think so."

Howard Koppelman sank down on the porch steps. The fight seemed to have been knocked out of him. "Jesus H. Christ," he muttered under his breath. "Game's over. Let's call the cops."

Chapter 7

*Blush no-no's: Never
smile and put blush on
the "apple" of your
cheeks. It can create a
clown-like appearance.
Never blush your nose.
Never apply blush to bare
skin. It should go over
your foundation for a
smooth, natural look.*

After seventeen years on the force, Detective Mark Trasker of the Neptune Township Sheriff's Office had witnessed his share of bizarre cases, including any number of unexplained disappearances: teenage runaways, rich businessmen who ran off to the Caymans with mistresses in tow, disgruntled housewives who walked out of their lives as easily as snakes shed their skin.

"Why'd they do it?" he asked rhetorically, tapping his pen against his spiral notebook. He was sitting in Anne's living room wearing a dark gray suit, one leg crossed casually over the other. His striped blue-and-crimson tie gave him a faintly preppy air. "Years of unhappiness, I'd suspect. Until one day, they thought: 'Aahhh, if I had a way out, things would be different.' Like a snake shedding its skin. And they *were* different, of course. Not better. Different. Still," he added, "those were the ones who went of their own accord, who weren't coerced, kidnapped, abducted. Or murdered."

He was in his late forties, tall and wiry, with skin the color of cocoa beans, and he reminded Anne of an actor in a movie she'd watched the other night on television. A Denzel Washington type. She didn't know what she'd expected in a detective—someone more rumpled, with nicotine-stained fingers. Not this self-assured man, with his cool impenetrable manner and a way of taking in his surroundings without seeming to care much about them.

"You think Mallory Loving vanished without a trace because she wanted a change of scenery?" Anne asked him.

"No, I don't," Detective Trasker said. His eyes rarely left Anne's face. For some reason she couldn't explain, it made her uncomfortable. "Although certainly, it's been known to happen. I had a case a few years back. Fashion designer vacationing in Spring Lake. You might have heard about it."

Anne remembered the story. It had been in all the papers. The designer had built an empire creating lacy, transparent dresses that showed undergarments beneath. He'd left his companion and a billion-dollar business and disappeared midway though his vacation, only to turn up seven months later on the Italian island of Sardinia, herding goats and extolling the virtues of a simpler life.

"And of course, there's the Pogue case."

Anne nodded. Lynette Pogue, a thirty-one-year-old Kmart sales clerk from Landsdown Park, had vanished four days earlier on her lunch break. When last seen, she had been leaving McDonald's with a Quarter Pounder, large fries, and a vanilla shake. Anne had read that Lynette was divorced, with no boyfriends to speak of, and no relatives except an elderly, retired uncle who lived in Freehold and was a permanent fixture at the Monmouth Park track. The police were still trying to explain Lynette's disappearance.

Anne tried to recall what she'd read in the papers. "She was sick, right?"

"Cancer. Her friends think she may have tried to kill herself. But there's no evidence of that, and no body." Detective Trasker shifted in his chair. "The Loving case is different. For one thing, there are the letters."

"Have you analyzed them?"

It struck Anne that the detective had been in her house an awfully long time. She'd told him about the woman she'd seen on the beach early yesterday morning, about her stolen notes. It hadn't taken long. So why had he been rambling on for nearly an hour, as if they were old college chums instead of virtual strangers? She got the feeling that he was playing some sort of game with her, weighing each of her responses. What did he hope to gain? She looked at Trasker closely. He gazed back at her. Anne could see him sizing her up, taking a mental inventory of who she was and what she wanted. Well, what she wanted most right now was to know Mallory's whereabouts. The actress had been gone for a day and a half. In the meantime, *Loving You* was still very much a go. In fact, according to Phil, Mallory's disappearance made the book more marketable. A hotter property, he'd called it.

"We ran the letters by our Threat Assessment Unit," said Detective Trasker. "They entered them into a computer system called MOSAIC. Grades the nuts who write these things in seven categories, from your garden variety neurotic to highly dangerous psychopaths. Wonderful little software program, actually." The corners of Trasker's mouth widened slightly in what passed for a smile. "Very thorough."

"And . . . ?"

"Since she's been in Oceanside Heights, Miss Loving
has received six of these letters in all. There have been
others over the years. Fan mail, mostly. Men who liked
her . . . uh, earlier movies, if you catch my drift. But
nothing serious. At least not according to the current
husband or her second husband, Mr. . . . ." The detective
consulted his notebook. ". . . Koppelman. The computer
grades the letters, so to speak, puts them through a series
of tests to try and get a personality profile of the writer."

Again, Anne wondered why Trasker was explaining
this to her. Because she was working on Mallory's autobiography? Because he knew more than he was telling? He *seemed* friendly enough, but she didn't trust
him. It was almost as though he were baiting a trap for
her, offering bite-size morsels of information.

"You know, Detective," she said, "for the past hour,
you've been looking at me like the cat who swallowed
the canary. Do you have a theory about what happened
to Mallory? What is it you're leaving out?"

"I'm just trying to get the facts straight," Trasker said
coolly. He was staring at her intently, as if he could see
right through her. To her horror, she felt herself starting
to blush.

"Do you have any leads?" she said, wondering why
he was able to unnerve her.

"We're canvassing all the hotels and motels within a
hundred-mile radius of here. But so far, there's no sign
of Miss Loving. In the meantime, the computer found
that the first five letters were written by someone who
fits the profile of a jilted lover. There's an obsessive
thread running through them. The writer seems to know
quite a bit about her. What she likes, what she doesn't
like. My guess is they were written by someone who
knows her. Or by someone who's read everything that's
ever been written about her."

"Could this person be dangerous?" she asked.

The detective leaned forward and rested his elbows

on his knees. There were neat, straight creases in his trousers. "That depends. Sometimes we find these types of people are caught up in what's known as eroto-mania. Their interest in the victim has little to do with sexual eroticism. It's more of a fantasy, really. They come home from work, have a glass of wine, light a few candles, and toss off a letter to the woman they're obsessed with. In the worst cases, there are threatening phone calls. Sometimes as many as fifty a day. There might be some destruction of property, threats made. That sort of thing."

"So you're talking about a stalker?"

"In a sense. Forty to fifty percent of all stalking cases are celebrity-related. Actors. Actresses. TV news personalities. Weather girls. In the most serious cases, there's some physical contact with the celebrity. Here, there wasn't. Or at least there hadn't been until Miss Loving disappeared."

Detective Trasker paused. He looked around the room, taking in the grandfather clock, the cherrywood cabinet, the quilt draped over the floral wing chair, all the old furniture she'd inherited from her mother. Dowdy, shabby stuff she'd lived with all her life. She wondered what he made of it, of her.

"Go on," she said.

"This last letter is different. We think it was written by someone else, someone unconnected with the other five. There's more anger in the last letter. More vulgarity and intent to harm. According to the computer profile, it was written by someone who posed a real danger to Miss Loving."

"Could this person have abducted her?"

"Possibly. Although usually there's more of a pattern, more letters sent over time. More threats." Mark Trasker looked around the living room again. "You mentioned earlier that your files had been stolen."

"Yes." Thinking about the break-in still made her nervous. She hated to imagine someone prowling around her house. What if she'd been home? Would she have been abducted, too? Or worse? "Ten days' worth of notes. My disk and tapes are missing. The stuff on the hard drive was erased."

"I'd like to take a look around."

"Sure." Rising, Anne led Detective Trasker to the small first-floor bedroom that she'd converted into an office. Along one wall was the Gateway 2000 computer she'd purchased the previous spring with half her advance from Mary Lou Popper's household hints book. It was a great improvement over her old machine. Her current software program had plenty of bells and whistles. It did everything but write books for her. The next thing she planned to buy was a color laser printer to replace her seven-year-old black-and-white ink-jet one. Only she'd have to wait for the second half of her *Loving You* advance check. Right now, she was flat broke.

"The last time you saw your notes was when, exactly?" the detective asked as he sat down in front of the computer.

Anne thought for a moment. Mallory had disappeared on Tuesday night. The last time she'd seen the red floppy disk containing taped conversations for *Loving You* was on Tuesday afternoon, several hours before Mallory's birthday party. "Two days ago."

Snapping open his briefcase, he took out a black kit. From it, removed a large fluffy brush, a vial of black powder, and a blank index card. "We would usually have a technician do this," Trasker explained. "But we've had some cutbacks in the department."

He dipped the tip of the brush into the powder, then brushed the dust lightly onto the surface of the keyboard.

"That's not going to damage the machine is it?" Anne said worriedly. She couldn't afford to replace the keyboard.

"It shouldn't. Are both doors usually locked when you're not here?"

"Yes."

He took a piece of tape from the kit and pressed down on the keys.

"Anyone else have access to the house?"

"My friend Helen has a key."

In one quick motion he lifted the tape and pressed it down hard on the edge of the index card. "She in the habit of using your computer?"

"Not that I know of."

He repeated the procedure with the powder, brush, and tape several more times. Then he took out a pen and wrote something on the index card. "What about the windows?"

"They wouldn't have been locked. But as you can see, my house is right across from the beach. Anyone trying to get in through the windows or break in forcibly would attract attention. I asked my neighbors if they noticed anyone entering or leaving my house Tuesday night. No one did."

Trasker nodded. "I'll need a set of prints from you as well."

He took hold of Anne's hand and pressed the second and third fingers onto what looked like a dark ink blotter, then transferred the prints to an index card and labeled them.

"And nothing else was stolen?" he asked. "Jewelry? Cash? Electronic equipment?"

"No."

He pressed her thumb and fourth finger onto the blotter, then did the same with the first four fingers on her left hand. Then he put the index cards and the kits back in his briefcase.

"Don't use the keyboard for a while," he said, "in case we have to come back and dust again."

Great, Anne thought. The last thing she'd written in longhand was a book report on the impact of the Industrial Revolution in Charles Dickens's *Hard Times*, back in twelfth grade.

"Do you have any idea who stole your notes?" Trasker asked.

"Well, Mallory was promising to dish a lot of dirt. That's the whole point of *Loving You*, why my publisher thinks it'll be a best-seller. She was giving readers the lowdown on her exes, her costars, the Hollywood big shots she'd met over the years." She told him what Mallory had said about Dakota's voice.

"You think the husband could be involved in her disappearance?"

"I honestly don't know."

Trasker looked around Anne's office. His eye rested on the black Royal typewriter on a stand in the corner. He walked over to it and ran his fingers lightly over the keys. "You had this long?"

"It belonged to my grandfather. He was a poet." Actually, she had great affection for the manual typewriter. It was a little like the Heights—old-fashioned, out-of-date, but endearing nonetheless.

Trasker took a sheet of blank paper from the computer table and rolled it into the typewriter. "You know, you could probably get a couple of hundred bucks for this baby. It's a genuine antique."

He hit the carriage a couple of times and began to type, hunt-and-peck style. She drew closer and looked over his shoulder at what he'd written: *The quick brown fox jumped over the lazy white dog.*

"Remember this one?" Trasker said. Bending over, he slid the paper out of the machine.

"What do you think they teach in typing class today?" Anne asked. "*Bill Gates will soon rule the world*?"

"Could be."

Trasker folded the paper neatly and put it in his breast pocket. Removing a card from his wallet, he handed it to her. "Here's where you can reach me," he said. "Remember to lock your doors and windows." She thought she detected a self-satisfied glint in his eyes. As if he were baiting her somehow. "Take care of yourself."

After the detective left, Anne went over the theft once more in her mind. Whoever had broken into her house on Tuesday night must have done so between the time she'd left to get her makeover at five o'clock, and the time she got home from Bradley Beach, at about two A.M. Trasker had found no sign of forced entry. Her front door had been locked when she got home, just as usual. The thief must have come through the back door or through a window. Either way, someone had managed to erase all traces of *Loving You.*

She went to the phone and dialed the number of the Central Bank of New Jersey. Helen picked up on the first ring. "Hi," Anne said. "It's me. Are you busy?"

"Not especially. I'm taking a coffee break. What's up?"

"Do you still have that extra key I gave you? The key to my house?"

"Sure. It should be right here, in my pocketbook. Hold on a sec." Anne heard Helen rustling through her bag. "Yup. Here it is. Right on my key ring."

"I thought so. But I wanted to check. I can't figure out how someone broke in here without anybody noticing and reporting a prowler."

"You're not kidding. Especially with the eagle eyes in our neighborhood. I swear, old Mrs. Torrance on my block manages to drop by every time Charlie and I have a fight. She does it deliberately. Eavesdrops on us from across the way, and then rings the bell to borrow a cup of sugar. Hah! I've told her a hundred times I use Sweet 'n Low. I bet she even knows what's in our garbage."

"My neighbors are the exact same way. They keep track of every date I go on, every package I get, every time I forget to water my geraniums. On the other hand," Anne mused, "you know how early everybody goes to sleep around here. Especially on a weeknight.

Maybe that's why I can't find anyone who saw anything."

"Maybe. Anyway, Annie. What do you make of Mallory's disappearance?"

"I can't help feeling it ties in with my missing notes somehow."

"God, I hate the thought of some guy breaking into your house. Want to stay with us for a while?"

Anne considered the offer. She might feel safer at Helen's house. But she wasn't about to let anyone drive her out of her home. "Thanks. But I'll be okay. I had the locks changed this morning, just in case. The locksmith's making an extra set for you."

"You think Mallory's okay?"

"No, I don't. She hasn't called or contacted anyone."

"Well, I hope she's all right, for both your sakes. Listen, kiddo. I've got to get back to work. I'll call you when I get home."

"Okay. Bye."

As Anne hung up the phone, she happened to glance out the window. The sun glinted off the waves, giving the ocean a metallic shimmer. Had she seen Mallory Loving yesterday morning? And if so, what on earth had Mallory been up to?

Chapter 8

Recipe for Yogurt Skin Cleanser: Place 1 teaspoon dried chamomile in a bowl and pour boiling water over it. Cover and leave to cool. Strain. Place 5 tablespoons of plain yogurt in a bowl and gradually beat in the chamomile and water mixture. Add 1 teaspoon of wheat germ oil. Store in the refrigerator and use within one week.

Sheila Lovitz came to the door carrying a plate of egg rolls. "Would you try one of these?" she asked Anne. "I'm going to a potluck supper to-night. Everybody's supposed to bring something."

"Sure," Anne said, following Sheila inside.

Sheila's apartment in the Landsdown Arms was small

but cozy. The living room was filled with books, stacked vertically, horizontally, and diagonally on shelves, and piled on the coffee table. A battered-looking oak desk held more books and papers, as well as a half-dozen framed photographs of children. In a wooden cabinet, painted barn red, was a collection of primitive stone carvings—vases and statues of animals, men in tribal makeup, women who appeared to be praying.

"Nice sculpture," Anne said. "Where are they from?"

"South America mostly. I'm dying to go. Argentina, Peru, Brazil. All the great ancient civilizations. Hey, maybe if I win the lottery, right?"

Anne sat down on Sheila's purple crushed-velvet couch. An Oriental rug, frayed at the edges, was shedding on the floor. In the middle of the rug sprawled a fat black-and-white cat, its chin resting on its paws. It stared at her with its one good eye.

"Anne, meet Harry," Sheila said. "The only male I've ever loved who's returned the favor. He's pretty old, in cat years, but he's completely faithful."

Anne forced a smile. She wasn't a cat person. They were too temperamental, too finicky, as though between eating, sleeping, and clawing up the furniture, they were simply waiting to be annoyed. She picked up an egg roll and took a bite. A burning sensation flooded her mouth. Tears sprang to the corner of her eyes, and she started to choke.

"Oh, God," Sheila said. "Too much hot mustard, right?"

"Yes," Anne gasped, fanning her mouth with her hand. "Can I get a glass of water?"

Sheila rushed into the kitchen and returned carrying two tall glasses. The cat looked up at Anne coolly, taking in her discomfort. "Sorry about that," Sheila said. "I lost the recipe. I was kind of recreating it from memory."

Anne gulped down the water. "What's in these?" she asked, pointing to the plate of egg rolls.

"Bean sprouts, water chestnuts, black mushrooms, jalapeño peppers."

"I think they could use a little tamari sauce."

Sheila's face brightened. "You're a vegetarian, too?"

"No. But I worked on a vegetarian cookbook once. I had to test all the recipes." Anne paused, remembering a certain spicy eggplant relish that gave her heartburn for days. "Personally, I'm more the burger and fries type."

Sheila picked up an egg roll and took a small bite. "Oh well," she said. "Maybe I'll just make a salad." She settled into a ratty brown armchair that looked as if it had seen better days. The cat leaped onto the chair and curled up in her lap. "I guess you're here about my sister."

"Yeah. I'm trying to track her down. Did the police contact you?" Anne said.

Sheila nodded. "They were here this morning." The cat stretched and rolled over. He had a white patch shaped like a star on his flank. Sheila stroked the cat's head affectionately.

"Have you heard from her?"

"Not since the night of her birthday party."

"You went to the party?" The news took Anne by surprise. She wondered how Mallory had reacted.

"I didn't intend to go," Sheila said slowly. "But after I talked to you, I started feeling guilty about not visiting my sister, when she's five minutes away in the Heights. So I drove through town on my way home and went by the house Marcia's renting. The lights were on."

"What time was that?"

"A little after two, I guess. The party was breaking up. Anyway, Marcia was there, drunk as a skunk. And a couple of other people were hanging around."

"Mallory was drunk?"

"It sure looked that way."

"Do you know who the other people were?"

"Let's see," Sheila said, picking at a scab on her elbow. "I was introduced to some girl named Jill. And the current husband. That was the first time I'd met him. But I'd seen his photo in the magazines. And a guy with huge muscles, like the after picture in those old Charles Atlas ads in the comics."

"Mallory's personal trainer. Anyone else?"

Sheila thought a moment. "Some blond chick, a Marcia wannabe."

"Caitlin Grey?"

"That's the one."

"What about Howard Koppelman?"

"Hubby number two? I didn't see him."

"How did Mallory seem?"

"Pretty out of it. I asked her how the movie was going. And she said it wasn't, basically. I guess they haven't been able to work very much the last couple of days." Sheila paused. She took a sip of water and set the glass back on the coffee table. "Actually, Marcia did say something strange. She told me someone was sabotaging *Dark Horizon*, somebody who was out to get her."

"Did she say who she thought it was?"

"She didn't know. And like I told that cop, I couldn't tell whether she was making the whole thing up. Marcia has such an inflated sense of her own importance. She always thinks everything's about *her*."

"Then what happened?"

"The movie folks were making me uncomfortable, with their insider jokes and their high-and-mighty attitudes. Then Marcia got this phone call. Like I told the cop, it really shook her up."

"Did she answer the phone herself?"

"Um . . . I think her assistant did."

"But you saw Mallory take the call?"

"Yup. Her face turned all pale. She looked spooked."

"Did she say anything to the person on the other end?"

"Not really. She was listening, mostly. When she hung up, she looked like she could use another drink."

"What happened then?"

"She kept saying she needed to be alone for a while. I got the feeling she wanted to get rid of me, so I left. The last I saw of her she was sitting on the porch swing by herself, hugging her knees to her chest, kinda rocking back and forth."

"Did you go to the beach in the Heights afterward?"

"What?" Sheila said. She looked surprised. "I went straight home. Why?"

Anne told her about the woman she'd seen on the rocks.

"That's weird," Sheila said. She looked at Anne closely. "What's going on? Where do *you* think Marcia is?"

"I don't know, but I want to check something out. Could we go for a ride?"

"Sure. But what about the food for the party? I have to show up with something, even if it's just a salad."

"No problem," Anne said. "We can pick up some lettuce on the way."

In the daylight, the old Lovitz house looked worse than it did at night. The front porch sagged. The siding was coming loose in spots, and the chimney was half-gone. Weeds grew waist-high on the lawn. The rest of the block was no better. None of the other houses looked lived in. Some were shells, the walls torn away in places. Debris littered the small, narrow yards. A rusted car parked across the street had been entirely stripped of parts. Even the trees were dead, their trunks scarred, branches bare.

The only trace of civilization was the sound of traffic out on Route 6, the old county road a half-mile away.

Anne parked the Mustang at the curb, and she and Sheila got out.

"In the past couple of years, practically everybody in the neighborhood's moved out," Sheila said as she unlocked the front door. "I know the house is a wreck, but I keep hanging on to it. I have this dream that one day it could be a clubhouse for the kids. The budget's been cut so much that the children have no place to go after school, no safe place to play."

Sheila led the way through the hall into what must have been the living room. The place was a mess. Layers of paint peeled off the walls; dirt crusted the windowpanes, obscuring the view. Anne looked up. She could see a patch of sky through the ceiling where the roof had collapsed.

"No matter how many times I have the windows boarded up, the homeless manage to get in here," Sheila said, sidestepping food wrappers and tin cans cluttering the dirty floor.

"They've got good taste," Anne said wryly. She bent down and picked up an empty ice cream container. It had a handwritten label glued to the front. Brand X from Nagle's on Crescent Avenue. Inside the container was a cigar butt, with a fancy peach-colored band and gold lettering that said *Avo*. Anne sniffed the container and read the label pasted onto the side. Brand X yogurt. Mallory's favorite. It smelled relatively fresh. Could it be a coincidence, something more?

"What's that?" Sheila said.

"A cigar band."

"You smoke cigars?" Sheila asked, sounding surprised.

"No. But a friend of mine does. He adores them."

Sheila wrinkled her nose. "Gross. I hate the smell."

"Does Mallory smoke?"

"She's smoked cigarettes for years. But cigars? I don't know. Are you thinking Marcia was here? I doubt it. There weren't exactly a lot of happy memories associated with this place."

Anne picked up a torn sheet of newspaper from the floor, and wrapped the cigar butt in it. "I don't know that she *did* come here. But it was worth a shot. Could I take a look at the rest of the house?"

Sheila showed Anne the bedrooms, the bath, and the tiny kitchen. Everything about the house was cheap, from the plywood paneling to the high, narrow windows that looked like they'd been installed in the early 1950s. On the floor of the larger bedroom were a couple of stained mattresses. A thick layer of grime clung to the broken-down furniture. Fuzzy gray dust bunnies clumped together in the corners.

"Believe it or not," Sheila said, "I've gotten calls from a developer interested in buying this place. But it's not for sale. This area is one of the few in Landsdown zoned for child care. Kind of ridiculous, considering there's no place for kids to go after school."

Anne took a last look around. "You sure have your work cut out for you."

"Don't I know it."

Outside, the street was still. A desultory breeze blew a green plastic garbage bag across the yard.

"Do you have any idea where Mallory could be?" Anne said. "Are there any old haunts she might have wanted to revisit?"

Sheila thought for a moment. "Sorry. I can't help you. My sister hated Landsdown. She wouldn't have come back here for the world. Besides, you don't really think she's in trouble, do you?" Sheila's tone was dismissive. "This is exactly the type of stunt Marcia would pull to get attention."

"Funny, her second husband said the exact same thing. Did the detective talk to you about the letters Mallory's been receiving?"

"Yeah. I guess when you're a movie star, it comes with the territory."

Anne slipped behind the wheel of her car. The Mustang had been parked in the sun, and the seat cushions were scorching hot. Sheila got in on the passenger side. "Ugh," she said, pulling her hair into a ponytail. "I can't stand the heat."

Anne turned toward her. "There's something I've been meaning to ask you," she said. Sheila looked at her expectantly. "What was it like when you got back together with Gerald Finch?"

"It was hopeless," she said glumly.

"How come?"

"He told me—" Sheila stopped and gazed out the window at the house she grew up in. She appeared lost in thought, as if replaying painful memories from her childhood. It occurred to Anne that Sheila might be better off if she sold the house and cut loose from the past. But maybe she couldn't. Maybe she took a perverse pleasure in holding on. Finally Sheila looked away from the house, staring straight ahead, her eyes fixed on the deserted street. "He told me I looked too much like Mallory."

Before she met Jack, Anne had never smoked a cigar and never intended to. Her Uncle Theo smoked cheap Tiparillos, and the smoke clung to his clothes, stale and smelly. Even as a child, she had held her breath when he'd bent down to kiss her cheek. But Jack had insisted that premium cigars were different, that she had to at least try one before she decided cigars were no good. Over the Fourth of July weekend, he'd brought two Churchill Partegas and a bottle of port. They'd sat outside on her porch, drinking and smoking and listening to the sounds of the waves crashing against the shore.

To Anne's surprise, she liked the Partegas. It was mild and creamy tasting with a faint spicy flavoring. She liked the ritual associated with cigars, how you sniffed the wrapper first, inhaling the cedarlike woodsy aroma, then carefully cutting the head off and toasting the end slowly over a flame, rotating it at a forty-five-degree angle. She liked the rings that floated up from Jack's Partegas and dissolved into the balmy night air. And she liked the fact that it took almost an hour to smoke, that taking your time was the point, unlike cigarettes, which people seemed to suck on in quick succession, barely noticing what they were doing. After a time, her mind slipped into neutral and she felt serenely calm. Jack was right. Cigars weren't half-bad. No wonder they'd gotten so popular lately.

Now, as she gazed at boxes upon boxes of cigars in various shapes, sizes and shades, she realized she didn't have the slightest idea how to pick out a quality stogie. She was in a narrow walk-in humidor in the back of the Cigar Shoppe, in downtown Red Bank, ostensibly to buy Jack a welcome-home present. The shop was elegantly appointed, furnished with Oriental carpets, a plush leather sofa and club chairs, and rich-looking wood paneling. Though the entire place was air-conditioned, the air in the humidor was cool and slightly misty.

"Need some help?" said a young man with sideburns, who had been reading *Cigar Aficionado* magazine by the old-fashioned wooden cash register when she'd first walked in.

"I sure do. I'm sort of new to all this."

The man smiled. His blond hair was cut short. There was light downy hair on his cheeks, like he was trying to grow a beard and failing. "Well, you came to the right place. Name's Luke. Are you looking to buy something for yourself?"

"It's for a friend of mine.

"Serious cigar lover?"

"Uh huh."

"Then there are a couple of things I'd recommend. One is a Macanudo." Luke plucked a longish cigar with a golden brown wrapper off one of the shelves. "Great body, very flavorful."

"Actually, I think he might like one of these." Anne

reached into her pocketbook and unwrapped the cigar, with its peach-colored band.

"Your friend's got good taste. That's an Avo," Luke said. "Aged for six to eight months before they're shipped to us."

"Do you carry them?"

"Right over here. Davidoff makes 'em. And we're the only shop authorized to sell Davidoffs in this part of Jersey." He pointed to one of the boxes on the top shelf. "You want that size?"

"I think so." Anne examined the Avo Luke showed her. It was the same width and the same color as the one she'd found. "Actually, I'd like two of them. I live over in Oceanside Heights, where they're making a movie and—"

"You mean *Dark Horizon*," Luke cut in. "Wow. That must be intense."

"It's been an *interesting* experience," Anne said with a smile.

"Did you get to meet Mallory Loving?"

"As a matter of fact, I did."

"Man." Luke sighed. "What a body. She's hot."

"Have you ever seen her?" Anne asked.

"I've seen, like, all her movies. You know my favorite? The one where she had amnesia and couldn't remember she was really a double agent. That was classic." He glanced through the glass wall of the humidor to the front of the shop, where two customers were browsing. "Shoot. I can't think of the name."

"*A Rose for Sierra*," Anne said. "I meant in person. Has she ever been in?"

Luke rolled his eyes. "I wish."

"Are you here all the time?"

"All day, every day. My dad's the owner. He's in the Dominican Republic right now. On a buying trip. So I'm kind of in charge."

"And these Avos, would you say they're pretty popular?"

"Can't stock 'em fast enough."

"About how many would you say you've sold this week?"

Luke looked at the shelf where the Avos were kept. "Oh, I don't know. A couple dozen, I guess."

Reaching into her bag again, Anne pulled out a *Dark Horizon* press kit, a turquoise folder with a picture of a stormy ocean on the cover. She pulled out several glossy eight-by-ten photographs and handed them to him.

"Could you take a look at these?" Anne said. "I was wondering whether any of these people had been in during the last week or so."

Luke leafed through the photos. Head shots of Caitlin, Dakota, and Howard Koppelman, as well as posed "action" shots of some of the other cast members. Anne had also stuck in a newspaper photo of Gerald Finch taken last fall, when he'd run unopposed for town selectman.

"The only one I recognize is him," Luke said, pointing to Dakota, who was flashing a huge grin for the camera.

"He was here, buying cigars?"

"No. I have a couple of his CDs. The last one was righteous."

"You've never seen any of the others before?"

"Nope. But we've had our fair share of celebrities. Bruce Springsteen, Eddie Murphy, David Letterman, Jim Belushi." He eyed her curiously. "What do you want to know for?"

"Just curious."

He handed back the photographs. "How many cigars did you want?"

"Two, please."

Luke plucked a pair of Avos from the box and opened the door of the humidor. "I'll be with you in just a sec," he called to the customers who were examining fancy carved wood humidors that looked like oversize jewelry boxes. "You need a cutter, too?"

"I suppose so." Luke handed her a metal object that looked like a pocket-sized guillotine. "How much is that all together?" Anne asked him.

"Sixty-one dollars, plus tax."

Wow, Anne thought, taking out her wallet. I hope they're worth it.

When Anne got home, the phone was ringing. She ran into the kitchen to answer it.

"Great, you're there," said the voice on the other end. "I was just about to give up."

"Jack," Anne said. She couldn't believe how incredibly happy she was to hear from him. "How are you? How's everything going?" She sat down at the kitchen table and began to doodle on a notepad.

"We've hit a construction snafu. Looks like I'll be in Portofino longer than I thought, at least till the middle of September. Any chance of you flying over and joining me? After you've done all your interviews for the book, you can write it here. My villa overlooks the Mediterranean. You can sit on the terrace and let the view inspire you."

She pictured Jack Mills's cornflower blue eyes, his beguiling grin. What she wouldn't give for a week with him on the Italian Riviera.

"Don't I wish." She sighed. "I'm stuck in ghost-writer hell. Talk about snafus!" She quickly filled Jack in on everything that had been going on, culminating in Mallory's disappearance.

"I don't like the sound of this," Jack said. "What if somebody tries to break in again?"

"There's nothing here to steal. I haven't even begun to reconstruct my notes."

"Just to be on the safe side, why not hop a plane to Milan? Portofino's not far, by train."

Ever since she'd first met him, Jack had been trying to get her to spend more time with him: *Come for a week, instead of the weekend*, he'd say. *Join me in New*

Orleans, Santa Fe, the Virgin Islands. Move to New York. But she didn't want to move. The Heights was home. She belonged here. Sometimes she thought about whether she'd still be with Jack if they were always together. Absence gave the relationship a sense of urgency, of missing each other, so every minute counted. Would things be the same if they spent twenty-four hours a day together?

Aloud she said, "I'd love to, if I had some spare cash for the plane ticket and if I didn't have to write this damn book."

"You know what they say," Jack teased. "All work and no play. Et cetera, et cetera."

"We'll have to fix that when you get back."

"Right you are."

She looked at what she'd written on the pad. *Loving You* enclosed in a concentric series of diamonds.

"One last thing before I sign off," Jack said. "Do you miss me?"

Anne grinned. "Only every day. I can't wait to see you."

"Same here. If your plans change, let me know."

"I will. Talk to you soon," she said, before hanging up.

She felt better, safer somehow. More connected. And Jack didn't sound as if he'd met a ravishing beauty on the Riviera. She looked up Nagle's in the phone book, dialed the number, and explained what she wanted to know. In response to her questions, Lenny Nagle said they sold so much Brand X yogurt a day, it would be impossible to track who had bought it. No, Mallory Loving hadn't come in. He would have remembered her. But movie people were in and out all day long, too many to count. So much for the yogurt connection. Grabbing a yellow legal pad and a pen off her desk, she went out on the front porch. She couldn't procrastinate any longer. Time to try and recreate what Mallory had told her, from scratch.

It was a hot, muggy afternoon. Across the street, at the Good Humor truck, business was brisk. A line of kids snaked halfway down the block. Anne leaned back against the cushions on the wicker swing. The air smelled of summer, sweet and faintly briny. It was so peaceful out here today. No film crew lugging equipment, no actors running around. They must be shooting *Dark Horizon* someplace else in town. Without Mallory Loving.

She picked up the pen and began to write. When she put it down, several hours later, she'd practically filled the entire pad. Her right hand ached. Daylight was fading from the sky, and the ocean had turned a smoky shade of gray. She went inside and reheated leftover chicken for dinner. After she'd finished eating, she took a bath and tidied up the house. Then she settled down on the couch with the mystery novel she was reading. It was set in South Texas. The heroine was an out-of-work accountant who got a job branding cows on a cattle ranch. After wading through the first two chapters, she put the book down. She couldn't concentrate. Images of Mallory kept surfacing. Mallory lying in an alleyway, passed out, clutching an empty vial of pills. If she was back on drugs, she could be practically anywhere. Anne closed her eyes. She felt incredibly tired. Without meaning to, she fell asleep. The phone woke her up, ringing insistently. She glanced at her watch. Eleven-fifteen. She'd been sleeping for nearly two hours.

"Hello," Anne said, feeling slightly groggy.

"Have you heard?" It was Betty Flugelhorn. She sounded breathless, upset.

"Mallory's been found?"

"They think it's her. They're not one hundred percent sure yet."

A knot formed in Anne's stomach. "What do you mean?"

"Mallory's car went off the road. Out by Route 6, between the Heights and Landsdown. The car went over an embankment and caught fire." Betty's voice was shaking. "There's a body in it. A woman. They haven't identified her yet, 'cause she's so badly burned. But the police think it's Mallory."

Anne took a deep breath to steady herself. "When did this happen?"

"About an hour ago. You think she was on something? Drugs, I mean."

"I don't know. How'd you find out about it?"

"It's all over the TV," Betty said, her voice breaking. "On every single channel. I can't believe it." Betty was crying. "I can't believe she's dead."

"Hang on."

Anne put down the phone and turned on the television. The local station had interrupted reruns of *The Honeymooners* and was showing footage of the burning car, interspersed with pictures of Mallory and clips from some of her movies. Anne stared at the screen. The anchor was talking about a "tragic life cut short by a fatal car accident." Oh, God. The car. Bright orange flames swirled up into the night sky. Mallory, reduced to a pile of ashes. It nearly made Anne physically sick.

"Betty," she said, into the phone. "I have to go."

Anne put the phone down and stared at the screen, her mind numb. Ten seconds later, the phone rang again.

"Anne, is that you? It's Phil. Have you heard?" His voice brimmed with barely contained excitement.

"Yes." She couldn't tear her eyes away from the TV. They showed Mallory's exquisite face, then the flame-streaked car. Face, car. Face, car.

"I want you to move on this," the publisher said. "We're rushing the book into stores by Christmas, so your deadline's been pushed up a month. I want comments from each of her exes. Talk to her costars, her family, the people who knew her when. Don't forget to throw in lots of local color. 'Her last days in a Victorian village'—yada, yada, yada. The hopes, the dreams, the drugs, the beauty tips."

"Phil—"

"We're checking the allegations about the husband's voice. Should know more in a couple of days."

"Phil, I—" Her throat felt thick.

"You can do it, Annie. It'll be a cinch. Work round the clock, if you have to. Fax me what you've got so far, first thing tomorrow. Don't worry about how good the writing is. Doesn't matter. Now that she's dead, we've got ourselves an instant best-seller."

"You don't have to sound so gleeful about it."

"Gleeful? I'm insulted. No, I'm hurt. I'm really hurt, Anne."

"Right. I can hear the pain in your voice," she said sarcastically.

"Fax me the first couple of chapters tomorrow. I don't care if it's rough. Or e-mail them to me. Work all night, if you have to. We've got to get our PR people moving on this."

He was pleased, happy even, that Mallory was dead. Publicity equals a bigger print run equals bigger sales. Phil Smedley's equation for success.

"I'm going now, Phil."

"Right. You go. You've got a lot of work to do, and I know you'll come through for us."

Anne hung up the phone, in a daze. On TV, firefighters were dousing the car with gallons of water. She glimpsed the black Lexus, reduced to a wrecked, twisted hunk of metal. The pretty auburn-haired newscaster was reviewing Mallory's career, showing brief clips of Mallory's movies. She registered mild concern about the death and just a hint of superiority. It was the same on every channel: *Fallen icon. Tragic death. Drugs and pills. Troubled beauty.* The message could be reduced to a sound bite. Live fast, die young. Mallory's incredible face stared at Anne from the screen, perfect as always. Smiling for eternity in radiant Technicolor.

Chapter 9

How to look great on camera: Don't put powder under your eyes. It can crease and make you look older. Slightly exaggerate your lip line with a pencil. This will create a mouth that "pops" out. Remember, light or bright colors will make your lips look larger. Dark color lipsticks will make them seem smaller.

The Antique Boutique on Main Street stocked all sorts of treasures from the nineteenth century. There were tufted sofas with claw feet, elaborately carved mahogany tables, scrolled mirrors, ottomans upholstered in rich brocades and silks, cherrywood four-poster beds with lace canopies, and an array of stately grandfather clocks that chimed hourly. Anne had a particular fondness for the bone china teacups displayed in the shop's plate glass window. They were exquisitely made, with bands of gold around the rims and delicate patterns—sprays of rosebuds, lush-looking fruit, overblown peonies clambering over leafy tendrils. She'd always wanted to collect something. It seemed like fun to hunt through antique stores and tag sales, searching for that special piece. Maybe she should start with teacups. She especially liked the royal blue one in the window, the one decorated with orchids on the inside.

She opened the door of the Antique Boutique and was immediately hit with a blast of cold air. The place was as chilly as a meat locker. It was Friday morning, so the shop wasn't jammed with tourists. On weekends you practically had to take a number to get in. Threading her way past dining room tables, settees, and china cabinets, she headed to the back, where the owner was seated behind an antique pine desk.

"Hi there," she said, trying to sound like a casual antiques lover out for a stroll. "I'd like to take a closer look at something in the window."

Gerald Finch looked up. He had on a long-sleeved white shirt, dark trousers, a plaid argyle vest, and a bow tie. "Hello Anne," he said. "How are you this morning?"

"Just fine. I was admiring one of the cups in the window. The blue one. Can I take a closer look?"

"Certainly. I'll fetch it for you." Gerald Finch got up from behind his desk. His dark hair was combed over his forehead, leaving a bald patch on the top of his head. He had thin lips and ears that stuck out prominently. Dull hazel eyes, a long, narrow nose, a dimple in his chin. In his mid-thirties, he had a formal, reserved manner more suited to a man twice his age.

Anne gazed around the shop. None of the stuff appeared to have price tags. She guessed that the high-backed burl chairs and delicately painted tables were well out of her price range.

"Here you are," said Gerald Finch. He handed Anne the cup and saucer. "Aynsley. Produced in England in 1923. The pattern is called Rhapsody in Blue."

"Lovely." She ran her fingers over the smooth cool china surface. "How much?"

Gerald Finch removed a slim volume from his desk and flipped through the book. "Yes," he said. "Here we are. One hundred and thirty-eight dollars."

Anne tried not to wince. "That's a little out of my price range."

"Very well." Gerald took the cup and saucer back and set them gingerly on the desk. In high school, he'd been a quiet, bookish sort, a bit of a loner. The other kids had nicknamed him "Finch the Grinch" and ignored him. Anne had always thought he'd wind up becoming a research scientist, working in a high-tech lab. Or a professor of sociology at an Ivy League university. Or perhaps an accountant, poring over spreadsheets and ledgers all day long. Instead he'd gone to UCLA and moved back to the Heights after graduation, working at different jobs, until six years ago, when he opened the Antique Boutique. He lived above the shop, in an apartment that was occasionally featured on the Heights's annual summer house tour.

"Terrible, isn't it?"

Anne pointed to the front page of the *Landsdown Park Press*, which was spread out on his desk. The headline read: ACTRESS KILLED IN CRASH.

"You remember those teenagers who died last year? The ones from Little Silver?" he said. "That accident happened at the exact same spot. The road curves suddenly. And there's no sign, no warning. The sooner they tear down Route 6 and complete the highway extension, the better off everyone will be. Even though the new mall will draw business away from Main Street." He picked up a stack of invoices and moved them from one side of his desk to the other. Anne saw that his hands were trembling. "They certainly don't have antique shops in malls. Only Bombay Company, and their merchandise is hardly vintage. But regarding the safety of Route 6, I'm calling a special town council meeting to address the matter. I trust you'll come.''

"I'll try," Anne said, knowing full well she'd rather watch paint dry than attend one of those boring town meetings. Not one word about Mallory. How curious. He didn't look at her when he spoke. Instead he busied himself straightening his blotter, smoothing down the pages of his desk calendar. The desk was obsessively neat, down to the pencils arranged according to height around the perimeter of a burgundy leather cup.

She sat opposite him. "I'm not sure if you heard about this or not, but I was in the middle of helping Mallory write her autobiography. Now my publisher's insisting that I continue the project alone. It's sort of a . . ." Anne paused, searching for a plausible explanation. Sort of what? A desperate move by a greedy publisher eager to cash in on a celebrity's death? A way she could earn a year's worth of car payments? Sometimes she wished she'd become a travel writer instead of someone who chronicled the ups and downs of other people's lives. ''A final tribute,'' she said lamely.

Gerald Finch stared down at his polished brown Oxfords. "How can I help?" he said suddenly.

She felt a twinge of surprise. She had thought he'd be uncooperative. Gerald was the kind of man who wouldn't reveal much beyond a stray comment about the weather. She knew him slightly from being three years ahead of him in school, and because everybody who lived in the Heights knew everybody else. But she didn't really know the first thing about him.

"Could you tell me a little about you and Mallory? About what it was like being married to her?"

"Certainly. I've spoken to several reporters already." He walked to the front of the shop and flipped the *Open* sign over to *Closed*. "Why don't we go upstairs?" Gerald crooked his index finger, beckoning to her.

Reluctantly she followed him into the back, up a steep flight of stairs. At the top she hesitated. It was awfully private up there. Mallory had been right about Gerald Finch. There was something about him that gave you the creeps. She followed him down a long corridor, with closed doors on either side. She had a sudden image of Anthony Perkins in *Psycho*, sequestering his mother in the basement of his house. He led her into a parlor that looked just like his shop, filled with expensive looking turn-of-the-century antiques. It was chilly up there, too. Gerald must have a thing for cold air.

She sat down on a camelback sofa, upholstered in pale blue silk. The lampshades in the room were made of similar blue fabric, as were the drapes. Pink roses bloomed in a cut crystal vase on the mahogany coffee table. In a corner of the room, she spotted a chair with a fanciful embroidered seat that looked identical to one she'd seen in the shop below. She wondered if the furniture up here was part of his stock, replenished as needed when pieces were sold off.

"Would you care for some tea?" he asked. "I have Earl Grey, chamomile, Darjeeling, English Breakfast, cinnamon spice . . ." He reeled off a dozen other flavors with the clipped diction of a maitre d' in a restaurant she couldn't afford to eat in.

"Earl Grey is fine."

After he excused himself, Anne wandered around the room. It overlooked a small garden of roses, petunias and impatiens. There was a wonderful view of the ocean, which gleamed like a glassy blue marble. Turning away from the window, she surveyed the furnishings again, trying to guess which piece cost the most. Her money was on an oversize leather wing chair, studded with nail heads. The chair was massive, regal almost. It looked like the perfect place to snuggle up with a good book. Next to the chair was an old-fashioned wicker magazine rack containing a dozen women's magazines—*Vogue, Glamour, Cosmopolitan, Mademoiselle*. Strange choices.

Anne picked up the issue of *Cosmo* and thumbed through it. She hadn't read the magazine in years, but it looked like the articles hadn't changed very much: "Frisky Fall Fashions Hot Off the Runway," "Where the *Good* Men Are (and How to Meet Them)," "When Sex Is Out of Sync," "The Lowdown on Breast Implants."

"Oh," Gerald said, entering the room. The saucer rattled against the cup unsteadily. He stuck his other hand out, barely saving the tea from splashing on the carpet. "Those aren't mine. I've been collecting fashion magazines for my niece. She's a freshman at the University of Pennsylvania. I'm going down to visit her later this afternoon."

He set the tea on the table, served in a dainty cup and saucer decorated with sprays of leaves and berries. "Here you are."

She noticed he hadn't made a cup for himself.

"Sugar? Cream?" he asked.

"No thanks." A plume of steam curled above the tea. She took a notebook and pen from her handbag. "Mallory's already told me a little about your relationship. She said you first met when you were teenagers."

"That's right. I was taken with her right away. She is . . . was," he corrected himself, "so very stunning. I met her at the Founders' Day Parade, right here in town. We were young, teenagers in fact, and we fell in love. We moved to California together and got married out there. I was studying film at UCLA at the time."

He addressed this entire speech to an inlaid enamel box on the coffee table. It usually didn't bother her when people refused to make eye contact. But in Gerald's case, it was a little unnerving.

"How many years were you married?"

"Three," he said, looking across the room. "We were quite happy."

"What happened?"

His left knee bobbed up and down, a nervous tic he

seemed unaware of. "What happened?" he repeated. "Any number of things." He stroked his chin, staring at an ornate settee upholstered in black horsehair.

"Like what?"

"I'd prefer not to discuss it." Then, anxiously, "What did Mallory tell you?"

"She mentioned you had a few habits she didn't care for."

"Did she elaborate?"

"She called you an eccentric." And a weirdo. And a phony, Anne added silently. But you didn't get people to reminisce about the past by insulting them. "Why don't you tell me a little about what your life together was like?"

"That detective who came to see me wanted to know the exact same thing. I'll show you what I showed him."

He crossed the room to a mahogany breakfront and took out a photo album with a crimson leather cover, handling the book gingerly, as if it were something precious that might break.

Sitting beside Anne, he opened the album to the first page. "Here we are on our wedding day," he said proudly. Anne looked at the picture. The couple was posed on a beach, in front of a raggedy palm tree. Mallory was wearing a short white dress and a wreath of daisies in her hair. She had a serious, almost stern expression. Gerald wore a white suit. Instead of facing the camera, he was gazing at her adoringly.

"Malibu," Gerald said, regarding the picture lovingly. "We drove up the coast for our honeymoon. It was a memorable, magical time."

Anne flipped through the pages of the book. There were Mallory and Gerald at Disney Land; in a tiny dorm room; surrounded by a group of college students; picking oranges in a sunny grove; standing in front of a teensy white house, with a dog and a yard. They looked happy enough.

"Did Mallory's career ambitions create problems in your marriage?" Anne asked tentatively.

"Not at all. I was entirely supportive of her plan to become an actress. In fact, I found her first agent. He was the second cousin of a classmate of mine."

"Did it disturb you when she began making pornographic films?"

Gerald's knee bobbed faster. With his index finger, he traced the curves of Mallory's face. "I know some men would have disapproved. But I realized she *had* to make those movies. They were only a stepping stone to bigger and better things, the first showcase, as it were, for her extraordinary talents."

Anne looked at him closely. He seemed sincere. When he talked about Mallory, his expression became more animated, his eyes took on the same adoring, eager look that Anne had seen on the faces of Mallory's fans. It seemed he had really loved her.

"Had you talked to Mallory recently?" Anne asked.

He snapped the album shut. "I've seen her, yes. Passing by the shop. Once I spotted her in Quilters, eating breakfast. But we never spoke."

She didn't know whether to believe him or not. On one hand, she could imagine Gerald mooning over Mallory from a distance. But she also sensed he'd want a closer look. It was one thing admiring a bone china cup on a shelf, and quite another to hold it in your hands, feeling the deliciously smooth porcelain glaze.

"That strikes me as unusual, considering how you seem to feel about her."

"We'd lost touch for many years." Gerald stood up abruptly. "Would you care for some shortbread? I just remembered I have some in the pantry."

"No thanks. Did you know that someone was sending Mallory threatening letters?"

Gerald finally met her eyes. His expression was tense, then his gaze slid away. "No, I didn't." His voice was a soft, brittle whisper. "The newspaper didn't mention it."

"It seems one of her fans was obsessed with her."

Could he have written the letters? Anne thought he could have, in a heartbeat.

"You have to understand, she had many admirers." His voice sounded almost worshipful. "She was a beautiful, beautiful woman."

"Except this particular fan threatened to harm Mallory. It was quite a violent letter."

He started toward her, and she involuntarily shrank away from him, her spine pressing against the back of the sofa. She felt her muscles tense.

Bending down, he retrieved the cup and saucer. "I'm sorry to cut this short, but I should be getting back to the shop. I'm expecting a lamp shipment any minute."

He glanced out the window, as if the lamps might already be on his doorstep.

Anne scrambled to her feet. "Thanks for taking the time to talk to me." She followed him back downstairs. When they were safely back in his shop, with its big plate glass windows and a view of Main Street, she said, "Oh, one more thing." He turned around. "I understand that before you married Mallory, you were dating her sister, Sheila."

"That's right," he replied with a tight smile.

"Sheila told me she'd tried to rekindle your relationship, but you weren't interested. Mind if I ask why?"

Gerald shifted uncomfortably. "I think Sheila felt that since they were identical twins, she could replace Mallory in my affections, and I'd regain exactly what I'd lost." He seemed unsure what to do with his hands, stuffing them in his pockets, then clasping them in front of his midsection, like an overage altar boy. "Unfortunately, that's quite impossible. They may be sisters, but they're not at all alike." He crossed to his desk and moved the stack of invoices back to their former position, taking care that the edges were lined up neatly. "I couldn't transfer my feelings from one to the other. It would be like substituting a bottle of Moet & Chandon champagne with a cheap jug of white wine."

It was a relief to step outside the frigid Antique Boutique into the steamy morning air. Anne saw the ubiquitous silver trailers parked a few blocks away, on both sides of Main Street. It looked like the press conference was just getting under way outside Baby Face, a shop that sold reproductions of porcelain Victorian dolls. They'd probably chosen the locale for its quaint appeal. Anne couldn't figure out how the shop managed to stay in business. Little girls didn't clamor for old-fashioned dolls with flaxen hair and tiny rosebud mouths; they wanted Cell Phone Barbie.

The doll shop was situated in a turn-of-the-century cottage, a narrow two-story rectangular building with an arched double-leafed doorway and a balcony beneath the gable on the second floor. Part of the sidewalk in front of Baby Face was blocked off, and the area fairly pulsated with activity. Smartly dressed men and women scurried back and forth, trying to interview anyone connected with *Dark Horizon*. Newspaper cameramen milled around, pointing and clicking incessantly. Inside the pink shop, with its fanciful gingerbread trim and its window boxes stuffed with bright pink petunias, the dolls stared through the display window with blank glass eyes.

Howard Koppelman was standing in front of a jagged row of television cameras as news jockeys thrust microphones at his chin. Anne recognized the anchor of one of the local news stations. Other reporters circled around Koppelman waving notebooks, pens, and tape recorders. They looked like brightly colored vultures, swooping down on their prey. Catching sight of Betty, Anne went over to her.

"Have you heard?" Betty said. She looked even more frazzled than usual, as though she hadn't had time to shower or comb her hair. "The body in the car, it was definitely Mallory. They matched the dental records."

"I heard it on the news." She'd been brushing her teeth, watching CNN, when Mallory's face flashed across the screen, and the serious-looking anchor announced that Mallory had been in the burning car. Anne had had a sick feeling in her stomach, and had turned off the TV just as the anchor was giving statistics on drug-related accidents.

Now she glanced around at the horde of reporters, with their steno books and microphones. It was ironic that Mallory was unable to enjoy all this attention. She would have adored standing where Howard stood now, basking in the media heat. It didn't seem fair, after all Mallory had done to claw her way back to the top.

"There are reporters here from all the networks," Betty said excitedly. "Plus the *New York Times* and the *Philadelphia Inquirer*. *Entertainment Weekly* sent someone. So did *People*. I heard we're going to be on *Good Morning America* tomorrow."

"They're not stopping production?"

Betty rolled her eyes. "Are you *kidding*? The buzz is tremendous."

Anne edged her way closer to Howard Koppelman. "We're trying to go on in light of this senseless tragedy," he was saying. "It's what Mallory Loving would have wanted, although we're all numb with grief, overwhelmed by a great sadness."

Koppelman didn't look numb. In fact, Anne thought he looked positively jubilant. He was freshly shaved, and his grin was as wide as the Raritan Bay. Just then, she caught sight of a woman emerging from Mallory's trailer. For a split second, Anne thought it was Mallory, back from the dead, and she blinked in surprise. Then she realized who the woman was. The blond was wearing one of Mallory's costumes, a tight black sundress festooned with tiny strawberries. She had on sunglasses and a straw hat with a black sash. As if on cue, the press descended on her, enveloping her in a swirl of cameras and microphones. All the newspeople were shouting at once, calling out her name.

Caitlin Grey threw open her arms, as if she were a queen embracing her royal subjects. "It's such a privilege," she exclaimed over the din, "to be filling Mallory's shoes. I hope I can honor her memory by giving myself body and soul to this role, as a final tribute to a superbly talented actress."

Chapter 10

*Don't be a fashion victim!
Designers like to push
something new each
season—ankle-length
dresses, mini-skirts, green
nail polish, dark brown
lipstick. Doesn't mean
you have to buy them.*

Reporters tossed questions at Caitlin for half an hour; she fielded them expertly. At one point Howard Koppelman joined her, and together they spoke about *Dark Horizon* and Mallory's tragic death and the need to move forward. The cast and crew would be spending an additional two weeks in scenic Oceanside Heights so the scenes involving Mallory could be reshot. Howard Koppelman expressed the utmost confidence in Caitlin. Caitlin expressed the utmost delight in her newfound stardom, tinged by occasional outbursts of grief at the loss of her "dearest friend and mentor."

"Nothing like free publicity to bring a smile to a mourner's face," Anne said to Betty as they stood off to the side and watched the press conference unfold. The reporters had pressed even closer to the doll shop, so all Anne could see of Koppelman and Caitlin were the tops of their heads.

"Ain't it the truth," Betty said. She was munching on a Devil Dog. Chocolate crumbs dotted her lower lip. "People are talking about *Dark Horizon*, and that means they'll see the film, whether it's any good or not. The same goes for your book. Hot damn, Anne. You've got yourself an instant best-seller."

"Not if I don't get it written. There are a lot of loose ends I need to tie up."

"Like what?"

"Like what Mallory had on her ex-husbands. I can't write a tell-all unless I know what Mallory was planning to tell."

"Well, if I can help, let me know," Betty said. "Right now I've got to get to work." She rolled her eyes unhappily. "Caitlin's already informed me she didn't like how I did Mallory's hair. Out of the frying pan, into the fire."

"Good luck. I'll catch up with you later."

Anne stood on tiptoe to get a better look at Koppelman. The director had taken off his trademark sunglasses, and his eyes were bright and animated. He looked like he'd just returned from a week at a deluxe health spa. It would be useless trying to talk to him now. She couldn't compete with *People* magazine. Her eyes roamed the crowd, searching for Dakota, but he was nowhere in sight. Why wasn't he up there, too? She thought he would have jumped at the chance for free publicity.

Grateful to leave the hubbub behind, Anne headed down Main Street, toward the beach. Although the day was hot and humid, there was a pleasant breeze off the ocean that caused wind chimes up and down the block to tinkle merrily. On the corner, two freckle-faced girls were selling lemonade and homemade peanut butter cookies. They'd made a big sign out of cardboard and crayons, advertising their wares. Behind them, the ocean fanned out like a turquoise carpet, flecked with foam. The smell of the surf was briny and pleasant, the scent of countless summer afternoons. Anne gazed longingly at the water. She had a sudden urge to go swimming, to plunge into the icy cold and forget about everything else she had to do. But she couldn't. Not today.

When she came to Olin Street, she turned right. It was even hotter away from the beach. The flowers in her neighbors' gardens seemed to droop. Light glinted off stained glass windows and doors. In front of the library, a group of elderly women were sitting on folding chairs, sewing under the shade of an elm tree.

"Hi Annie," one of the women called out. "Where've you been? You haven't stopped by all week."

"Sorry, Delia. I've been busy with the book."

Delia Graustark put down the piece of fabric she was working on and walked over to Anne. She was in her mid-seventies, with wide-set gray eyes and hair worn piled atop her head like a soft white cloud. Delia had been the Heights's librarian for half a century. But her real job was unofficial historian. If you wanted to know anything about anybody in town, Delia could tell you in less time than it took to check out a book, not in a mean-spirited way, but matter-of-factly, and with a certain amount of pride that her memory was still top-notch. Anne had gotten to know Delia even better over the last five years, ever since she started ghostwriting. She spent at least two afternoons a week in the library, researching books she wrote, with Delia at her elbow, offering advice and walnut pecan squares.

"You mean you still have to write it, now that Miss Loving died?" Delia said.

"Afraid so. How's it going?" Anne said, pointing to the sewing circle.

"Awful slow." Delia pushed her spectacles higher, so they rested on the bridge of her nose. "We'll never be finished by Sunday."

Anne smiled. Delia always had trouble getting the library float ready for the Founders' Day Parade. The parade was a big deal in the Heights. Each year the Ladies' Auxiliary stitched together a large flag in honor of the occasion. This one was going to depict an oversize bluefish, surrounded by clams, lobsters, and crabs, beneath the words *Seaside Spirit*. Dozens of cardboard floats replicated the town's most venerable institutions—the Church by the Sea, the library, Quilters, the Ocean Spray Inn, Moby's Hardware store, and dozens of others. Delia herself always rode on the library float, wearing one of the old-fashioned gowns that had once belonged to her grandmother. The mayor and members of the town council dressed in black frock coats, breeches, and fake beards. From a distance they looked like the Methodist ministers who founded the Heights back in 1896.

"Don't worry," Anne said. "The flag will be finished before the parade on Sunday."

"It won't be the same this year," Delia grumbled, "with all those show folks lurking about. Why, I wouldn't be surprised if our parade ended up in the movie. You can't walk down the street without tripping over a camera."

"I suppose not. Speaking of which, did you know Mallory Loving at all, when she was growing up?"

"No. But then I suppose she wasn't the sort to spend much time in the library. Gerald was a different story," Delia said, brightening. "I can't understand what he saw in that girl. Why, he used to stay here for hours, researching his book reports, doing his homework. It was hard on him, poor little fella, what with the other kids calling him egghead and such. He didn't have many friends, and his parents expected so much from him.

Now his sister, Becky, she hadn't the sense God gave a goat. I remember the time Becky caught a bunch of fireflies and tried to glue them onto her Halloween costume. That was the year Reverend Allbright broke his collarbone and Reverend Peaslip filled in for him. A trifle on the sickly side he was.''

Anne felt her mind wander. When Delia began reminiscing, she could yak for hours on end. And there was still so much work to be done on *Loving You*. Anne couldn't begin a draft of the book until she had more information. Like where Mallory had been for two days when she disappeared from the Heights, and where she was headed when her car had crashed through the guard rail on Route 6.

"Last I heard," Delia was saying, "Becky was living in Fort Lee, trying her darndest to find a husband. That dizzy girl always wanted to get married in the worst way." Delia sighed. "I suppose you've heard the buzz at the Mini-Mart? About Thelma Price on the evening news. Imagine. All because she got Miss Loving's autograph and they exchanged a few words when Miss Loving walked into the office the other day."

Anne snapped back to attention. "What?"

"It wasn't much to speak of. 'Hello, Miss Loving. I'm a big fan of yours.' Thelma's always been starstruck, if you ask me."

"Mallory was in Jim Finney's office? Why?"

Delia wagged her head. Her spectacles bobbed up and down briskly. "To draw up a new will."

"Where did you hear that?" Thelma Price worked part-time for Jim Finney, an estate attorney whose office was just off Main Street.

"I heard it from Lily Torrance. Who heard it from Carol Lapinski, who heard from Mary Lou Price. Thelma's Mary Lou's second cousin, don't you know. Not that Thelma should be working, with two little ones at home, mind you."

Anne could feel her heart rate speeding up. "Delia, you don't happen to know—"

"Of course I do," Delia finished, with a sly wink. "The fella who plays the guitar is out."

"Dakota?"

"That's right. Thelma made copies of the new will. Miss Loving left all her money to the Betty Ford Center, out in California."

Anne gave Delia a quick hug. It paid to be friends with the Heights's very own Hedda Hopper. The corners of Delia's eyes crinkled with pleasure. She looked like a cat who'd just polished off an especially tasty canary.

"I hope this helps you," Delia purred.

"You're the best," Anne said. "What would I ever do without you?"

"I honestly can't say." Delia patted her hair and tried to look modest. It didn't work. "Annie, I've got to get back to my sewing. If you need to come over after hours, go right ahead. I'll leave the key in the usual spot."

"Thanks."

Another interesting development, Anne thought. She wondered what had gone sour in Mallory's marriage to Dakota, and why the actress wanted to cut him out of her life so quickly. Did it have something to do with Dakota's alleged lip-synching? Maybe Mallory didn't want the negative press spilling onto the movie. On the other hand, as far as Anne knew, Mallory was the *source* of the Dakota scandal. Had she suspected Dakota of cheating on her? Was *she* cheating on *him* with Betty's Mr. Dye Job?

Crossing Primrose Lane, Anne turned left on Beechwood Avenue and stopped in front of Mallory's rented house. Trying the front door, she found it unlocked. Voices drifted from the rear of the house. She started to walk toward the kitchen, then changed her mind and climbed the stairs to the master bedroom. The room was sunny and spacious. The bed had been neatly made up, the drapes flung open. Some of Mallory's belongings were carefully laid out on a chaise longue. It looked as if she'd be back any minute. But it also seemed artificial—overly tidy, as though staged for effect.

Anne took a pad and pen from her pocketbook and began describing the scene. If worse came to worse, and she wasn't able to learn anything more about what Mallory was planning to divulge in *Loving You*, she'd have to pad the book with what Phil Smedley called "local color." She noted the four-poster canopy bed with its frilly white throw pillows, and the framed black-and-white portrait of Marilyn Monroe that Mallory had brought with her from California. *Marilyn, how sad. Another life cut short.*

Some of Mallory's things were grouped on the maple dresser: a silver hand mirror, a tortoiseshell comb, lots of Lancome lipsticks and eye shadows, a porcelain cup and saucer decorated with tulips, three bottles of tanning lotion, a glass paperweight shaped like a star. Anne peeked into the closet, crammed with dresses, skirts, and slacks, some with price tags still attached. Mallory had enough clothes to outfit a harem. There must have been at least forty pairs of shoes. Who would inherit them, now that Mallory was dead? Probably not her sister. Sheila would have no use for these fancy duds.

If Mallory had stayed in the Heights till Christmas, she wouldn't have had the chance to wear all these clothes. Still, Anne thought, it must be nice to shop till you drop and not worry about how you were going to foot the bill. She began to sift through the clothes, jotting down the designer names on the labels. She recognized a few outfits Mallory had worn during the past week—a black silk jumpsuit, a print cotton shift, an emerald green cardigan, white Capri pants. She slipped her fingers inside the pockets, encountering tissues, a lipstick, a few loose coins. She felt uneasy, embarrassed, like she was violating Mallory's privacy. Phil would love this. Going through the closet of a corpse. The black slip dress Mallory had worn at the party was missing. Had she been wearing that dress when she disappeared? At one end was a black satin blazer covered in plastic, with the dry cleaning bill still attached.

Anne glanced at the slip. Busy Bee Dry Cleaners in Neptune. Busy Bee was computerized. Mallory had brought the blazer in at 4:35 P.M. on Monday, and it had been delivered that morning, at 10:38 A.M. Anne lifted the plastic and rummaged through the pockets. Nothing. She folded back the lapel, checking the inside breast pocket. Buried at the bottom, something square and flat. She removed it carefully: a hot pink book of matches from a bar called the *Shady Lady* in Landsdown Park. On the cover was a drawing of a woman in a broad-brimmed hat, holding a martini glass. Anne flicked the matchbook open. Somebody had scrawled a name and a telephone number on the inside cover. Slipping the matches into her pocket, Anne closed the closet door. She walked over to the dresser and was just about to open the top drawer when she heard footsteps.

"What are you doing?" a voice demanded.

She turned to find Detective Mark Trasker standing in the doorway. His gaze was disapproving, almost stern. Behind him stood Jill Bentley.

"Conducting research, for my book," Anne said defensively.

The detective entered the room and stood by the bed, watching her. "Is that so?"

Trasker's arms were folded across his chest. He was staring at her like she'd illegally entered an off-limits crime scene. He wore tan slacks, a white cotton shirt, and a jaunty blue blazer, from which he removed a piece of paper.

"I was going to drop by your house later this afternoon." He handed her the paper. "Recognize this?"

She stared at the printed sheet. It was the page he'd typed out on her Royal. *The quick brown fox jumped over the lazy white dog.* She looked at him questioningly.

"That's a copy. I had the original analyzed."

Jill Bentley turned toward the detective. "What's going on?" she asked.

"That's what I'd like to know," Anne said angrily.

Trasker walked over to Mallory's bureau. Picking up the paperweight, he shifted it from one hand to the other. "Remember I was telling you about those notes Mallory got? How the last one was different from the other five. More violent, more of a threat." He put the paperweight back on the bureau and spun it around. "We analyzed the ink, the paper it was printed on. And we caught a break. The Y's are a shade lower than the other letters. A printer wouldn't make a mistake like that. It's what you'd find on a manual typewriter. I asked around, found out you own one."

Anne felt her face flush. Her eyes widened in disbelief. "Are you implying I wrote that obscene letter?"

"We analyzed the paper, too," Trasker said. "Easy to trace. Southworth Linen White, ink-jet stock. You purchased two boxes on August 19 at Peyton's Stationers here in town. The owner remembers you coming in. Said the paper was on sale."

"Don't you see what this means?" Anne said hotly.

"Yes, I do," the detective replied. "It means you're a suspect in the death of Mallory Loving."

Chapter 11

The little black dress is a classic. Every woman should own at least one.

Anne gazed incredulously at Detective Trasker. "A suspect?" she repeated. "I thought Mallory's death was an accident."

The detective's expression was grim. "There's a strong possibility she was murdered," he said.

"What do you mean?" Jill exclaimed. Her face was ashen.

"We're analyzing the tire tracks, the remains of the Lexus, how fast it went over the embankment, the damaged guard rail. So far, it doesn't add up to an accident."

"But that can't be." Jill gasped. "Everyone's saying Mallory was back on drugs. She must have lost control of the wheel. What about the brakes?"

"The car was too badly damaged to examine them properly. But I doubt there was a problem. When brakes don't work, a car tends to swerve wildly, as the driver loses control. And that wasn't the case here."

Anne's mind was racing. "You mean someone forced Mallory's car off the road?"

"Possibly," the detective said. He was watching Anne intently, almost scientifically, as if she were a fly whose wings he'd just removed.

"But that can't be." Jill gasped. "Someone would have noticed."

"Not necessarily," Anne cut in. "The place where the car crashed through the guard rail is at a bend in the road. You can't see it from a distance. And Route 6 isn't well lit. Besides, people don't use it much anymore, especially at night, not since they started building the new extension to the turnpike."

Her mind sorted through the possibilities. Anyone could have forced Mallory's car over the embankment—Koppelman, Dakota, Caitlin, anyone. She visualized the curve in the road. You'd have to work fast, but it could be done. Who had killed Mallory? The same person who broke into the house? And why did that person use her typewriter to compose an obscene threatening letter?

The detective leaned forward. His eyes were trained on Anne, as if he were trying to read her mind. "Did *you* type the note to Mallory and wrap it up as a birthday gift?"

"Of course not," Anne snapped. "What would I possibly have to gain?"

"Bigger book sales, for one. As it stands now, the sensational publicity surrounding Mallory's death means you'll sell millions of copies.

"Oh, please," Anne groaned sarcastically. "I'd like to be famous as much as the next author, but I'm not about to kill to land on the *New York Times* best-seller list. Whoever broke into my house must have used my typewriter—after they erased my files."

She studied Trasker, trying to determine if he believed her or not. If she had to bet on it, she'd go with no. But she also got the feeling he wasn't showing all his cards. She slipped her hand into her pocket, felt for the matches. If he wasn't telling everything he knew, neither would she.

"At this point we're not sure there *was* a break-in," Trasker said. "We couldn't get any clear prints off your keyboard."

"What does it matter now?" Jill interjected. "Mallory's dead."

"Until we can prove otherwise," the detective said evenly, "Miss Hardaway is a suspect." He headed for the door. "Don't leave town," he said pointedly to Anne. "I'd like you to be available for questioning as we continue the investigation."

"I don't believe this," Anne said to Jill after Trasker left. "He can't really think I'd kill Mallory."

"The whole thing is crazy," Jill said, flashing a sympathetic smile. She had on a taupe-colored pants suit and black sandals with thick wedge heels. Standard attire for Jill. But she looked worn out. Faint circles pooled beneath her eyes. Her close-cropped brown hair, normally blown dry to magazine-style perfection, was rumpled. "Mallory got into an accident," Jill said firmly. "End of story."

"No," Anne said slowly. "I don't think so."

"Why?" Her strong "Joizy" accent drew out the word into two syllables.

"A couple of things don't quite fit. You took the call Mallory got that night, didn't you?"

Jill rolled her eyes. "I am so sick of talking about that call. If I'd known it was going to be this important, I would have paid more attention."

"Was it a man or a woman?"

"A man, I think. The voice was kind of muffled."

"You screen all of Mallory's calls, right? Did you ask who was calling?"

"Of course I did." Her tone was annoyed. "The guy said he was Arnold Baker, so I called Mallory to the phone. He said it was a bad connection 'cause he was on his car phone."

Anne nodded. Arnold Baker was one of the men behind Pegasus Productions, the L.A.-based group that was financing *Dark Horizon*. Mallory would have taken his call no matter what time it was.

"But it wasn't Mr. Baker," Anne said, restating the obvious.

"No. Turns out he's in Hawaii. Least that's what the detective said."

Then the mystery caller had to be someone familiar with the film. Anne's gaze wandered around the room. Her eye was drawn to the cup and saucer on the dresser. "Where did Mallory get that?"

"In town, at her ex-husband's shop."

So Gerald had lied. Aloud, she said, "How do you know?"

"I was with her. I bought a cup, too. Only mine has little birds on it."

"When did the two of you visit the Antique Boutique?"

Jill thought a moment. "A couple of days ago, I guess. On . . . Monday."

"The day before Mallory disappeared."

"Yes. Why?"

"No reason. I went in there this morning and almost bought a cup myself. Did Gerald talk to Mallory much when the two of you dropped by?"

"They had a big fight," Jill said, almost too eagerly. "I guess there's some bad blood between them."

"What do you mean?"

"They went into the back while I was looking around. I could hear them yelling at each other. He sounded like he wanted to kill her."

It occurred to Anne that Jill was punching up the story and enjoying every minute of it. What for? She'd always assumed Jill was loyal to Mallory—the devoted assistant, working behind the scenes to ensure that Mallory got where she needed to go. Maybe Jill had secretly despised her boss.

"Did you hear what they were arguing about?" Anne said.

"It was about a dress. She claimed he sneaked in here and stole one of her dresses. I'd seen her wear it once. A Bob Mackie original, I think. Black with seed pearls at the neck and wrists."

Anne went over to the closet, peered inside. There were several black dresses, but none like the one Jill had described. "So they had this argument and then she ended up buying a cup from him?" Anne said quizzically.

Jill laughed. "Mallory didn't *buy* the cup and saucer. She took them after they quarreled. Of course, I paid for mine. Cost me an arm and a leg." Jill glanced at her watch. "Oh, God," she exclaimed. "I'm late. I've got to get back to the set." She beamed broadly, showing off a set of glossy white teeth. "You're looking at Caitlin's new personal assistant."

The Church by the Sea was the prize jewel in the Oceanside Heights crown. No other church on the Eastern seaboard was as large, as imposing, or as much of a tourist attraction. Situated directly across from the beach, the monolithic white building had three turrets, towering stained glass panels, and a twelve-foot-high cross on the roof. For nearly one hundred years, the cross had been lit at night. You could see it from thirty miles away, even out on the Atlantic. But it was dark now. Some of the bulbs had burned out, others were broken. And there wasn't enough money to fix it.

Still, the church was striking. It looked like an oversize house, with a wide sloping roof and shutters on the windows the color of sea glass. Just inside the massive double doors was a bronze plaque, bearing the mission statement of the town's founders: *To provide opportunities for spiritual birth and renewal through worship in a proper, convenient, and desirable Christian seaside setting.*

Anne had spent every Sunday of her early childhood sitting in the front pew. The wooden benches were smooth and cool and smelled faintly of cedar. Through the large window behind the pulpit, she had glimpsed the gentle rise of the dunes, the gulls wheeling and keening over the ocean. Her mother had sat beside her, wearing her best Sunday dress and a pair of white gloves fastened at the wrist. Anne had listened to the minister talk about faith and redemption, until Jesus became part of the sky and the sea, and she imagined the Lord's hand guiding the waves toward the shore, fashioning each shell, each tiny particle of sand. That was before her mother got sick and started acting crazy. Then she stopped going to church. It no longer held the power to comfort her, and she felt like an outsider among people in town. They'd withdrawn from Evelyn Hardaway little by little, like petals torn from a flower, until it seemed to Anne as though she and her mother were all alone.

Maybe if Evelyn had had cancer or heart disease, things would have been different. Anne had seen it happen, seen people rally around a sick neighbor—cooking, cleaning, acting kind and supportive. But Alzheimer's disease made her mother do strange things, strange un-Christian things, and the town had turned its collective back. The last time Anne had gone to formal services at the Church by the Sea had been eleven years earlier, for her father's funeral. But she sometimes went there at off hours, just to sit and think. Though she no longer sensed the presence of God, she still appreciated the tranquil power of the church, its simple understated beauty.

On her way home from the library, Anne walked by the church and heard angry voices coming from inside. She peeked through one of the side entrance doors. Several elderly matrons of the town were clustered in seats near the middle of the center aisle, along with Nathan Kurnetsky, Joe Vance, Bradley Herr, and a couple of others who owned stores on Main Street. Anne entered the church quietly and crept closer.

"We've got to put a stop to it," Eleanor Granville was saying, "get these movie people out of town before it's too late."

"I thought they'd be gone by now," Nathan Kurnetsky chimed in. "But I saw on the television they're fixing to stay even longer."

"Two more weeks!" bellowed Joe Vance. "Why, I'll practically be out of business by then. They been blocking off the sidewalk in front of the drugstore. My regular customers can't hardly get to the lunch counter. There's got to be a way we can pull the plug."

"But what about the money Mr. Koppelman's offering," said Bradley Herr, whose family had owned the Sandcastle restaurant for three generations. "You know how much it'll cost to electrify the cross? Ten, twelve thousand dollars. And he's offering twenty-five grand. I think we should let him film here."

Lucille Klemperer stood up. She wore a dowdy gray dress and a straw hat with plastic daisies on the brim. Lucille was so mad, the daisies were shaking. "Gentlemen, please," Lucille said. "How can you be concerned with money when our souls in mortal danger? They're talking about bringing their filthy cameras into church. The church, for pity's sake!"

"But Lucille," Bradley Herr protested. "The director promised he'd be real careful. Lots of folks feel the same way. I brought a petition." He waved a piece of paper at the group.

Lucille shook her head solemnly. "This is a historic building, a house of worship. It's wrong, plain as day. In man's eyes, if not God's." She placed a veined right hand on her breast. "I charge thee, fling away ambition. By that sin fell the angels." Her voice was trembling. "How can man, then, the image of his Maker, hope to win by it?"

"What we need," Joe Vance interjected, "is a plan. Does anyone have any ideas or should we just . . ." His voice trailed off as he spotted Anne. Everyone turned to stare. There was a long, uncomfortable silence.

"Is this a private party?" Anne said, coming toward the group, "or can anyone join in?"

Nathan Kurnetsky stepped forward. "That depends," he said, "on whether you're with us or against us."

"The movie isn't going to go away, just because you'd like it to," Anne said coolly. "They'll only be here another couple of weeks, and then everything will be back to normal."

Lucille shook her fist in the air. "Of course she's against us. Anne's in league with the movie folks. Why, she and that gal who died were thick as thieves. They were working on a book together."

Sunlight streamed through the stained glass. The huge pipe organ on the left side of the altar took on a burnished coppery glow. "Did any of you have anything to do with the disturbances on the set?" Anne asked, looking at each of them in turn. "With the damaged or missing equipment?"

No one spoke. Outside, Anne could hear the wind rustling through the beach grass and the distant tinkle of the Good Humor truck. Lucille Klemperer drew herself up to her full height. She marched down the bright red carpet in the center aisle and exited through the rear door. One by one, the others followed, until Anne was alone.

She sat down in a pew and picked up a thick black prayer book. She imagined her mother sitting beside her, hands clasped, eyes trained on the minister in the pulpit. Flipping open the prayer book, Anne idly turned the pages. She remembered the sermons of her youth, how the minister's voice would rise up and the congregation, nearly transfixed, had answered him with a hearty "Amen," responding as one, a united tribe. Her eye was drawn to a passage on the page: *And God shall wipe away all tears from their eyes; and there shall be no more death, neither sorrow, nor crying, neither shall there be any more pain: for the former things are passed*

*away. And he that sat upon the throne said, Behold, I
make all things new. And he said unto me, Write: for
these words are true and faithful.*

On her way home, she ran a few errands: dropping
Helen's film off at the One-Hour photo place, picking
up a container of skim milk at the Mini-Mart, buying a
birthday card for her Uncle Sidney, waiting on line at
the ATM machine, going back to the photo shop to pick
up the film. Funny how life rolled along, even in the
face of death. It felt strange to be gassing up the Mustang when Mallory's car was a smoldering wreck.
Strange and sad. It was 2:30 before she finally walked
in the door.

She checked her messages. The first one was from
Jack, who was about to fly to Venice for the weekend.
What she wouldn't give to be drifting down the Grand
Canal in a gondola with Jack instead of running around
the Heights, trying to find out what happened to Mallory
Loving. Another message, from Phil Smedley. More of
an order, really. *Where are those chapters? Fax them,
pronto.*

She made herself a tuna sandwich on rye and washed
it down with a Diet Coke and a powdered donut. All
she had for Phil were Mallory's beauty tips. Okay, she
told herself. The man wants copy. She sat down at her
computer and stared at the blank screen. *Chapter One*,
she typed. She drummed her fingers on the keyboard.

How would Mallory have wanted the book to begin?
With something self-aggrandizing, no doubt. *I've known
I was a star since I was six years old*, Anne typed. Mallory had said something to that effect once. *When I
played dress-up with my sister, I was always a famous
actress, and she was my maid.* Sheila had told Anne that
the other day. It was ironic that Sheila hadn't seen her
sister in years, and then Mallory was lost to her forever.
Sheila had said Mallory got a phone call right before she
disappeared, a call that had frightened her. Anne reached

into the bottom drawer of her desk and took out the phone book. She looked up the number for Bell Atlantic and dialed.

"Tina Lassell, please," she said to the operator.

"Just a moment."

Tina was a systems analyst for Bell Atlantic. She was also president of the New Jersey chapter of the X-Files Fan Club. Anne had met her last year when she was writing *A Viewer's Guide to Unauthorized Secrets of the X-Files*. After watching ninety-two episodes of the TV show, Anne had tried without success to talk to the producer and the actors, and had to settle for doing a clip job—rewriting magazine and newspaper clips about the show—along with interviewing a dozen people who knew more about alien abductions, UFOs and David Duchovny's love life than she had thought possible.

"Hi, Tina. It's Anne Hardaway."

"Anne. Hey, good to hear from you. Are you writing another book? Because I have such exciting news. We're starting an X-Files museum, right here in Camden. It'll be filled with stuff that's been on the show. Guns, autopsy equipment, special effects."

"That's great." Anne had stopped trying to figure out other people's obsessions a long time ago. As long as they didn't hurt anyone, what was the harm? "No, this time around, I'm writing a book about Mallory Loving."

"Oh my God. That's so cool."

"I was wondering if you could help me out."

"Sure. What do you need?"

"Mallory received a phone call around three A.M., on Wednesday, August 27, the morning she disappeared. I was hoping you could trace it for me."

"I could try. What's the phone number where she was?"

"It's 555-3131."

"Okay," Tina said. "I'll see what I can do."

"Do you need my number?"

"No. I still have it. And by the way, your book is

going to be on sale in the X-Files museum shop, as soon as we get everything set up.''

"Thanks. My publisher will be happy to hear it.''

After Anne hung up, she picked up the phone again and dialed the operator, who gave her the number for the Betty Ford Center in Rancho Mirage, California. It took about fifteen minutes to get transferred to the right person in the right department who was authorized to tell her what she wanted to know. After explaining who she was and what *Loving You* was about, she finally got the information she was looking for. Yes, they'd been notified about Mallory's bequest. It was extremely generous of the actress to have named the center the sole benefactor in her will. How generous? Anne wanted to know.

She was shocked by the answer. It turned out Mallory Loving's entire estate was worth a grand total of $12,500—barely enough money for an Oscar de la Renta original or a two-week stay at Canyon Ranch. In Mallory's world, this qualified as being broke! Anne had known that Mallory had fallen on hard times, but she had no idea things were this bad. In an article about Mallory's death, today's issue of *Variety* mentioned that because of her history of drug addiction, there was a clause in her *Dark Horizon* contract stipulating she be paid *after* filming had ended. She must have been banking on the money from the movie and the book in a big way.

Anne went back to her computer. *Chapter One* stared out at her from the screen. *It was going to be my big comeback*, Anne typed. *A starring role in a blockbuster movie that couldn't fail. I'd been waiting for an opportunity like this all my life. Here was a chance to prove everybody wrong, to finally come out on top.* Anne stopped typing. This was impossible. Her notes were gone. Mallory was dead. And she couldn't bring herself to make up the damn book as she went along. There was still too much she didn't know. And the movie people weren't any help. It was hard to know whether actors were lying or whether they'd simply memorized lines they thought you wanted to hear. She suspected she wouldn't get a straight answer from any of them. What she needed was a fresh pair of eyes.

She picked up the phone and called Helen at work.

"What are you doing tonight?" Anne said, when Helen came on the line.

"Nothing much. Charlie's working late. Wanna drive to that new Mexican place in Bradley Beach? I've been dying to try it."

"Some other time," Anne said. "How'd you like to be in a movie?"

Chapter 12

If you've got tired eyes, stay away from using eyeliner or mascara on the lower lid. Add pink or peach to the brow line to draw attention upward. Cold cucumber slices, moist chamomile tea bags, and frozen teething rings placed on the eyes can help reduce puffiness.

Although it was after dark, the canvas tents clustered around the Church by the Sea were bathed in white floodlights, which illuminated the arched doorways, the American flags hanging from the roofs, the tidy interiors filled with cots, rocking chairs, and TVs; baskets of geraniums on the tiny, narrow porches. The lights were so glaring that each feature took on an eerie, surreal glow. The tents hadn't been in the original script of *Dark Horizon*, but Howard Koppelman had asked the screenwriters to add a scene, incorporating their old-fashioned, rustic charm, and providing a quaint counterpoint to the high-tech plot.

When Anne was eight years old, she'd made friends with a girl named Penny from Jackson, Mississippi, whose family rented a tent during the summer. Anne had always found the tents enchanting, like miniature dwellings pulled from the pages of a fairy tale. While Penny's parents attended the church's summer programs—Bible hour, gospel sings, organ recitals, lectures by visiting clergymen on "Renewal of the Holiness Heritage" and "Prayer in a Christian World"—the girls played in the tent. Sometimes they pretended they were butterflies and hummingbirds in a magic hideaway deep in the forest. Other days a circus tent transformed the girls into clowns and lion tamers and glamorous aerialists who twirled above the big top, executing daring high-wire dives. Or they imagined a hospital tent, where they cared for wounded teddy bears and tree frogs that they'd capture, then release. Anne remembered coming home to the yellow cottage on Ocean Avenue at the end of the day and wondering why her family needed so much space. The tents were cozier, and much more fun to play in, even if their charm was spartan.

Now, in the blinding light cast by the movie equipment, the tents took on a larger than life quality. Caitlin Grey emerged from a white one trimmed with green and blue stripes. She wore skintight black pants, black open-toed pumps, and a red midriff top. Anne recognized the outfit immediately as one of Mallory's costumes. A production assistant offered Caitlin a mini spinach quiche, while a makeup assistant dabbed powder on Caitlin's face. Betty Flugelhorn hovered around the actress like a nervous moth, fluffing the ends of Caitlin's hair with a large round brush. Nick Fabien, Caitlin's newly acquired personal trainer, massaged her shoulder blades. In my next life, Anne thought, I want to come back as a movie star. Not a bit player.

She and Helen were herded together with three dozen other extras from Oceanside Heights and the surrounding beach towns. Koppelman seemed to have deliberately chosen eccentric types, whose main claim to fame was distinctively ugly features: obese women with double chins and mounds of doughy flesh, aging men with obvious toupees and Fagin-like beaked noses, people whose thick glasses, polyester pants suits, misshapen bodies, and freakish expressions branded them as losers who would feel right at home in a Diane Arbus photograph, a Fellini film, or a sideshow. Anne was surprised she had signed herself and Helen aboard so easily, considering they didn't have any obvious physical deformities.

"When do the extras get to eat?" Helen asked Anne.

"Beats me. I'm starved," Anne said. "It feels like we've been here forever."

Helen glanced at her watch. "Nine-thirty. God, we've been standing around for more than three hours. And I thought being a loan officer was boring! We should have eaten something before we came."

"I know," Anne agreed. Not only was she starving, she was hot and cranky, and she'd already gotten three mosquito bites that were itching like crazy.

It was a humid night. The air felt heavy, oppressive, as if it might rain. Bugs fluttered in front of the movie equipment, drawn by the steady white glare of the lights. From what Anne could gather, once filming started, they were each supposed to go to separate preassigned spots and pretend to be tent dwellers, taking care not to look at the cameras. But no one had told them where to stand, and efforts to find out how much longer they had to wait were met with blank stares.

"I'm going to try and steal us some grub," Helen whispered, pointing to a long table laden with hero sandwiches, cheese steaks, fruit, cookies, and diet soda, which was strictly for cast and crew only. "While I'm behind enemy lines, I'll see if I can find out anything."

"Good luck," Anne whispered back. "If you're captured by enemy forces, give a holler."

As Helen began circling the buffet table, Anne spotted Sheila Lovitz across the street, half-hidden by the trunk of a maple tree. She crossed Abbott Avenue and approached Sheila from the side.

"Hi," Anne called out.

Sheila jumped back. "Oh." She gasped. "You startled me."

Sheila was wearing the same outfit she'd had on the night Anne first met her at the bingo parlor: denim overalls, a short-sleeved white T-shirt, brown leather sandals.

"I've been meaning to drop by," Anne said, "to tell you how sorry I am about Mallory."

"Oh, thanks."

Anne peered through the darkness at Sheila. "What are you doing here? I didn't think you had much use for Hollywood shenanigans."

"I don't," Sheila said quickly. "It's just I heard there's going to be a memorial service." Sheila kept her voice low. Her face was partially hidden by her lanky brown hair.

"That's right." Betty had mentioned something about it.

"Do you know when and where?" Sheila asked.

"Not yet. But I can keep you posted."

Anne tried to get a better look at Sheila's face. Sheila's eyes were puffy and red, her skin slightly blotchy. She seemed distracted, stressed out, which was natural considering her sister had just died. Not so natural when you factored in the animosity Sheila had felt toward Mallory.

Sheila mumbled something under her breath.

"What?" Anne said.

"You going ahead with the book?"

"Yes. The pub date's been moved up."

"Well, good luck with it. If there's anything more I can do to help . . ."

"Did Detective Trasker contact you?"

Sheila took another step back. "Yes, why?"

"He doesn't think Mallory's death was an accident."

"What do you mean?" Sheila sounded frightened. Her hair covered her cheeks, partially obscuring her eyes, but not before Anne glimpsed her expression. Why did she look so grief-stricken, so tense, when all these years she'd hated her sister?

"Did the detective ask you where you were last night?"

"I'm not a suspect," Sheila said quickly.

A little too quickly, Anne thought. "Were you at home last night?" Anne said, trying to sound casual.

"Where else would I be?" Sheila said. "I have no life." Her tone wasn't sarcastic. It was matter-of-fact.

Across the street, technicians were dragging the wind machine into place. It started up with a low roar.

"Well," Sheila said, shuffling her feet. "I should be going."

"To bingo?"

Sheila's eyes were trained on the set. "Yeah," she said with a thin smile. "You gotta be in it to win it."

"I think that's the lottery."

"Same difference."

Anne spotted Helen waving at her near the food trailer. "I've got to go, too," she said. "Talk to you soon." But Sheila was already halfway down the block, moving fast.

Puzzling things over, Anne crossed the street and returned to the tents. The encounter had been odd. Sheila clearly resented Mallory, blamed Mallory for sabotaging her one true love. But could she possibly have disliked her sister enough to kill her?

Back at the tents, one of the production assistants was reading off a list of names, telling extras where to go.

"Here," Helen said, slipping Anne a chunk of foccacia bread. "This was the best I could do."

"Great." Anne took a bite. It was warm and tasted like fresh herbs.

"They assigned each of the tents a number," Helen said, "You're in 68. I'm in 15. And Caitlin and Dakota are definitely an item."

"What makes you so sure?"

"I happened to be eavesdropping on Caitlin's conversation just now. He bought her a ring. And I don't mean zirconium."

Anne glanced over to where Caitlin was consulting with the costume designer. A ring, huh? For a match made in heaven. If you combined both their egos, what you'd end up with could fill Giants Stadium. "When's the wedding?"

"She wants it ASAP. He's not in as big of a rush. Either way, sounds like they have great sex."

Anne tore off another hunk of foccacia. "You think she could have killed Mallory to get the part and the guy?"

"Absolutely."

"What about him?"

Helen grinned. "Let's put it this way, I don't think he got where he is by making nice. I heard a techie say he threatened one of the grips. Something about an overhead mike being too close to his face."

How *had* Dakota risen through the ranks? There must have been hundreds, maybe thousands of musicians who could play guitar and sing on key. Men who didn't need to lip-synch their lyrics. And where *was* he, anyway? She hadn't seen him since Mallory's birthday party. Which made it hard to ask him about the lip-synching.

"By the way," Helen said, "what's a grip?"

"The person responsible for maintaining the equipment on the set. They move things around, place props, build scaffolds, stuff like that."

"I don't know, Anne," Helen said, with a wicked grin. "The movie biz is starting to make banking look good."

Before Anne could think of a suitably witty come-back, she heard her name being called, and she and Helen had to race to their assigned spots. The whole process reminded her of going to the doctor, she thought, as she dog-trotted toward her tent. The receptionists always called a day in advance to confirm your appointment. But once you got there, you usually had to wait over an hour because doctors only valued their time, not yours.

Tent 68 was slightly west of the church. The windows were festooned with frilly pink curtains. Pink geraniums hung from woven baskets on the porch, and cabbages as small as toads grew in the tiny vegetable garden. Anne was fairly sure the tent belonged to a couple from Minnesota who had been summering in the Heights for years and were both pushing ninety.

She felt a hand on her shoulder. "Hiya, Annie," said a familiar voice.

She whirled around. "David. Hi."

David Chilton had a grin on his face the size of a Cheshire cat. His teeth fairly gleamed. "I didn't know you were going to be in this movie, too."

"Yup." She smiled. "Guess this is our fifteen minutes of fame."

Chilton was the town's resident dentist. He was six feet tall, with a square jaw, chocolate brown eyes, great-looking teeth. He was also unhappily married, and had given Anne every reason to believe he was going to leave his perky wife and three adorable children last year. Their affair had ended when it became apparent that the split was happening only in David Chilton's extravagant, very fertile imagination. The Heights was small, so Anne bumped into David practically every other day. It had gotten to the point where she was so completely over him that she couldn't recall what she'd ever seen in him. The love she'd once felt seemed as remote as a fever dream.

"I already had my moment in the spotlight," David

Chilton announced proudly. "You're looking at the man who provided the police with Mallory Loving's dental records."

"Did she go to your father when she was younger?"

"Yup. Pop treated practically everyone in Landsdown and the Heights. I saved all his records. Never knew they would come in this handy." David waved a mosquito away from his face. "How about all this excitement?" he said happily. "Isn't it something?"

"I'll say."

When she and David had been seeing each other, they'd had to sneak around, meeting in no-tell motels along the shore, far away from the prying eyes of the town. It hadn't exactly been easy hiding their affair, pretending there was nothing between them when she saw him in the deli aisle of the Mini-Mart or the reading room at the library. Looking back, she realized that was part of what had attracted her to him in the first place—the clandestine meetings, the secrecy and danger, the risk of being caught.

"You know what?" David said, flashing a smile. "I think we should talk to the mayor about promoting the Heights more. Hook up with the New Jersey Film Commission, get these Hollywood types to come here on a regular basis."

"How come?"

David Chilton laughed. "Because it's fun. Can you imagine sitting at the plex at the mall and seeing your face on the big screen?"

"We're extras, David. We'll be lucky if we don't end up on the cutting room floor."

"Still, I'm having a blast. You know what? This movie's even been good for business. I've treated a cinematographer, a sound engineer, and a gaffer, whatever that is. See that woman over there?" He nodded toward Jill Bentley, who was trailing after Caitlin while talking into a cell phone. "Came into the office the other day, just as I was closing up. She thought she had a cavity.

Turned out to be a false alarm. Hey, have you eaten yet? How about after this is over, we go grab a bite at the Sandcastle?''

Could he possibly be trying to start things up again? ''Where's Barbara tonight?'' Anne said pointedly.

''In Deal for the weekend. Visiting her mother.'' David grinned broadly. The man had no shame.

''Well, when she comes back, make sure you give her my best.''

''Is that a no?''

''Most definitely.''

''Suit yourself, Annie.'' He started to walk away, then turned back. ''You do look pretty scrumptious in the moonlight,'' he said, all but winking at her.

''Thanks, but no thanks, David.''

''Whatever.''

She watched him saunter off. God, what had she ever seen in that man? He was as subtle as a missing front tooth. She glanced at her watch. Ten o'clock. Obviously she wasn't cut out to be a movie star. The waiting around was maddening. She leaned against the porch railing and watched Caitlin run lines. From this distance Caitlin really resembled Mallory—same hairstyle, same clothes, same imperious manner.

''How much longer, Howard?'' Caitlin called out. ''If we don't get started soon, I'm out of here. I'm positively wilting in this heat.''

''We're almost ready, hon,'' Howard Koppelman said soothingly. He picked up a megaphone, and the actors finally got into position.

Just then Anne saw Betty waving at her frantically. There was something almost needy about her expression. Anne was about to go over to her when Koppelman shouted, ''Action,'' and a kid whose arms were covered with tattoos slammed a black metal clapper together and yelled, ''Take one.''

Anne's job was to walk from her tent to tent number 42. She tried not to look at Caitlin and the actress play-

ing Caitlin's sister, who were in front of tent number 1,
talking in hushed tones. Instead she pretended it was any
other summer night in the Heights, and she was out for
a stroll. Crickets sang in the maple trees. The stars were
out in glorious force, and the air smelled faintly of salt.
The wind machine caused the leaves to rustle gustily.

The other extras seemed to be trying to act just as
nonchalant—sitting in rocking chairs, talking with their
"neighbors," sauntering down the street. Out of the corner of her eye, she saw Helen walking an unfamiliar
Pomeranian. Pets as extras. Now there was a concept.

About a minute later, when the cameras stopped filming, Anne looked up and Betty was gone. Later she
wished she'd been able to talk to the hairstylist. She
would have liked to sip espresso at the Strange Brew
and listen to Betty gossiping and cracking jokes. The
way Betty looked that night came back to Anne at odd
moments. Her expression had been so peculiar, a curious
mix of delight and dread. But Anne had learned long
ago that hindsight was a waste of time. There was no
point in dwelling on what might have been. She couldn't
possibly have known it would be the last time she saw
Betty Flugelhorn alive.

Chapter 13

If you're long-waisted, don't wear long fitted tops. Choose looser styles that cover the waistline. Wear strapless or deep scoop-neck tops to make your body look shorter. No pants with cuffs. They'll make your legs look shorter. Hem lengths should break over the top of your shoes.

The Shady Lady was a dark, tacky little bar in a dark rundown alleyway in Landsdown Park. It smelled of beer and stale chips and sweat. The red neon sign in the window was broken, flashing red light onto the ripped Naugahyde bar stools, the row of liquor bottles over the bar, the half-open bathroom door. The room was crowded and noisy. Cigarette smoke floated up to the ceiling and settled there, like smog.

From an antiquated jukebox came the sound of the Drifters, singing "Under the Boardwalk." The Phillies game blared from an overhead TV.

Anne sat at the bar, nursing a vodka tonic with a twist, trying to ignore the men slouched over their drinks at the rickety wooden tables. She got the feeling that if she made eye contact with anyone, he'd slap a couple of twenties down and expect her to come home with him. Except for two barmaids, she was the only woman in the place.

It was ten minutes to midnight. After thirty-nine takes, Howard Koppelman decided he'd finally gotten the shot he wanted, and the cast and crew had called it a night. Helen had gone home; Anne drove to Landsdown.

"I'm looking for Veronica," Anne told the bartender. That was the name scrawled on the matchbook cover in Mallory's blazer. When she'd called the phone number written inside, she found it had been disconnected.

The bartender nodded at a busty, long-waisted brunette in her mid-thirties, who was depositing a round of drinks at one of the tables. Her face was leathery, too tan, like she'd spent every spare moment sticking it in the sun. Her uniform consisted of denim shorts that ended right below her crotch and a sky blue sleeveless shirt, tied in a knot at her midriff. Silver hoop earrings, dangling silver bracelets, silver platform sandals that harked back to the days of disco. Anne signaled to her.

"Need a refill?" Veronica's voice was low, husky.

"No, thanks. My name's Anne Hardaway. I'd like to talk to you." If she ever decided to stop waitressing, Veronica could probably make an excellent living selling phone sex.

"You a cop?"

"A writer. I was a friend of Mallory Loving."

Veronica clucked her tongue, then traced the sign of a cross in the air. "Tough break. Especially going the way she did, burned to a crisp and all."

"If you've got a minute, I have a couple of questions."

"Sure. My dogs are aching tonight." She sat down on the bar stool next to Anne and extended her hand. "Veronica Neal."

Veronica had a strong grip. Her fingernails were about three inches long, painted a pearly white. "Nice to meet you," Anne said.

Veronica reached into the pocket of her shirt and pulled out a pack of Winstons. "I can't believe Mal's dead. I just saw her last week."

"She came in here?"

Veronica laughed, a deep throaty chuckle. "Are you kidding? Mallory would never set foot in this place. She came over to my place. Right before my landlord evicted me." Veronica lit a cigarette and took a deep, hungry drag. "It's not what you're thinking. I didn't do anything illegal, unless you count not paying rent. I haven't had hot water since I can't remember when. He should have been paying me to live in that dump, not the other way around."

"Have you known Mallory long?"

"All my life. We grew up together. Fact, she's my inspiration. I followed her out to L.A., hoping to make it in pictures, like she did."

"And then . . ." Anne prompted.

"The dream died. It's tough out there. But I did okay for a while. Mallory helped me get my start. Fact, we were in a movie together."

"Really? Which one?"

Veronica tilted her chin toward the ceiling and blew four perfect smoke rings. "Trust me, hon. I don't think you've seen it."

Anne took a sip of her drink. The vodka tasted cheap and bitter. "I rented as many of Mallory's movies as I could get my hands on, including the X-rated ones. It's all going into my book."

"So you're the one doing Mallory's bio? Geez, I wish

somebody would write up my life. I got a million and
one stories. Swear to God.'' A man with thinning gray
hair and a sagging paunch walked by and swatted Veronica's rump. ''Hey,'' she protested halfheartedly.
''Watch it, Ed.'' She turned back to Anne. ''The name
of the movie was *Torrid Tori*. Directed by that jerk Koppelman. He really hit the big time, didn't he? I read in
the papers they're paying him a couple of million for
Dark Horizon.''

Anne looked at Veronica with interest. ''*Torrid Tori*?
You know, Mallory mentioned that movie to me. I called
around to video stores. But no one seems to have heard
of it.''

''You won't find it 'cause it never did get released.''

''Why not?''

Veronica appraised Anne carefully, taking in the
khaki pants, the short-sleeved cotton knit taupe shirt, the
white sandals with their low, sensible heels. Extras were
supposed to dress ''nice, but casual.'' This was the best
she could do on short notice.

''You sure you're not a cop?'' Veronica asked.

''Hardly. You want to see my membership card in the
Author's Guild? Or my checkbook? I bet you make a
lot more than I do.''

Veronica laughed harshly. ''Hon, that's impossible.
But you can't be too careful these days. Know what I
mean?''

''Hey, Ronnie,'' yelled a man at one of the tables.
''What's a guy got to do to get a beer around here?''

Veronica glared at him. ''Hold your damn horses. I'm
on a break.''

''Why didn't the movie get released?'' Anne persisted.

''Because there was a . . . problem.''

''What kind of problem?''

''Trouble on the set.'' Veronica lowered her voice to
a stage whisper. ''A gal got killed.''

Anne looked at her, surprised. Why hadn't Mallory

bothered to mention that little detail? Was she planning to? Mallory had a knack for editing out the parts of her life she most wanted to rewrite.

A cheer went up in the bar. On TV, one of the Phillies had hit a home run. She watched him trot slowly around the bases. "Go on," she said to Veronica.

"Gal's name was Linda LaRue. Only it wasn't. Nobody used their real names 'cause it was porn. Anyway, she was an illegal. She needed to make a few bucks so she could pay off some local yokel and get her green card."

"Linda was from Mexico?"

Veronica nodded. "She had a small part. Mallory was the star. Guess you could say I was the ingenue." Veronica pronounced it *engine-oo*. "Linda's character was supposed to like it rough. There was one scene where a guy was strangling her as they were getting it on."

Anne could guess what happened next. "And he got a little carried away."

"Right. She was gasping and yelling for him to stop. Her face turned all blue. We thought she was just acting."

Anne shuddered. "What did Koppelman have to do with this?" she asked.

"He kept urging the actor on, telling him what great stuff they were getting. Like he was Cecil B. DeMille or something."

"So it was his fault the girl died?"

"Him and the poor actor who was listening to him, yeah."

"What was the actor's name?"

Veronica thought for a moment. "Barry something or other." The men at the tables were getting rowdier, calling for another round of drinks. "Just a sec," Veronica shouted to be heard above the din. She turned back to Anne. "Barry Bigelow."

"When you saw Mallory, did she mention this Barry person at all?

"No reason to. He's six feet under. Died in a hit-and-run accident out in L.A. last year."

"Did Mallory seem upset about anything?"

"Not more than usual. She went on and on about Howard. How he was a hack, how this was the last time she'd ever work with him."

"Why *were* they working together? I could never figure that out."

"Mal said it was the studio's call. Koppelman has a development deal. But he doesn't really call the shots. It's up to the producers, the money men." Veronica winked and stubbed out her cigarette.

"You mean Mallory was having an affair with one of the producers?"

"Honey, it's not who you know. It's who knows you. In the biblical sense."

"You get his name?"

Veronica shrugged. "She never said. Some guy in L.A."

"Arnold Baker?"

"Honey, I couldn't tell you." The red light from the window played across Veronica's face. Leaning her elbows on the bar, she rested her chin in her hand. "I am so damn tired," she complained.

Anne nodded sympathetically. Veronica looked like she'd rather be anywhere else but in this rundown little bar, with the TV blaring and a half-dozen drunks calling her name.

"What else did Mallory say about Koppelman?"

Veronica slid off the bar stool and picked up her tray of drinks. "She said it was about time that sonofabitch got exactly what he deserved."

On her way back to the Heights, Anne stopped off at the Ocean Diner on Route 35. Built in the 1930s, it was a dull silver color, stubby and narrow as an old-fashioned railroad car. Spurred by its proximity to historic Oceanside Heights, the owners had tried to get the diner designated as a landmark building. But the state had turned them down, and they had to settle for a menu that featured "historic hamburger deluxe" and the "first establishment in Jersey to serve cheesesteaks." This last claim was disputed by a restaurant in Trenton, and the two eateries were forever squabbling, taking out newspaper ads to dispute the other's authenticity.

The diner was open all night, and Anne craved a cup of coffee and a chocolate frosted donut. Donuts were her weakness. She could eat them morning, noon, and night, as a snack or a meal. The diner had terrific homemade donuts. Light, not too sugary, nongreasy. She sat at one of the Formica booths by the window and ate two chocolate frosteds slowly.

She'd intended to go straight home and climb into bed. But she didn't feel the least bit tired. Her clothes smelled of cigarette smoke, and she couldn't get the taste of vodka out of her mouth. She wished she could put all the pieces together, so they made sense. If word got out in Tinseltown that Howard Koppelman had been involved in a young woman's death, he'd be ruined. No more multimillion-dollar movie deals. Mallory had the goods on her ex, all right. No wonder Howard had looked worried when he asked how the book was coming along. Howard had as much reason as Dakota for wanting Mallory out of the way.

Anne leaned her head against the back of the booth and closed her eyes. Delving into Mallory's life was like looking through the wrong end of a kaleidoscope. Images were out of focus, a confusing, scrambled blur. Things didn't add up. Little things. Like a cigar band inside a yogurt container. What was an expensive Davidoff cigar doing in a dirty, abandoned house? Had Mallory been holed up there after she disappeared? If so, with whom? And the woman on the rocks the other morning, the woman who was a dead ringer for Mallory or Sheila. Anne hadn't dreamed the woman up. She was real. But which sister was she? And what on earth was she doing there?

After paying her tab, Anne went back to her car. She was too keyed up to go home, so she got into the Mustang and drove through the Heights. The streets were deserted. Even on weekends, in the height of the tourist season, most of her neighbors were in bed before midnight. The stores closed at sundown.

Anne drove along the beach road. It was a hot night, hot and still. A thin sliver of moon hung above the ocean, like a crooked grin. The lights along the boardwalk shone on the empty lifeguard stands, casting long spidery shadows on the sand. She passed her house, continuing down Ocean Avenue another four blocks. When she reached Main Street, she made a right, cruising slowly through the center of town, past Advance Pharmacy and Moby's Hardware and Quilters. All the buildings were dark, their shutters drawn. Except one.

Anne cut the engine and parked across the street from the Antique Boutique. There was a light in the window on the second floor, in Gerald Finch's front parlor. Strange, since Gerald had mentioned he was going to be out of town, visiting his niece. A figure passed in front of the window, a woman from the looks of it. Anne suddenly thought of the break-in at home. Had this same woman broken into Gerald's place? She slouched down in the front seat, keeping her eye on the window. She could see part of Gerald's mahogany breakfront and one corner of the leather wing chair. Ten minutes passed. It was stuffy in the car. Mosquitoes whined in Anne's ears. The heat was so thick, you could cut it with a butter knife.

Anne was just about to call it a night when the light in Gerald's parlor went out. A minute later, a woman with dark shoulder-length hair emerged from the side door of the Antique Boutique, the door truckers used when Gerald received furniture deliveries. The woman was tall and thin. She wore a sweater and a long skirt, a pocketbook slung over one shoulder. In her other hand, she held a shopping bag. Anne couldn't see her face clearly, but something about her struck a familiar chord. The woman looked up and down Main Street, as if making sure no one was around, and then set off at a brisk pace, keeping her head down. Her high heels made a faint clicking sound on the pavement. Anne waited until the woman was a block away. Then she slid across the front seat and as quietly as she could, opened the passenger door of the Mustang, and got out. She hurried after the woman, staying on the opposite side of Main Street.

The woman walked purposefully, although she wobbled a bit, like her shoes didn't fit properly. Anne was glad she had low-heeled sandals on. They made less noise. She trailed the woman carefully, making sure to keep two blocks behind, as the shops gave way to small bungalows and cottages, and the scent of roses drifted from neatly manicured front yards.

When the woman reached Liberty Park, she stopped. Anne stopped, too, ducking behind a tree. The park was small, a square green plot with a couple of benches. The dark-haired woman glanced at her watch. Her back was to Anne. But Anne was sure she'd seen her somewhere before. The woman peered up and down the street, as if searching for something. As she turned in Anne's direction, her face was illuminated by a street lamp. Anne saw the woman's profile, the long aquiline nose, the jut of her chin. A tiny current of shock pulsed through her.

Before she could act, a silver BMW pulled up to the curb. The passenger door opened and Gerald quickly got inside. Anne strained to see the license number, but it was too dark. She stared at the car until it rounded a corner and disappeared from sight. Well, this certainly put a new spin on things. A whole new spin. She returned to the Mustang, looking up at Gerald Finch's darkened house. Then she drove around some more, thinking things over.

It was 2:30 in the morning when Anne finally pulled up outside her house. She checked the front doorknob reflexively. The new locks were in place, but she couldn't shake her nervousness.

She turned the key, then flicked on the light in the living room. Before she'd left, she'd closed all the windows, and the house felt as hot as a sauna. Now she threw the windows open, letting the sea air stream in. She was a light sleeper. If someone tried to break in during the night, she'd hear it. She sank onto the couch and checked her phone messages. There were three. One from Jack, calling from Venice. He was staying at a hotel off Saint Mark's Square with pink marble floors and a king-size Jacuzzi. Tomorrow he was going on a walking tour of the city, and then he planned to sketch the pastel-colored palazzos along the Grand Canal. *I wish like hell you were here*, he said.

"You're not the only one," she said aloud.

The second message was from David Chilton, asking if she'd like to have brunch with him the next day. In your dreams, Anne thought. It was over between them, had been for more than a year. But his wife was out of town. And he couldn't resist the opportunity to cheat. Anne knew she hadn't been David Chilton's first extramarital affair. She probably wasn't the last, either.

She listened to David talking about how he still cared about her, how there was still something between them. Hadn't Anne felt the pull, too? He had a low, silken voice, like a late-night radio announcer. Seductive, in a smooth, understated way. It was one of the things that had first attracted her to him. After what seemed like forever, the machine cut him off. There was a long beep, followed by the last message. Tina Lassell, the *X-Files* fanatic who worked for the phone company.

"Hey," Tina said. "You know that call you wanted me to trace? I found out something kinda strange. Turns out the house Mallory Loving was staying in had two phone numbers. A call came in on the number you gave me at 3:11 A.M. on August 27. It was made from the other number, which means the person who Mallory talked to that night must have been calling from *inside* the house.''

Chapter 14

If you're a redhead, choose warm makeup tones, such as rust, copper, bronze, and gold. (But don't be afraid to use shades of pink.) Freckles can make makeup look splotchy. To cover yours up, cleanse your face with a moisturizer and use heavier, oil-based cream or stick foundation.

Oceanside Heights had one of the lowest crime rates in the state of New Jersey. Maybe it was because the Heights was only one square mile. Or because the population was minuscule, a mere 703 people. Or because it was a dry town, and high school and college kids went farther down the shore to gulp Jell-O shots and glass after foamy glass of beer. A wholesome feeling pervaded the Heights. Though the stately, sometimes quirky architecture recalled the Victorian era, the period the town evoked most was the 1950s, a time of innocence, neighborliness, clean streets, fresh air, and sturdy, old-fashioned values.

The Church by the Sea attracted God-fearing, upstanding folks from around the country. Religious tourists, if you will, whose idea of a good time was a gospel sing, followed by a hearty, home-cooked supper. The Heights was a family-oriented town, a close knit town, the kind of place where you knew whether your neighbors preferred instant or freshly ground coffee, and where the houses were so close to one another, you could reach out and pass a slice of blueberry cobbler from one porch to the next. A gentle town. Scenic, restful, and safe.

That could be why the following morning, when Anne looked out her bedroom window to watch the sun steal across the sky, leaving rosy, bashful streaks of pink, and saw the body lying on the sand, her first thought wasn't murder. It was that the person would probably be slapped with a $50 fine. Sleeping on the beach was strictly prohibited, as was barbecuing, playing the radio, dog walking, and littering. The beach didn't officially open until 9 A.M., when the three wooden gates on the boardwalk were unlocked, and fresh faced teenage girls collected beach passes from tourists and locals alike.

It was still partly dark outside. Anne could just barely make out that the person was lying facedown, dressed in a hooded sweatshirt and jeans. She felt the morning breeze whisper against her face. Anne glanced at the person on the beach. She couldn't tell if it was a man or a woman, just that the person was overweight. Sleeping probably, a large dark figure sprawled on a broad expanse of sand. The sun flung golden light onto the ocean, casting a glittery net. On the dunes, grass rippled in the wind. As she watched, the beach grew more distinct—the wooden lifeguard stands, gulls scavenging for food amid the tangle of seaweed and mussel shells at the water's edge, waves cresting lustily against the shore. Her eyes kept drifting to the sleeping form. There was something odd about the angle of the body. Something wrong, like it had been jerked—no, twisted—into position.

Dressing quickly, she hurried out of the house, across Ocean Avenue, and over the gray wooden planks of the boardwalk. When she came to the chest-high gate that separated boardwalk from beach, she swung herself over it, landing with a thud on the other side. She trotted down the steps leading to the sand, her eyes trained on the body. It was a woman. She could see that now. A large motionless woman. The sun had inched a little higher, and the sky was shot through with pink. Anne sprinted the last thirty feet, then stopped abruptly as she realized what she was looking at.

Betty Flugelhorn lay in a crumpled heap. One arm was bent at the elbow, folded behind her back with the palm facing up. The other arm was extended, as if she were reaching for something. Her feet were bare. Anne knelt down and gingerly turned Betty over. Betty's head flopped to the side. There was a dark eggplant-colored bruise on her neck. She gazed up at the sky, unseeing. During the night, sand had stuck to the whites of her eyes, which were now a gritty shade of brown. Anne shuddered and rocked back onto her heels. She felt her throat tighten, struggled to catch her breath. A sudden chill passed through her. What did the kids say? Someone was walking over her grave. Leaning closer, Anne bent over and closed Betty's eyes. Her eyelids felt thin and papery.

Anne sank down next to the body. There was a throbbing in her ears. The sand felt cool against the backs of her legs. On the horizon, the sun was climbing over the ocean, announcing the start of another hot, beautiful day. The beach was still deserted, but behind her she heard cars whizzing by on Ocean Avenue, windows being thrown open, the creak of screen doors, sounds that meant the town was awakening. In a few minutes she'd have to walk back to her house and call the police. They'd send an ambulance, and the medical technicians would zip Betty into a plastic body bag and strap her onto a stretcher. Someone would have to call Betty's family in California. Anne remembered Betty mentioning an older brother in Santa Monica.

She pictured herself making the call, listening to the phone ring in a house across the country, the confused, pained voice of Betty's brother on the other end, as she delivered the news. It didn't feel real. She felt a quick *buh bum, buh bum* beating in her neck. Her pulse. She couldn't look at Betty. She couldn't not look at her, either.

Everything was bright, too bright. The ocean had turned a deep turquoise, dappled with sunlight. Spray from the waves reared up, hissing onto the shore. She saw the mark made by the high tide, staining the sand a shade darker. It seemed surreal, the dead body on the beach, like a scene from *Dark Horizon*. The director would yell cut and Betty would pick herself up, brush the sand from her eyes. Anne felt the tightness again in her throat. She was slightly dizzy. She closed her eyes, counted to ten. When she opened them, Betty was still crumpled beside her.

Anne noticed a black canvas tote bag next to the body, with the words *Dark Horizon* written in red. Anne reached for the tote. Each member of the cast and crew had received one. A freebie, Betty had called it. A movie perk. Anne turned the bag upside down and dumped the contents onto the sand: keys, lipstick, a miniature bottle of hair spray, tissues, pocket mirror, two combs, a brush, a blank postcard of scenic Oceanside Heights, half a roll of mints, and a Ring Ding wrapper. No wallet. Anne blinked back tears. Betty never could resist Ring Dings. She was always going to start dieting tomorrow. Now tomorrow would never come

Later, it would hit her that Betty Flugelhorn's body

lay directly across the street from her house, opposite her front door, like a message meant especially for her. A message or a warning.

Once again, Detective Mark Trasker sat in Anne's living room, with his legs crossed, studying her like she was a fly who had wandered into the web of a waiting spider. It was another sweltering day. The air smelled clean and faintly salty. Out the window, Anne could see a stream of tourists, loaded down with hampers, umbrellas and chairs, crossing Ocean Avenue. They wouldn't be able to use this part of the beach this morning. It was cordoned off with bright yellow police tape. A half-dozen cops walked back and forth, searching the sand for clues. Where Betty had lain, the outline of her form had been traced with a stick. From where Anne sat, it looked like a child's drawing.

"We believe she was the victim of a mugging," Detective Trasker said.

"A mugging," Anne repeated.

"Yes. The victim was taking a walk along the beach when she encountered a person or persons who demanded money. Miss Flugelhorn must have refused, put up a struggle. And that's when the killer strangled her."

"What about her shoes?" Anne said wearily. It was only 10 o'clock in the morning, but she felt like she'd been up all night.

"What?"

"Betty wasn't wearing any shoes."

"So?"

"So usually when people walk on the sand, they take their shoes off, and hold them in their hands or leave them up on the boardwalk. There weren't any shoes there. I checked. Plus, Betty's rental car is still parked where she usually left it, halfway across town. Most people don't take long walks barefoot."

"Meaning what?" He was studying her in that cool, deliberate way of his.

"I don't think Betty was mugged on the beach. If she had been, there would have been some kind of struggle, like you said. Maybe she would have screamed. Someone would have heard something, seen something. The boardwalk is lit at night. It would be very risky to commit a violent crime in plain sight."

Detective Trasker drummed his pen lightly against his notepad. "All right. I'll bite. What do *you* think happened?"

"I think Betty was killed someplace else. She was staying at the Yard Arm Inn, right?" Trasker nodded. "Let's say she was in her room at the Yard Arm, lounging around in jeans and a sweatshirt. It's late. There's a knock at the door. Somebody comes in. They talk for a while. Maybe Betty turns her back for a second, and that's when the person strangles her. I've been in the room where Betty was staying. It's on the ground floor in the back, right next to the rear door that leads out to the parking lot. It'd be easy for someone to shove Betty in a car, drive the five blocks to the beach, carry her onto the boardwalk and down the steps, then dump her body on the sand. If anyone noticed, it would look romantic, not threatening. A man carrying his girlfriend down to the beach. But the killer was in such a hurry to get out of there he forgot to put shoes on her."

"Are you certain Miss Flugelhorn would open her door late at night and start chatting with whoever was on her doorstep? Even in cozy little Oceanside Heights?"

Something in his tone struck a chord. She wondered if it was hard being a black cop investigating two deaths in lily white Oceanside Heights. Oh, there wouldn't be any obvious signs of prejudice. Only a subtle coolness, like mist rising off Grassmere Lake. She stared at the detective, trying to determine what he was really thinking. But he was a difficult man to read.

Aloud, she said, "Betty may have opened the door to someone she knew."

"Why would this person go to all the trouble of moving her body?"

"To make it look like a random mugging, not premeditated murder."

The detective leaned forward ever so slightly. His expression didn't change. It was stuck in neutral. "I have a few more questions."

"Okay. But I'd like to ask you something first. Yesterday you said you were analyzing the tire tracks left by Mallory's car the night she died. Could you tell me what you found out?"

Detective Trasker's face was impassive. She got the impression that very little fazed him, whether it be the remains of murder victims or the messy business of dying. "This is for your book, I presume."

"Yes. I could contact the police department directly, go through the usual channels. But I'm pressed for time."

"I see," he said evenly. "Well, I suppose it will be in the papers shortly. The tire tracks were barely visible. No skid marks, nothing that would indicate Miss Loving's car was forced off the road by another vehicle." His tone was polite, almost disinterested. Yet his eyes never left Anne's face. "From the angle the car went over the embankment, we believe it was pushed from behind."

"Then Mallory may have already been dead when the car went into the guard rail," Anne said excitedly. "She could have been killed someplace else. Strangled, even. Like Betty."

Detective Trasker smiled. It was a thin, joyless smile, and it made Anne suddenly afraid. "Where were you at about ten o'clock the night Miss Loving was killed?" he said slowly.

Anne's eyes widened in surprise. "At home."

"Can anyone corroborate that? Did you have friends over that evening? Did you speak to anyone on the phone?"

"No. I made myself dinner, I started reading, and I fell asleep. I woke up a little after eleven, when Betty called to tell me Mallory had been in an accident."

"I see."

"What exactly do you see?" Anne demanded.

"A witness has come forward, a witness who claims to have seen a young woman with long red hair driving away from the scene of the crash in a red '68 Mustang convertible."

"Well, whoever this person saw, it wasn't me," Anne said angrily.

Long red hair. A wig, maybe? Like the wigs stolen from Betty's trailer?

She tried to collect her thoughts, but they bolted off in different directions. Wig. Mustang. Typewriter. Break-in. She could feel her heart galloping in her chest. She had a bad feeling about this. Somebody was working awfully hard to make her look like a murderer. "I was here all night," she insisted. "I saw the crash on TV."

Mark Trasker was staring at her as if he didn't believe a word of it. "I see," he said again.

"No. You don't. Otherwise you'd realize someone is trying to frame me."

"Now who would want to do a thing like that, Miss Hardaway?"

"I don't know. But I intend to find out."

Chapter 15

Makeup doesn't last forever. Liquid or cream foundations may separate or discolor with age. Mascara is usually the first to go. It should be replaced every three to four weeks, since the accumulation of bacteria can cause eye infections. Most other makeup can last up to two or three years.

There were fourteen rental car places in Monmouth County. Anne called every single one and got the same response: None of them had a '68 red Mustang. It was the same with local used car dealers. No way, no how. And since Trasker had refused to tell her the name of the witness who claimed to see her driving away from the scene, Anne was at a loss. Someone might have broken into her house, but it was unlikely he or she drove her car Thursday night, and then thoughtfully brought it back.

Near the end of her futile search, Phil Smedley phoned, turning up the pressure. Over the past two days, he'd left messages alternately cajoling, badgering, threatening and pleading with Anne to send him what she had, and now he'd decided to play hard ball. In his last message, he'd announced that if she didn't fax him the first few chapters immediately, if not sooner, he was bringing in another writer to "help" her out.

When she reminded him that he hadn't amended her contract to include a deadline change, he pitched a fit.

"I don't need this aggravation, Annie," he shouted. "There are other writers out there. Good writers. Fast writers. Hell, you know what I read in the paper this morning? There are three other unauthorized biographies in the works right now. What does that say to you?"

"Absolutely nothing. Look, Phil. I'm the one who actually talked to Mallory. I've got the inside track."

Or I did until all my notes were stolen, she added silently. It was a factoid she'd neglected to share with Phil Smedley for obvious reasons. She did some quick math: If Phil took her off the project and she never got the second half of her advance, she had enough money in the bank to pay her property taxes, electric bill, and living expenses for three, maybe four months. Terrific. That was just terrific.

"I've got it covered," she said aloud, trying to sound convincing. "Just as soon as I tie up some loose ends. Did I mention I was an extra? How's that for an angle?"

"I don't care if you're nominated for an Oscar. I want the damn chapters and I want them *now*."

He slammed the phone down before Anne got a chance to tell him she couldn't possibly get any writing done today. Not with Betty dead. Not while someone was trying to frame her for murder. And not with a half-dozen trailers, Porta-Pottys, and sound trucks parked outside. The noise was distracting, to say the least: cameras and cables being dragged into place, excited tourists screaming for autographs, assistants scurrying around, barking orders into cellular phones and walkie-talkies. Most of the cops had left, but the crime scene on the beach was still cordoned off with official yellow tape. Anne had walked over to the Yard Arm Inn earlier, hoping to look around Betty's room. Two police cars were parked out front, and when she went inside and walked down the corridor leading to Betty's room, she saw the yellow tape stretched across the door.

Anne tried to block the sight of Betty's body from her mind. After she made her last Mustang call, she sat in the white wicker swing watching a grounds crew scrub Hannah Morton's front steps. They'd hosed down the violet exterior of Hannah's Victorian house, repaired a wobbly newel post on the porch, and trimmed the grass on the tidy front lawn. Anne figured Hannah had just saved an extra five hundred bucks on home maintenance and repairs. Not to mention the $1200 the Mortons were getting because their house was going to be in a movie for all of eight seconds.

Anne watched as the production manager combed the lawn for unkempt pieces of grass, as if she were hunting for malformed Easter eggs. Last week she'd knocked on Anne's door. A nervous, rabbity-looking woman with a pencil stuck behind each ear and a habit of blinking her eyes when she spoke, she'd examined Anne's Victorian cottage with some trepidation, as if the yellow shingles, clapboards, and siding might suddenly come loose and hit her on the head. Minutes later she'd announced she'd have to "pass" and had headed next door to Hannah's. Meaning Anne's down-at-the-heels home wouldn't be getting a free facelift anytime soon.

Now Anne went to the computer and printed out a list of Mallory's beauty tips: *Sweeping blush in the crease of your eyelids warms up your face. Your concealer should be a shade or two lighter than your foundation. You can find the best makeup brushes in art supply stores. If you have close-set eyes, apply medium to dark shadow on the outer third of the eyelid. Never wear white lipstick. Don't dry your nails under a blow dryer. (Heat causes the polish to expand and lift away from the nail.)* And on and on. Double-spaced, they totaled nine pages. She scrawled a note on the top of the first page. *Phil, start with this, more to come.* Then she faxed him in North Carolina, and went out on the porch so she didn't have to hear the phone ring when he called to chew her out.

It was so humid outside, it felt like a sauna. A breeze blew hot air up and down the street. The ocean stretched out invitingly, smooth as polished glass. Anne scanned the set for Dakota, but he was still playing the role of Invisible Man. She spotted Caitlin Grey emerging from her trailer a block away, holding a script. Anne had read the script in its entirety, courtesy of Mallory. In this particular scene, Caitlin's character was supposed to walk down the street and come to an abrupt stop in front of Hannah Morton's house, where she spied a pink flamingo lawn ornament made of sandstone. The sight of the flamingo caused Caitlin's character to remember that the password to a top-secret Internet site was *Audubon,* a memory surge that sent the character racing for her laptop. Since the Mortons didn't happen to own a pink flamingo lawn ornament, it arrived courtesy of two beefy prop guys. Anne half-resented the bird. The Heights might be tiny, but it certainly wasn't tacky.

She wondered how the original owners of the Morton place would feel if they knew the Victorian house would be featured in a movie. In the early 1960s, before she'd gotten sick, Anne's mother had collected everything she could find on the past owners of all the houses on the block. The house next door had been built back in 1898 by a sea captain who lost his fortune and then his life to the whims of the Atlantic Ocean. When his widow realized he wasn't coming back, she found salvation in God, spending most of each day at the Church by the

Sea. The widow never remarried, becoming what Anne's mother called a "fire and brimstone Christian." She definitely wouldn't be pleased by the gratuitous sex and violence in *Dark Horizon*. Not to mention the fact that the young women working as production assistants pierced as many parts of their anatomy as was humanly possible.

Spotting Howard Koppelman, Anne scrambled down the porch steps and went over to him. "I need to talk to you," she said. "It's important."

"Haven't got time," he announced, barely glancing at her. As usual, he was dressed in black, except for his mirrored silver sunglasses. He was looking through a camera that was strapped onto another man's body. Anne followed his gaze. In the camera's viewfinder, the Morton house looked larger than life, almost grand, like a restored Queen Anne "painted lady" down the shore in Cape May.

"I think you'd better make the time. It has to do with Linda LaRue."

Koppelman stepped away from the Steadicam. His whole body seemed to tense up. "Meet me at the Lobster Shack. Nine-thirty tonight," he said, under his breath.

Before Anne could answer, he had moved off and was busily conferring with a sound engineer and the cinematographer. The assistant director told Caitlin to get in position for a run-through.

"Not now," Caitlin said petulantly. "My contact lens is killing me. And I've got to go to the john." Since taking over Mallory's role, Caitlin had gone from grateful ingenue to pushy prima donna quicker than you could say "star billing."

"Could I use your bathroom?" Caitlin said to Anne. "My Porta-Potty is all backed up."

"Sure." Caitlin fell into step beside Anne. There were six other bathrooms on wheels—one for each of the other cast members—but Caitlin apparently didn't want to avail herself.

"How's everything going?" Anne said.

"Fabulously. I was born to play this part, and the proof is in the pudding." Caitlin giggled. "I mean, on the screen."

"Have there been any more mishaps on the set? Stolen or broken equipment, freak accidents?"

"Nope," Caitlin said blithely. "Not since Mallory died. It's like she was a jinx or something. Now it's smooth sailing." They walked up the steps to Anne's porch. "Could I possibly get something cold to drink? A Diet Coke? Perrier?"

"I have iced tea," Anne said, opening the front door.

They were in the small entryway, leading to the living room.

"Fine. Whatever." Caitlin made a sharp left turn and entered the guest bathroom next to Anne's office, closing the door behind her.

Anne stared at the bathroom door. The windows in the living room were open. A slight breeze drifted in off the ocean, providing some relief from the heat. Outside, two production assistants were deconstructing the nuances of light and shadow in film noir. She heard the toilet flush, followed by the sound of running water. As if in a daze, she went into the kitchen and poured some iced tea into a tall plastic cup.

Retracing her steps, she saw Caitlin standing in front of the hall mirror, fluffing her blond hair with her fingertips.

"Here you are," Anne said, handing her the drink.

Caitlin took a sip. "Thanks. You still going ahead with your book?"

"Uh huh."

"Must be tough, now that Mallory's dead."

"It is," Anne said, forcing herself to sound polite. "Actually, I need to get started. Would you excuse me?"

Anne ushered Caitlin out the front door, then went to the window and watched her cross the street, where she conferred with Howard Koppelman and his assistant director. Anne waited until she saw Caitlin begin to block out the scene in front of the Morton house. Three cameras followed her every move. Behind her were two silver photographer's umbrellas, mounted on stands with inset lights, to help reflect the sun and fill shadows. Anne knew she didn't have much time. Ten minutes, tops. But it would have to do.

She slipped out of the house, locking the door behind her, and headed toward the trailers parked farther down the block. Caitlin still used her old trailer, perhaps because the police had declared Mallory's off-limits. But she'd evicted the two other actresses she used to share it with. Anne paused outside the entrance. She could swear the red star on the door had gotten bigger.

Turning the handle, she went inside. The trailer seemed larger than the last time Anne had been in it, probably because the other women had cleared out. There was only one cot, a dressing table, a kitchenette. Caitlin had added a retro-looking chaise longue, upholstered with oversize daisies, which brought to mind the mid-1960s. Costumes hung from a rack against the wall.

Anne glanced out the window. A small patch of beach was visible, but she couldn't see Caitlin from this vantage point. She went over to the dressing table and opened the drawers. Brushes, combs, lipsticks, powders, eye shadows, the usual tricks of the trade. Moving quickly, she searched the kitchenette, examining the microwave, the shelves where Caitlin kept Cap'n Crunch cereal and red zinger tea and Triscuits. Still no sign of it. She opened the mini-refrigerator and was immediately greeted by a sour smell. A hunk of cheese was moldering next to a rotten potato that had started to sprout white tubers. Between the bread of an ancient-looking deli sandwich were two pieces of greenish meat. She shut the door quickly.

Outside she heard a radio counting down the summer's top twenty hits from 1967. "Windy," by The Association. Anne slid her hand under the mattress of the cot, tracing its perimeter. Nothing. She knelt down and peered under the bed. All she saw were a pair of espadrilles and a tweed suitcase. She took out the suitcase, threw it on the bed. There were zippers on either side of the case. She unzipped them hurriedly. The bag was crammed with white tissue paper. Her mother would have approved. Evelyn believed in putting tissue paper between each and every article of clothing to be packed. Anne took the tissue paper out and laid it on the bed. A pouch was sewn onto the lining of the case. She put her hand inside and felt around. Immediately she encountered something hard and square. She pulled it out, a sealed white envelope, and slit it open with her fingernail. Inside was a red floppy disk. She'd have recognized it instantly, even if it wasn't labeled *Loving You*, in her own familiar scrawl.

She went to the door of the trailer, opened it. On the other side stood Caitlin Grey. Caitlin's mouth formed an O of surprise. "What . . . ?" she began angrily. Her eyes fell on the red disk. "Shit," she said softly. "You found it."

Chapter 16

> *To refresh your makeup,*
> *don't apply more until*
> *you've misted your face*
> *with mineral water. While*
> *your face is still moist,*
> *use a Q-tip to clean*
> *mascara that has flaked*
> *or run and eyeliner that*
> *might have bled. When*
> *your face is dry, add*
> *more blush and freshen*
> *your lips.*

"How did you know?" Caitlin said, slamming the door of the trailer behind her.

"My house is built funny," Anne said, slipping the disk into the pocket of her shorts. "Especially the first floor. My mother used to call it the House of Doors, because there are so many. When you come into the house, there are five, right next to each other. People go into the wrong room a lot, mistaking the bathroom for a closet, or a closet for my office or the spare bedroom. But you went straight into the bathroom, like you'd been in my house before. It got me thinking."

Caitlin's jaw was set. A thin trickle of sweat streaked her brow. She wiped her hand across her forehead, smearing her foundation makeup. Anne could see she was debating whether she could lie her way out of this.

"Why'd you steal my notes?" Anne said quietly. She was still ticked, but now that she had the disk back, she also felt relieved. She'd be able to reconstruct Mallory's life and possibly uncover the circumstances of her death.

Caitlin sank down on the cot. She looked as skittish as a long-tailed cat in a room full of rocking chairs. "I didn't want you to write that junk Mallory said about me. It wasn't fair."

"Where are the tapes?"

"I threw them away."

It could be worse, Anne thought ruefully. She'd transcribed most of the tapes to the disk already.

"How'd you get inside?"

Caitlin stared out the window. Though she was wearing Mallory's costume, she didn't have Mallory's larger-than-life presence, her unadulterated glamour. She was just another beautiful blond in a business crawling with pretty faces. "The door was unlocked."

"Like hell it was. Caitlin, breaking and entering is a serious offense. Either you come clean or I'm going straight to the cops."

"Okay. Okay. A friend of mine picked the lock," Caitlin said. Her voice was a high-pitched whine.

"And who might this friend be?"

Caitlin was silent a moment. "I can't say."

Anne took two steps toward the door. "If you change your mind, I'll be at the police station, talking to Detective Trasker."

"Wait," Caitlin said frantically. "I'll tell you anything you want to know. Only please don't go to the cops."

Anne turned back. Caitlin was perched on the edge of

the cot, her hands stretched out beseechingly. She looked as though she were auditioning to play Juliet. Anne let her sweat for about twenty seconds, then said, "I'm listening."

Caitlin took a deep breath and exhaled noisily through her mouth. Another deep breath, then out through the mouth. Was this what they taught at Stella Adler? "Dakota picked the lock." She sounded half-glad to be tattling, glad she wasn't the one who'd committed a felony. "He used to break into houses when he was a kid. You can check for yourself. I think he has a record."

"Go on."

"He was worried about what Mallory was going to say about him in her book. We decided if we took your notes, it'd cause a big delay. Maybe convince you to drop the whole thing."

"Why did you use my typewriter to write Mallory the threatening note?"

"That was Dakota's idea."

The gamble had paid off. Caitlin was so busy confessing, she didn't seem to notice Anne hadn't a shred of proof when it came to the typewriter.

"Mallory told him about these anonymous letters she'd gotten. She was even bragging about them—how other men found her desirable and stuff." A note of irritation crept into Caitlin's tone. Even dead, Mallory annoyed her. "He thought it'd be funny to take her down a peg. A pornographic letter for the porn queen. As a joke."

"Some joke."

"Well, they weren't too fond of each another," Caitlin said defensively. "They were getting divorced."

"Only you didn't feel like waiting, did you? With Mallory out of the way, you could move right in."

"So I slept with him. So what? It's not a crime. We're engaged now, anyway."

"Whose idea was it to kill Mallory? Yours or Dakota's?"

"What!" Caitlin exclaimed. She looked surprised, but it was hard to tell if she was acting or not. Anne doubted Caitlin experienced many emotions that weren't scripted in advance. "I didn't have anything to do with Mallory's death," Caitlin protested.

"Really? Where were you the night Mallory's car crashed?"

"In my room. Fast asleep."

Anne turned toward the door.

"Where are you going?" Caitlin said nervously.

"To find your boyfriend."

In Oceanside Heights, fishing was more of a recreational sport than a serious commercial endeavor. The three wooden piers off the ocean each had a shack where tourists could rent tackle and rods, and buy bait for a nominal fee. But the pickings close to shore were slim. At most, you could catch a small fluke or flounder, not worth bothering about, barely large enough to cook for supper.

Across town, at the marina, the bay was filled with pleasure craft moored at the docks: sailboats, motorboats, the occasional yacht. People spent leisurely weekend afternoons on the water, downing six-packs of ice-cold Budweisers, with the radio blasting away while they soaked up the summer sun. The only charter boat in the marina was *The Daredevil*, a forty-seven-foot-long craft owned by Captain Red Holbrook, who took fishing parties out himself or, when business was slow, dropped anchor at an inlet he particularly liked and landed enough flounder to last a week.

When Anne got to the marina, the bay was already freckled with pleasure boats. It was 1:30 in the afternoon and the sun glinted sharply on the water. Thin, wispy clouds threaded the horizon, like a blue-and-white spin art drawing. Anne hurried over to the slip where *The Daredevil* was moored. Red Holbrook was about to cast off. His passenger sat in the stern, next to a fishing rod

and a tackle box. Dakota glanced up just as Anne
reached the charter. She clambered over the fiberglass
gunwale, feeling the boat pitch beneath her.

"Is there room for one more?" Anne called to the
captain, who was standing in the cockpit. Holbrook
shrugged and took the wheel. The engine turned over,
and with a deep thrumming sound, *The Daredevil* left
the dock and skimmed across the bay, heading south.

Dakota didn't look all that surprised to see her. He
had flipped open the built-in adjustable seat on the port
side of the boat, so it converted to a lounge chair, and
his sneakers rested against the maroon leather cushions.
He wore a black short-sleeved golf shirt and tan shorts.
A cigarette dangled from his mouth. The skin around his
eyes had crinkled into faint lines.

"You're a hard man to track down," Anne said, taking a seat across from him. "Where've you been the last
couple of days?"

"Around," he muttered.

"There's a PA on the film who admires you a lot.
Tall, redheaded kid with aviator glasses. Owns all your
CDs."

"Kevin." His tone was sullen.

"Seems Kevin's a big fan of yours. He doesn't mind
being your personal go-fer—buying you cigarettes,
mailing your letters, taking messages for you. He thinks
if he acts helpful enough, you'll help him break into the
music business." Anne smiled. "Kids can be so naive.
Anyway, Kevin's the one who told me where you've
been the past four days. In New York. At the Royalton
Hotel."

He reached over and tugged the large trolling rod that
hung from the side of the boat. "So?"

The pungent odor of fish wafted from the bait prep
center in the middle of the boat, equipped with cutting
board, tackle, pail, and sink with spray hose.

"What were you doing in New York, when you're
making a movie here?"

Dakota's mouth twisted into a sneer. "Visiting the Empire State Building."

He got up, tossed his cigarette into the bay, and went through the sliding door leading to the cabin. Anne could see a U-shaped galley, complete with curved mahogany wet bar, a double stainless-steel sink, and inset laminate counters. Sandwiched against the far wall was a microwave, an oven, and a full-size refrigerator/freezer. *The Daredevil* was state-of-the-art, all right.

The boat was cruising toward Bay Head at about thirty-five miles an hour, leaving a trail of sailboats and catamarans in its wake. From this distance, the candy-colored Victorian houses in Oceanside Heights looked fake, like an old-fashioned picture postcard. Along the banks of the bay, tall grasses flattened in the breeze.

When Dakota came back, he was holding a bottle of Amstel Light. He took a long swallow, keeping his eye on the trolling rod. "You got yourself a nice little bay here," he remarked conversationally, as if Anne were the president of the Visitors and Convention Bureau.

"Let's skip the small talk, shall we?" she said tersely. "You went to New York to safeguard your career, to plug any leaks about the lip-synching."

"I don't know what you're talking about," Dakota said flatly. He glanced uneasily at Red Holbrook in the cockpit, but Red didn't appear to be listening.

"At her birthday party, Mallory told me that your voice is shot. She said you lip-synched the words to your last album."

Dakota pursed his lips, as if tasting curdled milk. "She would say something nasty like that. If you print it, I'll sue your pretty behind."

"My publisher's been checking the allegation," Anne said. "He has contacts in the music business."

A Jet-Skier in a black wet suit zipped by on the starboard side, sending up plumes of foamy spray. *The Daredevil* gradually slowed. They were about five miles south of the Heights. Anne could see a blue water tower farther south. It looked like a large bulbous spider. Red Holbrook cut the engine, and the boat glided to a stop, rocking back and forth. "This spot is as good as any," Holbrook called to Dakota. He began to clamber down the steps that separated the cockpit from the deck.

"That's okay," Dakota said, waving Holbrook back. "I got it covered."

"Suit yourself," Holbrook said. Turning his back on them, he picked up a newspaper and began to read.

Dakota went over to the prep center. Scooping a minnow out of a pail of water, he hooked it to the end of a wire rig that had a chartreuse lure attached to it. The minnow jerked back and forth, thrashing helplessly in the air.

"I had a long talk with Caitlin. I know the two of you broke into my house and stole my notes. I found the disk in her trailer."

Dakota's eyes slid over Anne's face, then returned to the distant shoreline. "You can't prove I was involved."

"But I *can* prove you wrote that obscene letter to Mallory. Your fiancee just ratted you out. I think she'd talk to the police, if it meant saving her own skin."

The change in Dakota's expression was striking. His face clouded over. His dark eyes narrowed. He looked as mean as a wild dog who'd just gotten bit on the hindquarters. Anne remembered what Trasker had said about the threatening note. It was written by someone who posed a real danger. Could Dakota have killed Mallory? Strangled Betty?

"What do you want?" Dakota scowled, casting the rod into the water.

"Answers."

"For that damn book of yours?"

"Partly."

"How do I know you won't go to the cops?" Dakota said, keeping his voice low.

"You don't. But if I were you, I'd try to get on my good side right about now."

"And what you said before, about my voice?"

"If you're telling the truth, you've got nothing to hide. Right?"

"Right." He didn't look especially convinced.

"I just have a couple of questions about Mallory's disappearing act," Anne said. "Tell me about the phone call she got the night of her birthday party."

Dakota grabbed hold of the rod. With a flick of his wrist, he cast it into the bay. The minnow churned like an egg beater across the flat surface of the water, then dove under. "What about it?"

"Who else was around?"

"Caitlin, Howard, Nick, Jill. We were sitting around the kitchen table, shooting the breeze. Mal's sister came in, and the two of them went out on the porch. A little bit after that, the phone rang."

"Who took the call?"

"Jill, I think."

"You were all in the kitchen?"

"No. The party was breaking up by then. I was in the bathroom, trying not to puke."

"And the others were still in the house?"

"How the hell should I know?" Dakota tugged impatiently at the rod. There was a thin white mark on the fourth finger of his left hand, where his wedding band had been.

"After the party, where did you go?"

"I was wired, so I drove around some."

"Where, exactly? You didn't check into the Royalton until the following morning."

"My, Kevin's been a busy lad," Dakota said sarcastically. "Down the shore, toward Spring Lake. Not on Route 6, if that's what you're implying. Not that it's any of your business."

"And last night?"

Dakota glanced up, his eyes alert. "What's that?"

"Where were you between midnight and 5 A.M., when

Betty Flugelhorn was killed? You checked out of the Royalton yesterday afternoon.''

"You think I mugged a hairdresser?'' His expression was disdainful. ''Puh-leeze.''

Water lapped at the side of the boat. ''So where were you?''

"Asleep. Look, I came out here to fish, not face an inquisition.''

"I only have a couple more questions. You and Mallory had an argument on the beach last Tuesday afternoon. What were you fighting about?''

Dakota's smile was forced. ''Her sexual appetite. If you must know, La Loving was cheating on me.''

"With whom?''

"I never found out. But she was definitely having an affair.''

Anne studied his face. It was angry, almost cruel. ''You obviously didn't love her anymore. What did you care?''

Dakota laughed harshly. ''I don't like when someone makes a fool out of me. My wife was a cold, selfish bitch. I wanted to give her a taste of her own medicine.''

It was payback time, pure and simple. But how far would he go to safeguard his honor, or salvage his unraveling career?

Aloud, she said, ''Next time you get the urge to write an obscene letter, leave me out of it.''

"There won't be a next time.'' Dakota jerked the reel, as if willing the fish to bite. ''And if you mention any of this in your trashy little book, I will make your life a living hell.''

Chapter 17

*Caught out in the rain?
Hair spray's not going to
help. If you have curly
hair, put a tiny bit of gel in
the palm of your hands.
Then take your hair and
scrunch it up. And next
time remember
your umbrella.*

Was there one pivotal moment when your life
veered off course? One event that shaped your
destiny, determining whether you'd be successful, happy, dead at thirty-two? Or was there only a series
of small choices you had to make, stumbling blind, one
wrong step a catalyst for disaster?

Anne sat in front of the computer, poring over the lost
disk. Her notes brought Mallory's story to life again—
the abusive mother stinking of gin and despair; the ab-
sent, idealized father; the high school boys with their
grabby hands; the junkies and pimps of Landsdown

Park; downing fistfuls of colored pills and partying till you lost consciousness; the overhead lights in the emergency rooms melting into the hot white light of the camera; waking up next to some guy whose name you didn't want to remember.

Maybe the disk would unmask Mallory's killer. Then again, maybe not. The notes were a jumble of dates, times, places, snatches of the past. Images leaped off the screen to grab Anne's attention: Mallory marrying Gerald Finch on the beach in Malibu. Mallory at eight, cowering beneath the sheets as her mother's boyfriend stared down at the bed. Mallory slathered with body paint in a six-page spread in *Vogue*. Mallory on a bus to Hollywood, nose pressed against the dirty glass pane. Mallory doing situps on the beach the other day, toning, toning, endlessly toning.

Anne closed her eyes. At some point, she'd have to try and put the notes in chronological order. God, she was tired. All day long, she'd been trying not to think about Betty. How Betty lay crumpled on the sand, her eyes trained on the sky. Anne didn't believe Betty was the victim of a random crime. She didn't think for one minute that Betty had gone for an early morning walk on a dark, deserted beach. If Betty was having trouble sleeping or needed to clear her head, she'd have driven to an all-night 7-Eleven and stocked up on barbecue flavored potato chips and Ring Dings. Or she'd have knocked on Anne's door, armed with a box of double fudge brownies and all the latest gossip.

What had Betty been trying to tell her yesterday? Had she found out something that had gotten her killed? Anne's mind wandered back to the woman she'd spotted on the beach Wednesday morning. Was it Mallory? There was something so familiar about the woman. As if she'd seen her before in the exact same spot. Had it been a dream? A memory? The image was so vivid: A woman. The ocean. Her back to the shore, her arms stretching to embrace the water . . . Anne's eyes snapped open. She scrolled through her notes again, the type blurring on the screen. Where was it? Damn, if only she'd put this stuff in some kind of order.

She slowed the cursor, searching for the passage she wanted to reread, the part where Mallory was talking about leaving home, going out to Hollywood to reinvent herself. Before she'd gathered her savings and packed a suitcase, before she boarded a bus she'd thought would transport her to La La Land, Mallory had done something else. Aahhh, here it was. Here was the paragraph. Anne read it over, hearing Mallory's silken voice:

It happened the summer I turned seventeen. I woke up the morning of my birthday, when it was real early, still dark outside. I took my ma's car and drove to the beach. I didn't know what I was planning. I only knew I'd had enough. I couldn't take anymore. I took my shoes off and walked into the water. It wasn't like I was planning to kill myself or anything. But I wanted to die. I really did. I figured I'd swim out as far as I could and stop. I could have done it, too. It'd be days before they found me, if they ever even did. There weren't any waves. The surf was dead calm. I waded in till the water got up to my neck. It was icy cold, so cold it hurt. Tears ran down my cheeks. I was all crazy mad inside. About to die and nobody cared. Nobody at all. And then, I know it sounds nuts, but I had, like, a vision. The sun started to come up, the light sprinkled on the water, like gold. I felt this . . . presence. Like there was someone watching over me. An angel. Or God. I don't know. I stretched out my arms as wide as I could, and suddenly I wasn't cold anymore. And I knew. I knew what I had to do. Leave this backwater town and go to Hollywood. Don't you see? It was the only way out. When I waded back to shore, I practically bent down and kissed the ground. I felt like I'd been reborn.

Anne stared at the computer screen and read the passage again. She'd assumed Mallory had meant the beach in Landsdown Park. But now she wasn't so sure. Even back in the seventies, the mile-long strip of beach in Landsdown was dangerous, especially after dark. The teenage Mallory must have come *here*, to the Heights. Anne got up and went to the window. The light was fading, the sky a deep indigo that would soon give way to night. She couldn't see the mossy rocks jutting into the ocean. They were only visible during low tide. She thought back to the woman she'd seen on the rocks the other morning. It had to have been Mallory. The woman's shape, the way she held herself, had looked so much like her, even though her face was hidden. It made sense. August 27 was Mallory's birthday. What better time to reenact a pivotal moment in her life? Only this time, Mallory wouldn't wade into the Atlantic Ocean and get wet, she'd walk on the rocks that formed a makeshift path.

But if Mallory had been abducted, there wouldn't have been time for a side trip to the beach. Anne tried to retrace Mallory's steps. At 3:11 A.M., on the morning of August 27, Mallory had received a phone call that shook her up, a call that was placed from inside her own house. Assuming the woman on the rocks was Mallory, Anne had seen her two hours later, alive and well and in no apparent danger. Not only that, Mallory had been dressed oddly. The baggy jeans, the sweatshirt, the base-ball cap—they weren't exactly the kinds of clothes the actress favored. When Anne had looked in Mallory's closet, she'd seen nothing but elegant fabrics, cut to reveal the actress's curvy physique. Even when Mallory worked out, she dressed provocatively, in Spandex thong unitards and low-cut crop tops that left little to the imagination. Anne didn't think she owned a pair of baggy jeans.

It was as if Mallory were in disguise. Which meant she hadn't been abducted from the house on Beechwood Avenue. She'd disappeared of her own free will.

                    *   *   *

On the way to Sheila Lovitz's apartment, it started to rain. The heat that had been building up all afternoon finally broke and the sky split open, pelting the ground with drops. Anne pulled the Mustang over to the side of the road and put the top of the car up. It didn't help. By the time she'd closed the windows and the top was firmly in place, she was soaked to the skin.

She flicked the windshield wipers on high. It was pitch black outside, and the darkness and rain made it hard to see. She turned on her brights and crept along at fifteen miles an hour. Sheets of water struck the car. As the storm raged over the ocean, waves pounded the shoreline, crashing noisily against the beach. In Landsdown Park, rain pounded the garbage bags piled on the curb and drove the teenage boys with their boom boxes inside. The windswept streets were dark, deserted. Neon lights on bars and restaurants melted into a wet, fuzzy blur.

Anne parked across the street from Sheila's building, locked the Mustang, and dashed into the small vestibule. The outer door of the Landsdown Arms was propped open with two soaked New Jersey Bell phone books. Shaking droplets of water from her hair, Anne pressed the button for apartment 4B. She hugged her arms to her chest and waited. The rain had cooled the air temperature to about fifty degrees. She felt cold and damp, like a wet stray dog.

"Come on up," Sheila called through the intercom, before Anne had a chance to identify herself. The inner door buzzed and Anne pushed it open. Oh well. She hoped Sheila wouldn't mind if she dripped all over the rug.

As Anne tramped through the lobby, her sneakers made a squishing sound. She caught a glimpse of herself in a large oval mirror and laughed aloud. Her curly red hair was plastered to her forehead, her jeans and T-shirt were soggy. She got in the elevator and pressed the button for the fourth floor. Someone was cooking. The building smelled like cabbage and boiled potatoes.

Sheila answered the door dressed in a pink terry-cloth bathrobe. When she saw it was Anne, her mouth dropped. She took a step backward. "What in the world . . ." she stammered. "What . . . what are you doing here?"

"I tried calling first, but the line was busy," Anne said. "I wanted to go over a couple of things with you."

From inside the apartment, Anne heard the sound of a man's voice.

"Now isn't the best time," Sheila said. She was wearing powder blue eye shadow and deep pink lipstick. Her hair was piled on top of her head, loosely fastened with a silver clip. Her cheeks looked flushed.

"This'll only take a minute," Anne said, trying to see inside. Did Sheila have a date?

A buzzer sounded. Sheila gave a little jump and sneezed. "Oh," she said. She shifted her weight, but made no move to answer the intercom. Her arm stretched across the doorway, blocking Anne's view of the living room.

"You expecting someone else?" Anne said.

"Um. The delivery guy. I thought that's who you were. I ordered some Chinese food."

"Look, can I come in for a sec? Just so I can dry off a little before I face the monsoon again."

"Sheila?" the man inside the apartment called out.

Sheila turned uncertainly, and Anne took the opportunity to peer over Sheila's shoulder. The living room was half-dark. For a second, Anne thought the storm had knocked the power out. But no, a small brass lamp near the window was lit, giving off a weak light. She could see the shape of a man on the sofa, talking on the telephone.

She half expected it to be Gerald Finch, but it didn't look like Gerald. Or his female alter ego, for that matter. The man on the sofa looked up. Their eyes met. Nick

Fabien. What was he doing in Sheila's apartment? Sheila didn't seem like his type.

Nick's face registered surprise. The smile he offered was paper-thin. But then his features softened. "Hiya, Anne," he said, with a wave. "What a storm. You must be soaked."

The buzzer sounded again, longer this time. A long, loud trill.

Sheila sneezed noisily. Reaching into the pocket of her robe, she pulled out a tissue and wiped her nose. "Yes. Come in," she said, opening the door wider.

"Thanks." Anne stepped inside.

The living room was a mess. Books that had been arranged in neat piles on Anne's last visit were scattered haphazardly on the desk and coffee table. Dirty cups and plates littered the dining table. Clothes covered every available surface—the purple crushed velvet sofa, the armchair, the desk chair, even the radiator. Two suitcases flopped open on the floor, spilling out more clothes and shoes. It looked like Sheila had saved every single outfit she'd ever owned in the last twenty years. Ragged blue jeans patched with peace signs, skinny tube tops, halter dresses, Huk-a-poo shirts, suede buckskin maxiskirts, cowboy boots, peasant dresses. There was enough stuff here to outfit a small thrift store. Or to interest a certain playful cat. Anne looked around for Harry. But he wasn't in sight.

"Taking a trip?" she asked Sheila.

"Just cleaning out my closets." Sheila edged over to the intercom on the wall by the kitchen and pressed a small white button. "Come on up," she said loudly.

"Then we're square," Nick was saying into the phone. He wore white jeans and a tight white cotton T-shirt that showed off his bulging biceps to advantage. He had one arm flung over the sofa as if he owned the joint. "Great. See ya Monday. Nine sharp." He hung up. "Anne, how are ya? Geez, it's a helluva night to be driving around."

"I needed to talk to Sheila about something," Anne said. "Actually, I'm surprised to find you here. I didn't think the two of you knew each other."

Nick crossed his arms over his chest. In the half-light, with his square jaw, pumped-up physique, and dark coloring, he reminded Anne of Bluto, the blowhard bully in the Popeye cartoons. "I came by to tell Sheila about Mallory's memorial service on Monday."

Anne felt a small pang of guilt. She was supposed to have let Sheila know when the service was being held. But she'd completely forgotten about it.

"I also wanted to see if Sheila's going to the parade tomorrow," Nick said. "*Dark Horizon*'s got a float. Some of us were talking, and we thought it'd be nice if Sheila went in Mallory's place."

Some nice free publicity. Anne could picture the headlines now: GRIEVING SIS TAKES STAR'S PLACE. Only she didn't seem to be grieving very much, did she? Sheila kept crisscrossing the room, eyes darting here and there, like a bird taking stock of its nest. Anne watched as Sheila plucked a heap of clothes off an armchair and dumped them in a plastic laundry basket. Strands of hair had come undone from the clip and hung loosely by her cheeks. She seemed . . . what? Hyperactive. Nervous. Definitely nervous.

Nick said, "So how about it, Sheila? You feel up to a parade?"

"I . . ." The doorbell rang. Sheila let out a series of short staccato sneezes. "I have a cold," she said to no one in particular, before hurrying to the door as if grateful for the interruption.

Anne sat in the armchair Sheila had cleared off. The seat sagged in the middle. The arms were worn thin.

Nick leaned forward. "Poor kid," he said, lowering his voice and hooking a thumb toward Sheila, who was paying the Chinese delivery boy. "It's been rough on her losing her sister so sudden."

Sheila closed the door and carried the white take-out

bag into the kitchen. Anne's stomach growled softly. The food smelled spicy and good. She glanced at her watch. Almost nine o'clock. She'd skipped dinner and now she was starving.

"So," Nick said. "How's your book coming along?"

"It's hard to write it without Mallory. There are pieces of her life I can't seem to put together."

Sheila reentered the room but hung back, standing in the doorway as if she was scared to enter.

"Speaking of which," Anne said to Sheila, "I have a few more questions for you." Sheila leaned against the wall, shifting her weight uneasily, her eyes trained on the floor. She looked like a suspect in a police lineup. Anne said, "The summer Mallory left for California, before she and Gerald eloped, did your sister try to kill herself?"

"I, um . . . I really don't know," Sheila said in a low voice. "Why?"

"Because I saw a woman on the beach by my house early Wednesday morning. Now I think it was Mallory."

"Really?" Nick cut in. He stood up and went over to the window. The rain was still coming down in slashing torrents. "That's funny. Why would Mallory be at the beach?"

"It was her birthday. I think she was trying to reenact a pivotal moment in her life. The moment she decided to become an actress, instead of drowning herself in the ocean."

"I don't get it," Nick said. He had grabbed hold of the cord to the venetian blinds and was twirling it between his fingers. "I mean, what's that got to do with anything?"

"I'm not sure." Anne turned to Sheila. "Could Mallory have been hiding out in the house on Pitt Street?"

Sheila stared at her. "What?" she blurted out. "No. No way. Mallory hated that dump. She wouldn't go back there in a million years."

Nick Fabien was watching Anne intently. "What are you getting at?" he said.

"I don't think Mallory was kidnapped after all. I think she was lying low for a while. Maybe that phone call scared her off and she decided to hightail it out of the Heights."

Sheila shrugged. Her shoulders were hunched. "I doubt Mallory's been in that house in years."

"It does seem like a stretch," Nick agreed.

"Ya know," Sheila said, fidgeting with her hair. "I'm real tired. And I've got a cold. Actually, if you both don't mind, I'd like to eat my dinner and get to bed."

Nick grabbed his leather jacket from atop a pile of skirts on the couch. "Hey, sorry for barging in here," he said to Sheila. "Thanks for letting me use the phone. If you feel like riding on a souped up float, we'll be in front of Quilters tomorrow, around one."

He headed for the door, sidestepping the clothes strewn around the room. Anne got up. She sensed Sheila couldn't wait to get rid of her. She just didn't know why.

Sheila rubbed her eyes, then jammed her hands into the pockets of her bathrobe. "I'll call you," she said, without looking up.

Somehow Anne doubted it.

Chapter 18

*Always remove your
makeup before you go to
sleep. During the day, tiny
particles of dirt and
pollutants cling to your
face, on top of your
makeup. If you don't get
them off, they can be
absorbed into your skin.
Plus your makeup will
clog your pores,
and you'll wake up with
a smudged pillowcase.*

"You heading home?" Nick said, in the elevator. At close range, his cologne was overpowering. It smelled sickly sweet, like cough
medicine mixed with peppermint.

"Not yet," she said. "I'm meeting Koppelman in
about fifteen minutes."

Nick made a sound of disgust. His jaw worked up and
down.

"Koppelman's a piece of work. He acts like he doesn't give a shit Mallory died. Kinda cold, when you consider he was nailing her."

The elevator creaked to a stop and the door slid open.

"Howard and Mallory were sleeping together?" Anne said incredulously. "I thought she hated him."

"Hell, no," Nick said. They walked through the lobby, past an Oriental-style lacquered chest and two artificial ficus trees coated with dust. "That was just a put-on. I probably shouldn't be telling you this, but the two of 'em were hot and heavy right up till the day Mal died. Fact, I heard she was fixing to leave Dakota and go back to Howie."

Anne stared at him. She couldn't believe Mallory would have an affair with Howard Koppelman. There was too much malice between them, too many scars that hadn't healed. "How do you know?" she asked.

"I saw 'em one time. Right after her workout. They were going at it hot and heavy in her trailer."

Anne studied Nick Fabien carefully. At first he'd struck her as a muscle-bound ex-jock whose main interest was pumping up his pectoral muscles. But maybe he was smarter than he looked. He'd held on to his job, training Caitlin each day on the set of *Dark Horizon*. Did he have an ax to grind against Koppelman? Against Mallory?

"Sounds like the best-kept secret in the business," she said skeptically.

"Not for long. These things got a way of leaking out."

They reached the vestibule in the front of the building. Anne peered outside. The wind had picked up, tearing through the trees in gusts. The temperature had dipped even more. She shivered, wishing she'd brought a sweater.

"Later," Nick said, zipping up his leather jacket. "Maybe I'll see ya at the parade tomorrow."

He ran to his car, keeping his head down. As she

watched him drive away, she thought about what he'd just told her. It didn't add up. Mallory despised Howard Koppelman for any number of reasons. For ditching her to take up with a much younger actress. For being a player. For his success in mainstream movies. For getting her hooked on cocaine. And most of all, for luring her into porn flicks in the first place, a stigma she never could seem to live down. There was no way in hell Mallory would begin sleeping with him again. Would she?

Anne made a dash for the Mustang. Rain struck her shoulders hard. The street was laced with puddles, and she felt as if she stepped in every single one. In the car, she turned on the heat and headed back toward the Heights. The storm showed no signs of letting up. It was pouring in heavy sheets; the wind still caterwauled. At the intersection of Spray Street and Ocean Avenue, a flashing yellow streetlight swayed unsteadily. A tree branch had landed in the middle of the road. Slamming on the brakes, Anne navigated around it.

At 9:45 P.M. she pulled into the parking lot of the Lobster Shack, a ramshackle wood building slapped together with weathered gray planks. Inside, fishing nets were tacked to the ceiling, sagging above the creaky wooden tables and chairs. The walls were plastered with black-and-white photos of dead entertainers—Burgess Meredith, Harry James, Lawrence Welk, Dean Martin. As far as Anne could tell, none of them had actually eaten at the restaurant, but the owner seemed to feel it was beside the point. In the far corner was a large aquarium filled with dozens of lobsters stacked three and four deep, their claws taped shut, squirming and jostling as if sensing their fate.

Anne looked around. The place was half-full, tourists mostly, older couples who'd been married so long they no longer spoke to each other while they chewed, families with sleepy toddlers in tow. She spotted Howard Koppelman at a table in the back. Sliding into the seat opposite him, she picked up her napkin and used it to dry her damp hands and face. Howard didn't look the least bit inconvenienced by the rain. He was dressed immaculately, outfitted head to toe in his customary black. His dark hair looked like it had been blown and styled. Did he use hair dye? Hard to tell.

"I already ordered," he announced. "Hope you like stuffed crab."

"Crab's fine."

Howard signaled to the waitress, a girl, young enough to have a smattering of pimples on her cheeks and chin. "I'll have another scotch and soda. And the lady will have . . ."

"A margarita," Anne said. "Extra salt."

After the waitress ambled away, Howard rested his elbows on the table and leaned forward. His eyes were the color of the ocean on a cloudy day. "So," he said, "let's cut to the chase. You know about Linda."

"Yes. I spoke to Veronica Neal."

"Well, now that you know, I'd like you to refrain from mentioning it in print."

He removed a white envelope from his jacket and slid it across the table. Anne picked it up. Inside was a stack of crisp hundred-dollar bills. Twenty, maybe thirty in all. Was this what it felt like to find a wallet stuffed with cash? Shock, then elation, a thrill of guilty pleasure followed by the sobering realization that you had to give the money back.

"Sorry," Anne said, pushing the envelope at him. "No can do."

"This is just a down payment," Howard said quickly. "I was thinking along the lines of fifteen, twenty thousand."

Twenty thousand dollars! Enough to pay for new storm windows and to fix the leaky pipes in her house. Enough to fly to Milan, rent a Fiat, and be sipping Bellinis with Jack on a moonlit balcony. Enough to finally get a master's degree in creative writing and start working on that novel she was always tinkering with in her head. But not enough—it could never be enough—to forget about Mallory and Betty and the horrible way they died.

"I don't want your money," Anne said. She was surprised to find she felt relieved by this noble declaration.

"Then what?" Howard demanded. "What *do* you want?"

She thought a moment. God, there were so many things. For Mallory to walk through the door, explaining it was all a ridiculous publicity stunt. She wanted another job, as a travel agent or a music teacher maybe, even though she couldn't play a note, anything but digging into people's private, secret lives. She wanted Betty not to be dead.

"The truth," she said finally.

Howard slammed his hand down hard on the table. "About what?" he yelled. An elderly couple at the next table turned to gape.

"Were you and Mallory having an affair?"

Howard stared at her for a moment. Then he threw his head back and laughed. It was a harsh rasping sound, like he was getting over a cough. He laughed so hard he doubled over. "Are you for real?" he said when he'd finally caught his breath.

"Nick Fabien claims he walked in on you and Mallory. In her trailer."

"He said that? He's crazy!"

"Then it's not true."

"Of course not," Howard sputtered. He dabbed at his eyes and gulped down some water. "She hated my guts. And the feeling was mutual. I only agreed to work with her again because the studio insisted."

The waitress brought their drinks. Anne took a sip of her margarita. It tasted like it was made from a mix. She said, "Did you offer Mallory money not to dredge up the Linda LaRue business in the book?"

"No."

"Why not?"

"I didn't need to. Mal wanted to put the porn flicks in the past. She would never have mentioned Linda's death in that damn book of yours. The less said the better. Otherwise she wouldn't have gotten the roles she wanted." He stirred his scotch and soda with a plastic mixer shaped like a lobster. "You know what Hollywood thought about Mal's past? They thought it was kinda cute. A paragraph in a magazine story. That's all. Reborn from porn. She'd risen above it. Beaten the odds. Overcome her addiction."

"That wasn't the word on the set. And you're the one who warned me she'd been acting high-strung."

"Rumors spread." He picked up a knife and started buttering a stale-looking dinner roll. "I never actually saw Mal take any pills. I just heard she was using again."

"From whom?"

"I can't remember. Now, regarding my little offer, if you don't need money, I might be able to help you out another way." He put down the knife and studied Anne, taking in her almond-shaped eyes, the cascade of red hair tumbling over her shoulders. "You ever thought about acting?"

Now it was her turn to laugh. "Not interested. Look, Mallory's biography is going to be published whether you cooperate or not, and what I'm after right now are the facts."

"Whose facts?" Howard said angrily. "Yours? Mal's? This sordid little chapter in my past doesn't have to be part of your great literary masterpiece."

Anne could hardly miss the fact that his voice dripped with sarcasm. "You're right," she said. "It doesn't. Not if you clear up a couple of points for me."

"Fine," he snapped. "What do you want to know?"

"Do you own a green plaid shirt?"

He looked at her curiously. "No."

"Have you ever been to Mallory's childhood home, in Landsdown Park?"

"Nope."

"I read in today's *Variety* that the film will actually benefit from Mallory's death. The 'morbidity factor,' they called it. The gross is expected to double."

Howard shrugged. "Nobody ever accused the American public of having taste and decorum."

"But her death seemed to come at a particularly opportune moment, didn't it? You've got more publicity than you can handle. And the producers are pouring money into *Dark Horizon*, instead of pulling the plug."

"What are you implying?" Howard said caustically. "That I engineered her death to be number one at the box office?"

"I'm just reviewing the facts. The article also pointed out that your career is riding on this movie. The guy who wrote the piece pointed out that your last picture went way over budget and flopped."

Howard's upper lip curled into a half-smile. It was cold as the ice melting in their water glasses. "In La La Land, people don't fail; they fall up. Sometimes you have to think big, to risk everything in the name of vision, of artistic creativity."

"For a while there, it looked like somebody was out to destroy that vision," Anne said. "But the incidents on the set—the thefts, the broken equipment, the cut cables—they seemed to have stopped once Mallory vanished."

"I suppose."

"What about the business with the wigs? Did Betty Flugelhorn tell you about the wigs missing from her trailer?"

"I heard some things got misplaced. Happens all the time." Howard pushed his chair back. "Okay, I've answered your questions. Now are you going to write about Linda or not?"

"I haven't decided." It was true. She hadn't.

He glared at her and stood up. "Do it and I'll make you sorry you ever met me." He threw two bills on the table and left, just as the waitress brought their food.

Anne glanced at her plate. The crab was nestled on a slab of coleslaw, next to a mound of French fries. She picked up her fork.

What the hell. She was hungry.

By the time Anne got home, it was after midnight. Six in the morning in Italy. Too early to call Jack. She changed into an extra-large T-shirt that doubled as pajamas and curled up on the couch in the living room. Rain thrummed against the windowpane, a steady melancholy beat. She liked the beach in the rain. The air smelled cleaner. The tourists stayed inside. If she stood on Fisherman's Pier and watched the waves try to lick the sky, it was almost like being part of nature, like the storm was enfolding you in a swirling, wild embrace.

It was cold in the house, cold and damp. She pulled a quilt around her, tried to empty her mind. But she couldn't. All she kept seeing were Betty's eyes, riddled with sand. The eggplant-colored bruise on Betty's neck. She considered getting up, making herself a cup of strong coffee, going over her notes again. It required too much effort. She was tired. Her body felt weighted down with stones.

She leaned her head back, closed her eyes. In minutes, she was asleep. She dreamed she was wading through waist-high dune grass, the sun a yellow button stitched on the sky. The grass made a sweet rustling sound. Up ahead lay the ocean, a fat silvery ribbon. The brightness hurt her eyes. At the water's edge, a woman looking out to sea. Long, curly red hair, her black dress billowing out behind. Anne called to her, but the wind swallowed her words. She walked faster, nearly stumbling. The grass was taller now, to her chest. Anne had to reach the woman, to tell her something before it was too late. She watched the woman go into the water, knowing the woman would drown, though the sea was smooth as porcelain. The grass climbed to Anne's chin. It was thick and coarse and smelled like hot tar.

Slowly, the woman turned. A black velvet mask covered her nose, hiding the skin around her eyes. The woman waved once, twice. A final good-bye. She bent low, the water swirling over her head as she disappeared under the waves. *Wait*, Anne cried out. *Come back.* The grass tore at her mouth. Not grass. Vines. Thick, ropy vines cutting into her body. She glimpsed a piece of the water, felt her knees buckle as she fell.

She woke in a sweat, heart pounding. The morning sun streamed into the room. Above the ocean, the sky was the color of stale eggshells. On the table next to the sofa, the lamp was still on. A loose shutter banged against the side of the house. Outside, the rain had finally stopped.

Chapter 19

To darken your hair naturally: Place a tablespoon of dried sage leaves and a teaspoon of tea leaves in a saucepan filled with 1 cup water. Bring to a boil. Cover and simmer for ten minutes. Strain while still hot. Pour mixture into a bowl, beating in one egg yolk. Beat in enough kaolin powder to make a paste the consistency of cream. Section your dry hair, then cover each section in sage paste. Wrap your hair in aluminum foil and leave for between thirty minutes and one hour. Rinse the paste out with warm water. Shampoo and rinse.

The boardwalk was deserted when Anne went for her three-mile run. She had her Walkman on, tuned to a station that played nothing but Sinatra on Sunday mornings. "Fly me to the moon," Frank sang, as Anne's feet thudded against the wooden planks. She had no energy today. And Phil had already left her a message, his voice laced with anger, which she'd screened while flossing her teeth. He was brief, but to the point: Either he got a full outline by 5 o'clock today, or she was off the book. Permanently. He must have been desperate to call before 8 A.M. on a Sunday, when he normally slept until noon. She had to stall him somehow: *My computer malfunctioned. My fax is on the fritz. My brain isn't functioning. The dog ate my homework.* No, that one wouldn't work.

When she got home, she did a few cool-down stretches and took a quick shower, then slipped into shorts and a T-shirt, her standard weekend attire. Helen phoned at 9:30 A.M., just as Anne was gulping down the last of her breakfast. Cereal, cinnamon glazed donut, coffee. She filled Helen in on everything that had happened yesterday, including the dream.

"Sounds like your subconscious is trying to tell you something," Helen said. "The mask is interesting. Does it mean Mallory was hiding something?"

"You got me," Anne said, a note of exasperation creeping into her voice. "It's getting so I can't tell what's real and what's not anymore."

"You think Koppelman killed Mallory so the movie would get lots of play?"

Anne considered the question. "He's certainly capable of it. I think he'd sell his firstborn for a bigger gross."

"But why kill Betty?" Helen asked. "Unless she somehow found out about it."

Anne finished the last bite of her donut. "I can't figure out what Betty was trying to tell me the other night. I recognized the expression on her face. It's a certain look she had when she'd just discovered an especially juicy bit of gossip."

Helen let out a sigh. "I think you're right about one thing. She probably knew her killer. She let him into her room at the Yard Arm. Then he strangled her and dumped her body on the beach."

"What makes you think it was a man?"

"The nature of the crime, I guess. You have to be pretty strong to kill someone with your bare hands."

"I suppose." Anne gazed out the window. Her kitchen faced a tiny patch of yard in the rear of the house, where her mother had once grown tulips, freesia, and prize-winning roses. Now the strip was bare. "I can't help feeling like I've overlooked something," she said absentmindedly.

"Come on, Annie. You're the most thorough person I know. You practically footnote every piece of information that goes into your books."

"True," Anne laughed. "But this time I've missed something."

"Okay, let's review," Helen said. "The killer might be Dakota. Or Caitlin, for that matter. She benefited big time from Mallory's death. Or Koppelman, of course."

"You know what I don't understand? If Koppelman's telling the truth; if he wasn't sleeping with Mallory, then why would Nick want me to think they were having an affair?"

"Beats me."

Anne stacked the dishes up on the table. "You met all these folks. Who do *you* think is lying?"

"Probably all of them, one way or another. Hey, I almost forgot. Are you going to the parade?"

"I guess. You?"

"Wouldn't miss it for the world." Helen chuckled. "I heard the Mummers are going to be here this year."

"Wow. That's a coup. Score one for the tourist office." The Mummers usually performed at bigger, more important events, in Philadelphia. The Founders' Day Parade was small potatoes. "You want to come over around one-thirty? That's about when the first float usually goes by my house."

"Sounds good," Helen said. "I'll bring over the batch of sugar cookies Aunt Tiny made last night. If I don't share them, I'll wind up eating every single one myself."

"Okay. See you later."

After Anne got off the phone, she did the dishes and straightened up. Something nagged at her, something she'd forgotten to do. Grabbing her pocketbook and car keys, she headed out the door. As she passed the hall table, her eyes fell on the cigars she'd bought in Red Bank. They were tucked inside a slim forest green box with gold letters on the cover that said *The Cigar Shoppe*. Next to them was the cutter Luke had sold her. Anne was so sure Mallory had been holed up in the old Lovitz place, holed up with someone who smoked Avo cigars, someone she knew. Just as Betty had known *her* killer. But then why hadn't Luke recognized any of the cast or crew?

Anne opened the cardboard box and removed one of the cigars. It was hand-rolled, fairly thick, with a mild woodsy aroma. Jack would love one of these babies, but tease her mercilessly for buying them. She could hear him now: *You're going to smoke cigars! Miss I-Hate-Cigarettes. The woman who's always telling me I should eat healthier and exercise more*. It was true. She did encourage Jack to cut down on junk food and eggs, a perfect example of do-as-I-say-not-as-I-do. Jack had high blood pressure and high cholesterol, and she didn't want him to have a heart attack and keel over on his way to work, like his thirty-eight-year-old cousin had four months ago. Jack wasn't overweight. But the most exercise he got was bending over to retrieve the *New York Times* from the mat outside the door of his apartment. She was always trying to get him to go running with her. She'd even bought him a video called *The Armchair Athlete*, with exercises you could do while reclining in a Barcalounger. He'd watched it once, then tossed it onto a shelf. *I'm just not into fitness*, he'd told her. *I'll never be one of those muscle men who love bragging about how many pounds they can bench press.*

Anne started to laugh, then abruptly stopped. Muscle men. Like Nick Fabien. She hadn't shown Nick's picture to Luke because Nick wasn't mentioned in the press kit. It was a long shot. But what the hell? If Nick was with Mallory in Landsdown Park, he knew more than he was telling.

She picked up the cigars, went to the phone, and dialed the number on the box. It was Sunday. The Cigar Shoppe would be closed. But maybe they had an answering machine.

To her surprise, a woman picked up on the other end.

"Is Luke around?" Anne said.

"We're closed today. I'm his sister, Kim. Can I help you?"

Briefly, Anne explained why she was calling.

"I'm about to lock up," Kim said. "I just stopped by to drop something off. But Luke might be in a little later. He said something about taking inventory. I'm not sure what time."

"Do you have a fax?" Anne asked.

"Sure do."

"Great. I'll fax it right over. Could you leave Luke a note telling him to look out for it?"

"No problem."

After she hung up, Anne went into her office and took

out the pictures she'd had developed. Flipping though them, she removed the photos she'd shot Tuesday on the beach. There was Mallory, in full Fitness Queen mode— lifting her perfectly shaped legs off the mat, under the close supervision of Nick Fabien.

Luckily, Anne wasn't a great photographer. Several of the pictures were off-center, showing more of Nick than of Mallory. He was on his knees, his face turned toward the camera. Instead of watching Mallory, he appeared to be gazing at something in the distance. Anne took the picture over to the small copier she'd bought for $49 when the Sandy Lane Salt Water Taffy store had folded and announced that "Everything Must Go."

She placed the picture facedown on the glass, experimenting with different settings—enlarging, lightening— until she was satisfied she had a good likeness. Then she faxed the page over to the Cigar Shoppe, to Luke's attention.

As the copy slid from her fax machine, Anne picked it up and stared at it again. The copier had emphasized tonalities, dividing the image into stark blacks and whites. Nick's hair was dark as motor oil. A little hair dye went a long way.

All along Main Street, preparations were being made for the parade. Although stores were officially closed, shopkeepers crowded the sidewalks, putting the finishing touches on their floats. It looked like almost every establishment had one: Quilters, Baby Face, Moby's Hardware, the Enchanted Florist, the Pelican Café, Bea's Kite Shop, even the Mini-Mart. The shops at the marina had pooled their resources to create a sailboat float, complete with rudder, mast, and striped orange-and-yellow sail. And of course there was the library float, a sky blue replica of the Victorian building, laden with books.

Anne spotted the float from the Antique Boutique when she was still several blocks away. It was at least ten feet high, built in the shape of a mahogany Federal-style highboy chest, which towered over the other floats on the block. When she got closer, Anne could see the chest was made out of papier-mâché, with golden spray-painted "brass" pulls on its drawers. Glued to the sides of the float were tissue paper cutouts of teacups and saucers, in bright floral designs. Anne recognized some of the cups as exact replicas of china patterns in the window of the antiques shop.

When Anne reached the float, Gerald was putting the finishing touches on his sign. His clothes were protected by a long gray bib that reminded Anne of what the workers at the taffy shop used to wear as candy rolled by on the production line.

"Hey there," she said. "Nice float."

"Thanks," he replied, adding a curlicue to the E in *Boutique*. "I might actually have a chance of winning this year. If Kurnetsky doesn't beat me. I think his clamshell is rather shabby, don't you?"

Anne glanced down the street at the Moby's Hardware float, where Nathan Kurnetsky had fashioned a giant clamshell from Pepsi bottle caps. Nathan's fifteen-year-old daughter was decked out as a mermaid. Her scaly tail, cobbled together out of hammers, nails, screwdrivers, and other small tools tied together, looked like it weighed a ton. "It's okay," Anne said. "Disney does it better."

"Exactly. Know what I think?" He put down his paintbrush and wiped his hands on his bib. "The entire competition is rigged. Last year Nathan promised a free Weber grill to anybody who voted for him. He won, remember?"

"Oh, yes. The buried treasure float." Featuring silver "doubloons" and glass "diamonds" made from scrap metal and recycled jelly glasses.

"It should never have come in first," Gerald said disparagingly. "Oh, well, if you'll excuse me, I've got to get cleaned up before this big shebang starts."

He picked up his paint can and headed toward the

back of his shop. Anne trailed after him. The sun was just starting to peek out from behind a bank of gray, low-lying clouds. A butterfly fluttered near the holly-hocks lining the walk.

When Gerald reached the side door, he turned and looked at her inquiringly. "I'm closed, today, Anne. If you'd like to look around, come back Tuesday morning."

"The thing is," she began, "I was driving by your apartment late Friday night and all of a sudden the lights came on. I thought I saw someone prowling around. Somebody broke into my house last Tuesday and I was concerned it was the same person. So I sat in my car for a while, and after about fifteen minutes a woman came out this door." Anne pointed to the side entrance. Gerald put the paint can down on the steps. His mouth had gone slack. His eyes had the startled, pained look of a mouse caught in a sticky trap.

"Come in," he said in a low voice, moving toward the door leading to the shop.

"If it's all the same to you, I'd rather talk in the garden. It's cooler." And safer, she thought suddenly. Could Gerald be dangerous?

He nodded and led her around the corner of the house to the small garden Anne had seen from the upstairs parlor. Petunias nodded gently in the breeze. The smell of roses was overpowering. Gerald took a seat on a cedar bench, covered with blue-and-white plaid gingham cushions. Anne sat in an adjoining Adirondack-style cedar-wood chair.

"I appreciate your concern," Gerald said. He managed a strained smile. "But you needn't have worried. The woman you saw was my cousin Grace. She's been staying with me for a couple of days. She's gone home, to Wisconsin."

"I followed you to Liberty Park," Anne said carefully. "I saw the car pick you up. A silver BMW."

Two bright spots of color had appeared on Gerald's

cheeks. His right knee jiggled up and down. "I'm afraid I don't know what you're talking about." His voice shook slightly. His hands had clenched into balls.

"I'm talking about the fact that Mallory knew you liked dressing in women's clothes. Delia Graustark told me your sister never married. You don't have a niece who goes to Penn. The magazines I saw upstairs. *Cosmo*. *Glamour*. They belong to you." Gerald twisted his hands in his lap. He appeared to be willing himself not to panic. "Mallory apparently accused you of stealing a Bob Mackie dress from her closet. You were terrified she was going to reveal your secret in her book. That's why you caused all those mishaps on the set of *Dark Horizon*."

"I didn't . . ." Gerald sputtered.

"Both Mallory's assistant and her hairdresser told me you've been hanging around the set early in the morning. I didn't put it together at first. But it's not easy to jam a camera shutter or cut the cable on a generator. You have to know what you're doing. And you told me yourself you studied film at UCLA."

Gerald wrapped his arms across his chest. Although the temperature was in the eighties, he was practically shivering. "Please don't tell anyone." He stopped. Anne could see he was struggling to contain his emotions. "If it got out about the dress, about what you saw in Liberty Park," he said haltingly, "I'd have to move away."

It was true. Anne knew it as well as he did. People in the Heights didn't have much patience for what they didn't understand. Or for anything different from their definition of normal. Dressing in women's clothes would be looked upon not only as a perversion, but as a sin against God. In no time at all, the news would spread, until even the tourists had heard. At best, he'd be a curiosity. At worst, an abomination. Either way, his standing in the community would sink faster than a stone tossed into Grassmere Lake. His business, his reputation, would sicken and die. Anne looked around at Gerald's immaculate garden—the neat rows of flowers, the out-door furniture arranged just so. There was a desperate look in Gerald's eyes, desperate and faintly dangerous. She wondered how far he would go to protect his secret.

"I have no intention of telling anyone," she said finally. "I only want to ask you a few questions."

He licked at his lips as if his mouth was dry. "Well?"

"The incidents on the set. You were responsible, right?"

"I needed to buy some time." His voice was tight. "So I could convince Mallory not to tell."

"Did you break into the hair and makeup trailer?"

"Yes," he said, almost defiantly.

The sun emerged from behind a cloud, illuminating Gerald's flowers. The roses were overrun with bees, crawling up the pink and salmon petals.

"What'd you take?" Anne said.

"Not much. Some cosmetics. I just messed the place up a bit."

"The broken light meter. The missing equipment. You were behind them."

"There wasn't much damage," Gerald said sullenly. "It's not like they couldn't afford to replace things."

"Did you take a red wig?"

"A wig? No."

She studied him carefully. His face was slick with sweat. His knee bobbed up and down, a quick, jittery motion. When she'd seen him in Liberty Park, he'd been wearing a dark, shoulder-length wig. Who knew how many other hairpieces were upstairs in his bedroom?

"You're sure you didn't take a red wig?

He smiled acidly. "Quite sure. Red's not my color."

"Where were you Thursday night, around ten-thirty?"

"At home, asleep. If you're trying to imply that I had anything to do with Mallory's death, you're dead wrong."

A bee flew over to where they were sitting. Anne

shooed it away with her hand. In the distance, she heard a band warming up for the parade, the peal of trombones, drums, brassy trumpets.

"I believe Mallory was going to reveal everything she knew about you," Anne said. "She told you as much, didn't she? On Monday. The two of you had a big argument in the back of your shop."

"She walked off with one of my teacups," Gerald whined. "I'd like to see you put that in your book. The late great Mallory Loving, a common thief."

The bee circled Gerald's head, letting out a faint droning sound. Without warning, he reached out and clapped his hands together. The bee fell to the grass, a black and yellow dot. Gerald wiped his hands on his bib. "If I were you, I'd let it alone. You wouldn't want to do something you'll regret."

Chapter 20

The sun ages your skin. Period. That's why it's important to use an SPF of 15 or above. When you're shopping for moisturizers, choose one that contains sunscreen.

Although the Founders' Day Parade wasn't scheduled to begin for another hour, most of the participants were already congregating outside the Mini-Mart. There were nine junior high and high school bands from various schools in Monmouth County. Plus members of the Ladies' Auxiliary, volunteer firemen, Neptune Township selectmen, Friends of the Library, the Oceanside Heights Historical Preservation Society, the Camp Meeting Association, a group of teenage lifeguards, the Church by the Sea Choir, a handful of Coast Guard members, three barbershop quartets, employees of the Main Street Launderette, the Oceanside Heights Fishing Club, a half-dozen postal workers, the Chamber of Commerce, Boy Scout Troop 41, and of course, the Mummers, decked out in candy-colored costumes and winged headdresses like it was the first day of Mardi Gras.

A line of floats snaked down Trinity Lane, rounded the corner onto Seaside Avenue, and spilled over onto Crestwood Street, where they backed all the way up to Route 35. The *Dark Horizon* float was the grandest one of all. About a half-block long, it featured cameras on tripods and a life-size poster of Caitlin and Dakota embracing in front of a tumultuous, roiling ocean. Cutouts of automatic weapons and laptop computers dangled from a cord high above the float. An overhead banner proclaimed: *Murder, Mayhem, & More on the Shore*. Anne figured it was supposed to entice you to see the movie. But it struck awfully close to home. Mallory, not Caitlin, would have been the star on high, waving to her adoring public. Bad girl makes good. Mallory would have eaten this up with a spoon.

Anne surveyed the phalanx of floats. She couldn't believe how many there were this year. Even David Chilton, dentist and philanderer extraordinaire, had one—a huge tooth (a molar? a bicuspid?) mounted on what looked like a pink sheet of aluminum foil the size of a kiddie pool. Anne spotted him next to the tooth, doling out wrapped hard candies to children in the crowd. Wasn't that a conflict of interest? Like a teacher handing out cheat sheets.

"Annie," she heard a voice call out.

She turned to see Delia waving at her from the Friends of the Library float. Delia was wearing her parade finery, an ankle-length lavender dress with long puffed sleeves and a bustle at the back. She had on white leather boots that laced up the front, and she held a lavender parasol, dripping with ribbons. Her white hair was pulled into a tight bun.

"Wow," Anne said, drawing closer. "Fabulous dress."

"It was one of Grandmother's favorites."

"You look like you stepped out of an Edith Wharton novel."

"Thank you kindly," Delia said. "Hop on up. The view's better from here."

Anne climbed onto the float. Under a white lacy canopy, protected from the sun's glare, sat five elderly ladies. Each wore a different solid-colored gown and held a matching parasol in white gloved hands. The ladies nodded to her and continued their conversation, something to do with a gingersnap recipe. Behind them towered a cardboard replica of the library's sky blue facade and piles of real books, arranged in neat stacks. Poetry, history, the classics, nineteenth-century literature. Forget the parade! She would have loved to spend the afternoon curled up in a hammock with Jane Austen or Charles Dickens.

From this vantage point, she could see the length and breadth of Main Street. People were lined up three and four deep, cameras at the ready. One of the tourists had shimmied up a lamppost and was videotaping the scene for posterity.

"I swear," Delia said. "Founders' Day is turning into a regular circus. Why, I remember the very first time we celebrated the occasion, back in 1936. I was twelve years old at the time. My mama let me wear my hair long, instead of in braids. And she sewed sailor suits for my sister and me to wear. There couldn't have been more than sixty folks marching back then."

"Do you have any pictures? I'd love to see them."

"Sure. You know what? You should write that book, the historical book you used to talk about doing."

"Mmmmmm," Anne said, with a smile. "Maybe." There wasn't much of a market for a history of Oceanside Heights. She could just hear Phil Smedley now: *You gotta be kidding. Nobody would pay a plug nickel for it.*

Thinking about Phil reminded her of the deadline.

How was she supposed to get an outline to him by the end of the day? She couldn't do it. Period. She couldn't write about Mallory's life until she'd figured out how Mallory died. Only Phil didn't want to hear it. Not when he could make big bucks if he rushed the book into stores by Christmas.

"Now, back in '45," Delia was saying, "we had a pie-eating contest at the end of the parade. And the prettiest float got a blue ribbon, not a grill from Moby's Hardware. I think they ought to revive those traditions, don't you?"

"I certainly do. Especially if you're doing the baking." Delia made the best sweet potato pie in Neptune Township. Everybody said so.

"Why don't you stay and ride with us?" Delia asked. "You're entitled. You use the library more than anyone in town, with your research and such. Besides, there's plenty of room."

"I'd love to," Anne replied. "But I'm supposed to meet Helen back at my house in . . ." She glanced at her watch. "Half an hour."

"All right. Be sure to clap nice and loud when we go by."

"Will do."

Anne climbed down off the float. With a backward wave, she headed home. Main Street was so crowded that she cut over to Primrose Lane, then doubled back on Lattimore Street. The Victorian-style homes on Lattimore were among her favorites. Painted in two tones— mustard yellow and blue, blush pink and scarlet, pale green and jade—they had clapboard facades and octagonal shaped turrets crowned with finials. The Carpenter Gothic windows on the third stories were surrounded by fish-scale shingles. Stained glass panels shimmered in the afternoon sun. In honor of Founders' Day, American flags hung above nearly every door. Bright-colored bunting festooned the porches. On the white porch railings sat large pots of marigolds, hydrangeas, and geraniums.

Her own house, by contrast, was not as festive. She didn't own a flag, she never gardened, and the last time the porch had been decorated with crepe paper she'd been celebrating her eighth birthday. Oh, well. She sighed. The house still had a faded charm. She wouldn't want to live anywhere else. This was home sweet home, for better or worse. She unlocked the front door and went straight into the kitchen. She removed a pitcher of iced tea from the refrigerator and set it on a white wicker tray, along with two tall glass tumblers. She rummaged through the cupboards, taking out paper napkins and a large flowered ceramic plate for Aunt Tiny's sugar cookies. Helen's aunt weighed two hundred pounds and could bake like nobody's business.

On her way out, she went into her office. Jack had sent a fax. She set down the tray and picked it up. One page only, a drawing of a couple in a gondola, floating down a canal under a starry sky. The gondolier wore a striped shirt, trousers, and a funny hat tied with a ribbon. The woman seated in the prow of the boat had long, curly hair and a contented smile. Underneath the picture, Jack had written one word: *Well*?

If Phil carried out his bluff and hired another writer, she could scrape together her savings and meet Jack in Venice. Wouldn't it be something to surprise him unannounced? The thought of his face, beaming and pleased, made her smile.

She checked the answering machine. Two messages. She hit the *Play* button, and the tape rewound. It took a while. Phil Smedley, demanding a progress report. *Sorry, Phil. No can do.* She fast-forwarded to the second message. "Luke here," the voice said. "Got your fax. The guy in the picture is one of our regulars. He comes in once, twice a week. Likes Avos. But he also buys Partegas and Macanudos. I'm heading out to the beach. But I'll be here tomorrow morning at 10, if you need to reach me. Hope you're enjoying the cigars."

So Nick Fabien smoked Avos. Interesting. Maybe

he'd been at the Lovitz place with Mallory. Hell, maybe he was the one who'd been having an affair with her. Anne grabbed paper and pen from her desk. *Have gone on an errand,* she wrote. *Back soon.* Holding the tray in both hands, she went out onto the porch. She set the tray on the wicker table and taped the note to the front door. Helen should be there soon. In the meantime, there was something she needed to do.

Although the parade didn't go down Embury Street, the front of the Yard Arm Inn was decorated with pink-and-blue bunting. Large helium-filled balloons fluttered from the porch railing. Someone had strung a sign underneath the cornice that said: *Happy Founders' Day to You.* A couple of tourists were rocking on the porch, reading the Sunday paper and taking pictures of each other wearing pointy paper birthday hats.

Inside, other guests were polishing off the last of the free continental brunch: blueberry muffins, banana bread, fruit salad, juice, coffee. A teenage girl with pouty lips sat behind the front desk, filing nails the color of espresso.

"Hi," Anne said. "Is Nick Fabien around?"

The girl put down her emery board and scanned a ledger notebook on the counter in front of her. "He's in 308, right?"

Anne nodded. She and the girl both turned to look at the row of wooden cubbyholes lining the wall. Box 308 was empty.

"Looks like he's out," the girl said. "Wanna leave a message?"

"No thanks. But could I use your bathroom a minute?"

"Sure," the girl said, turning her attention back to her cuticles. "Top of the stairs. Second door on your left."

Anne clambered up the stairs to the second floor, then rounded the corner and climbed to the third story. The hallways were decorated with early American furnishings—pine blanket chests, corner cupboards, a tall case clock with a crescent moon on its face. Room 308 was in the back of the inn, facing away from the ocean.

Anne tried the door. Locked. She peered down the hall. Then she put her ear against the door and listened. No sound from within. Reaching into her wallet, Anne pulled out her Visa card. It was the only credit card she owned, and she'd vowed not to use it again until she'd finished paying off the Gateway computer. Holding the credit card in her right hand, she slid the top edge in the lock and jiggled it back and forth. She applied a little more pressure, feeling the card rub against the cylinders. Gripping the doorknob in her left hand, she continued working the lock. She'd gotten into her own house countless times this way, back when her mother, in the worst days of the Alzheimer's, locked all the doors and began screaming that Anne was out to get her. One time she'd broken in seconds after her mother had set the rug in the guest bedroom on fire.

Anne forced the image from her mind and concentrated on the lock. She jiggled it gently, pressing the card up and in. Just as she heard a faint click, the door across the hall swung open. Anne turned the knob of Room 308 and slid the credit card into her front pocket. Turning, she saw a heavyset man in a golf shirt and white slacks emerge from the room across the way.

"Hi there," Golf Shirt said. "Beautiful day for a parade."

"Sure is," Anne agreed. She had her hand on the door and had pushed it halfway open.

"Last time I was at a parade was Thanksgiving, in the Big Apple. The Woody Woodpecker balloon got caught in a tree. Shot it just as Woody's leg deflated." He tapped his camera bag. "I'm from Del Ray Beach, Florida. But me and the missus spend the summer up here. Too darn hot in the Sunshine State. Where you from?"

Anne hesitated. ''North Jersey.''

''Is that right? We've got a nephew lives up there. Paterson, I think. He's my wife's nephew, by marriage. Lives about forty minutes outside the city. We visit him every year except when there's—''

''Excuse me,'' Anne cut in. ''I'd love to chat, but I'm running late.''

The man smiled broadly. ''Nice talking to you. Happy Founders' Day.''

As he turned away, Anne gave a sigh of relief. It was a good thing the man didn't know she lived in the Heights. Tourists usually had dozens of questions about the town's curious traditions and history. She slipped inside Room 308, shutting the door behind her. As far as breaking and entering went, she was right up there with Dakota.

Nick's room was smallish. Along one wall was a full-size bed, covered with a pale blue and red quilt, flanked by two nightstands. An oval mirror in a mahogany frame hung on the opposite wall, above a mahogany double dresser whose top was strewn with papers. The heavy crimson drapes were pulled shut, but sunlight peeked through the sides of the window. She'd better hurry. The last thing she wanted was for Nick to walk in and find her here. What could she possibly say if he did? She was in the market for an aerobics instructor?

Just as Anne stepped toward the dresser, she was startled by a rustling noise. Turning toward the adjoining bath, she saw a black and white form streak into the room. Her heart leaped into her throat, but the next second she broke out laughing. A fat black and white cat leaped onto the bed and studied her with one quizzical oval eye. Harry? Anne walked over to the bed and stroked the animal's back.

The cat rubbed itself against Anne's leg. She put her hand under the animal's face and stroked the underside of its chin. No collar or identification tags. Anne tickled the cat's belly. It rolled over playfully, stretching its legs. Sure enough, there was a white patch shaped like a star on its flank. It had to be Harry. What was Sheila's cat doing in Nick's room? The inns in the Heights didn't allow animals. No pets. No children under the age of two. No smoking on the premises. No alcohol. No exceptions.

Anne walked over to the dresser. From his perch on the bed, the cat watched her. She began leafing through Nick's papers: A rental car agreement. A map of New Jersey, photocopied from an atlas. A series of exercises, also photocopied, on strengthening abdominal muscles, inner thighs, and buttocks. A take-out menu from the Happy Land Chinese restaurant in Landsdown Park. A *Dark Horizon* press kit. No, two press kits, in identical Mediterranean blue folders, with a picture of a storm-tossed ocean on the cover. She picked up the top one. Inside was the familiar press release and black-and-white glossies of the cast. Anne noticed that Mallory's picture had been taken out, and Caitlin had been upgraded from a five-by-seven to an eight-by-ten enlargement.

She closed the press packet, put it back on the pile. The second kit was tucked beneath it. Why did Nick need two? She opened the second folder. The heading on a document stuck inside the right-hand flap jumped out at her. *THE CITY CLERK. The City of Trenton— The State of New Jersey.* She eased the paper out of the flap and scanned it. *This license permits the bride and groom to be married anywhere in New Jersey State only* . . . She stared at the page, taking it in. Nick and Sheila, married last Wednesday. The day before Mallory died.

Why would two virtual strangers decide to tie the knot? Anne remembered what Sheila had said about men at the Blue Marlin. *You can't live with 'em. And you can't pretend they don't get on your nerves.* Not the sentiments of a woman anxious to get hitched. Anne's gaze returned to the press kit. Lodged in the left-hand flap was a thick document held together with a large paper clip. She took it out, leafed through it. A contract of some sort, a bill of sale. Her eye alighted on the purchase price, $1.8 million. The buyer was Telco Property Management Ltd., in Landsdown Park. And the seller was . . .

Anne drew in her breath. There was no way Sheila Lovitz would sell the house on Pitt Street. Not for anything. Unless . . . Anne could almost hear the cylinders tumbling in her brain. Unless . . . Was it possible? Yes. There was no other logical explanation.

The lock clicked audibly. Anne looked up, just as the door swung open. Jill Bentley stood on the threshold, dressed in a beige pants suit and carrying a brown leather pocketbook and a leather briefcase.

"What are you doing here?" Jill exclaimed, shutting the door behind her.

"Mallory's not dead," Anne announced. "The whole thing was a setup. A double switch."

"What?" Jill said. "That's crazy."

"No," Anne said excitedly. "Mallory's been impersonating Sheila for days. Sheila's body was in the car that went off the road." Anne waved the press kit in the air. "The proof's right here. Nick and Mallory got married on Wednesday. They sold Sheila's house to that company, Telco, the ones behind the new mall that's going to be built. Telco needs the house to build the highway extension. Sheila and Nick stand to gain millions."

Jill put her briefcase on the floor and opened her pocketbook. Anne looked around for the phone. There wasn't one.

"Come on," Anne said. The cat jumped off the bed and rubbed against her ankles. "We've got to go downstairs and call the cops."

She started for the door, then stopped when she saw what Jill was holding. A small silver gun pointed directly at her chest.

Chapter 21

If you suffer from allergies, put mascara on only your top lashes, since the bottom ones may tear. Opt for waterproof mascara, and darken the eyelid slightly. It will make you look less puffy. If your skin has red, blotchy spots, use a greenish toner to even it out. And remember to play up your mouth. It's probably the only part of your face that isn't suffering!

"Sit down," Jill said.

Anne backed into the room and sat down hard on the bed. She couldn't take her eyes off the gun. It was shiny stainless steel, with a two-inch long barrel.

"You shouldn't have been snooping," Jill chided.

Anne could feel the blood rushing to her face. Her breathing was shallow, her mouth felt dryer than the Negev Desert.

"Are you related to him?" she managed to say. Her legs felt like Jell-O. She put both hands on the bed to steady herself.

Jill laughed. "Let's just say we're close friends."

"Close enough to get a cut of a $1.8-million pie?"

"Let's just say I won't be fetching coffee or setting up lunch dates anymore."

"You'll never pull it off." Anne's heart felt like it was beating loud enough to burst. "If I figured it out, the police will, too."

"The police don't usually break in and rifle through private papers. Unless they've got a search warrant."

Jill sounded more confident than she looked. A thin bead of perspiration had formed on her upper lip. She still held the gun straight out in front of her, but Anne noticed her hand was shaking.

"You switched the dental records," Anne said. "David . . . Dr. Chilton . . . told me you were in his office the other day, complaining about a cavity. But there was nothing really wrong with you."

Jill couldn't shoot her here. The gun would make too much noise. If she could keep Jill talking, maybe someone would come, take the gun away. But the bed was already made up. The only one likely to walk through the door was Nick Fabien, and he wouldn't be much help.

Jill bent her elbow slightly, inching her arm closer to her body. The gun was aimed at Anne's head. "Gee, Sherlock," Jill said sarcastically, "looks like you've got the whole caper figured out."

"Not everything." The cat yawned, stretched, and rested his chin on Anne's thigh. "I don't know why

Mallory wanted her sister dead. She was making a lot of money on the movie. Why get greedy?''

"Mallory's clueless," Jill said with disdain. "She thinks her 'stalker' killed Sheila by accident. And if he knew she was still alive, she'd be next."

Anne's mind was racing. So Mallory wasn't in on the plan.

"Is she in love with him?" Anne asked. If she kept talking, kept trying to puzzle things out, it would take her mind off the gun, off the look on Jill's face. A scared, strange look that said Jill wanted her dead.

Reaching in front of her, Jill put her free hand on the gun, steadying it. "Doesn't matter. In about ten minutes, Mallory's going to die. For real this time."

"What?" Anne could feel the tension in her back, her knees. Her stomach was twisted in knots. She leaned forward and stroked Harry's coat. "What do you mean?"

"Mallory's got hay fever, asthma, all kinds of allergies. She takes antihistamines three times a day, like clockwork. Took the first one at eight this morning, back at the apartment. In ten minutes, she pops the next one. Then it's bye-bye baby."

"Why?"

"It's not allergy medication."

"But an autopsy—"

"—will reveal nothing," Jill finished. Her eyes were as cold and hard as the metal on the gun. "Nick switched the pills. He used to work in a pharmacy. Bet you didn't know that. There's a drug called Phrenoxadol that's lethal if you have asthma and perfectly safe if you don't."

Anne kept her eyes trained on the gun. She felt light-headed, shaky. Her heart was beating a tattoo against her chest. "Sheila didn't have asthma."

"Bingo," Jill said slyly. "They're not even going to know what to look for."

"Then Nick doesn't feel like sharing the money."

"Only with me."

Jill's hands still trembled slightly. Her right index finger rested lightly on the trigger. Anne prayed the safety was on. Did the gun even have a safety? She could see Jill didn't know what to do next. Their eyes locked.

"Why did Nick kill Betty?" Anne said, stroking the cat's back.

"The hairdresser? She recognized Mallory the other night. Nicky warned Mal to stay away from the set, but she had to see how they were doing without her." Jill forced a smile. "Want to know what tipped the hairdresser off? Mal's mousy brown dye job. Guess it wasn't too professional, huh? Betty got all excited. We told her it was a publicity stunt, but you could see she was dying to tell."

Anne remembered the look on Betty's face. *I've got a secret. I've got a secret.* Her eyes on the beach, clotted with sand.

Fear skidded through Anne's body, like a skater tumbling on an icy lake. And beneath the fear, white-hot anger.

Aloud, she said, "How'd you kill Sheila? Was she dead when the car went over the embankment?"

Jill started to answer, then stopped. "Enough questions," she snapped. "I've already told you too much."

Anne pulled her gaze from the gun and focused on the cat lying contentedly in her lap. What next? Jill had to get her out of here. But how?

As if she were thinking the exact same thing, Jill said, "Get up. Slowly. With your hands where I can see them."

Anne didn't move.

"Did you hear me?" Jill barked. "Get up."

Anne looked at the gun again. It was pointed at her larynx. She made as if to rise, and as she did so, she gave the cat a sharp pinch. Harry sprang forward with a wail. Startled, Jill took a step back. Anne lunged for the gun. As she caught Jill's wrist, wrenching it upward, the gun went off. A loud pop, like a car backfiring.

The two of them crashed sideways, banging into the dresser. Anne smelled perfume and sweat. She had both hands on Jill's wrists. But Jill held on to the gun. Jill spun around and Anne spun with her, holding tight. Anne felt her hip hit the corner of the dresser, just as Jill kicked her in the shin. She stumbled, held on. Her right hand closed on the gun. Pop. The shot cracked the mirror. Someone pounding on the door. Anne wrenched at the gun, cold metal against her fingers. Her left elbow swung against Jill's face. "Ow," Jill screamed as the gun sailed across the room. Jill wrestled her to the floor, yanking her hair. Voices outside the door, louder now.

Anne's breath came in ragged gasps. Her shin throbbed. Jill's talonlike nails dug into her. She kicked her legs hard. The blow connected with Jill's stomach, catching her off-balance. Anne struggled to her knees. Where was it? Bed, chair, dresser. Where? Out of the corner of her eye, she saw Jill stagger to her feet.

Anne rolled toward the window. There was a rag rug by the chair. Near the fringe, a glint of silver. Anne reached for the gun. She felt for the trigger, found it, and aimed at the chair, just as Jill grabbed her leg. Pop. Jill released her and fell back. Struggling to her feet, Anne pointed the gun at Jill, who was lying on the floor, looking dazed. The cat had leaped onto the bed and was eyeing Anne reproachfully. Anne edged toward the door, unlocked it. Half a dozen people were out in the hall.

Anne spotted the teenager who'd been sitting behind the front desk. "Is there a door in this place that locks?"

"Closet," the girl stammered.

"Where?"

The girl pointed feebly down the hall.

Anne turned back to Jill. "Let's go," she said.

Jill got up slowly, blinking a few times, as if unaccustomed to light. The fight had drained out of her eyes. Wisps of hair were plastered to her forehead. Her suit jacket was wrinkled, two spots of color flared on her cheeks.

The people in the hall stood back to let them pass. No one uttered a word when Jill stepped inside the closet, and Anne locked the door behind her, propping a chair under the knob for good measure.

"Call the police," Anne said to the teenager, who couldn't take her eyes off the gun. "Tell them a woman on the *Dark Horizon* float is about to die. Her allergy pill has been tampered with."

The girl stared at her blankly, rooted to the spot.

"I'll do it," said the man in the golf shirt whom Anne had spoken to earlier. "The *Dark Horizon* float?"

"The woman's name is Sheila Lovitz. Blue eyes. Shoulder-length brown hair."

The man made an A-okay sign with his thumb and forefinger, puffing his chest out like he'd just been deputized.

Anne started for the staircase, then wheeled around. "One more thing. Don't let that woman out. She just tried to kill me."

Before Golf Shirt could respond, Anne was hurrying down the stairs, taking them two at a time. Outside, it had gotten hotter. Sunlight glinted off the pavement. The air felt thick, weighted down. There was no breeze at all. The pink-and-blue bunting decorating the Yard Arm sagged in the heat.

Making a left at the corner, Anne jogged down Mount Tabor Street, which ran parallel to Main. The parade always began on Main Street, wound its way north for seven blocks on New Jersey Avenue, then turned toward the water at Broadway until it reached Ocean Avenue, where it proceeded south, past Anne's house to Fletcher Lake. She glanced at her watch. Ten of two. The parade had started twenty minutes ago. She didn't know where the *Dark Horizon* float would be. The Heights Association usually alternated the floats with marching bands, and she had no idea if the movie float was among the first to promenade or was being saved for the grand finale.

As she drew closer to the main thoroughfare, the streets got more crowded. Tourists were out in full force, waving their cameras, jamming the sidewalks. For the most part, the townspeople preferred to hang back, gathering on one another's front porches and balconies, with cold pitchers of lemonade and plates of homemade goodies. The sound of the crowd mingled with the music from the marching bands. Sousa music. Trombones blared. The heat seemed to rise off the pavement in waves.

At Main Street, she tried to glimpse the floats, but her view was blocked by a solid wall of bodies. She plunged into the wall. Bodies pressed up against her. Arms, elbows, faces. Bits of color and skin flashed by, she heard angry mutterings as she tried to break through. Her vision narrowed: a Rolex watch, a child's sneaker, brass buttons, a hairy arm, appearing and disappearing in quick succession. She was jostled and pushed, shoved sideways, nearly knocked to the ground by people who wanted a better look at the parade. And then suddenly she was shaken loose from the crowd and standing on the curb, opposite a row of blue sawhorses that separated sidewalk from street. Without thinking, she ducked under one of the sawhorses and found herself face to face with the Oceanside Heights Historical Preservation Society. They were dressed in much the same manner as Delia and her friends had been. The women wore ankle-length, solid-colored dresses, with puffed sleeves and high collars. The men had on gray morning coats over trousers, vests, and crisp white cotton shirts. They carried signs that said: *Preserve Our Precious Past. Don't Ignore, Restore*! *History and Houses: A Perfect Fit*. Anne thought they must be wilting from the heat.

She peered down Main Street. No sign of the float. They must be ahead of her. No cops either. She fell into step beside the Preservation Society. What the hell? She lived here, too. And right now she needed a prop.

Spotting Lucille Klemperer, Anne hustled over. The elderly woman wore a pale lavender dress under a frilly white apron. Her hands and forearms were encased in white gloves. A parasol was draped in the crook of her elbow. In her other hand, she carried a sign that said: *Proud to Be Historically Correct.*

"Your sign looks heavy," Anne said, shouting to be heard above the crowd. "Need a hand?"

"No, thank you," Lucille said coldly.

She and Lucille had never been especially fond of each other. But things had gotten even worse last summer when Lucille became a suspect in Jack's brother's murder.

"Actually," Anne persisted, "it would mean a lot to me. My house is nearly a hundred years old. And . . . well, you know I'm not a member. But I'd like to be. I thought this could be the first step." Anne tried her best to look sincere. Her house needed so many repairs. The Preservation Society had never bothered asking her to take part in the annual house tour.

"Restoration is our civic duty," Lucille said sternly.

"Oh, I know. Marching in this parade would be a real honor."

"In that case . . ." Lucille gingerly handed over her sign.

Anne hoisted it above her head. "Thanks. I'm going to run on up ahead. Spread the word our group is coming."

As she sprinted away, she caught a glimpse of Lucille's shocked expression. Oh, well. She'd write the society a check tomorrow. Volunteer to be a docent on the next walking tour. Donate her majolica teapot to the shop 'n' swap.

Up ahead was the float from Bea's Kite Shop, its pink streamers hanging from a kite as high as a lamppost. She jogged past, weaving in and out of marching bands, with their fresh-faced baton twirlers and overweight boys lugging tubas and drums. The music ripped at her ears. She spotted David Chilton perched next to his tooth and pretended not to notice when he signaled to her. The sign wasn't heavy, but it slowed her down. It was hard to run while waving it in the air.

There looked to be twice as many spectators pressed behind the sawhorses, a wall of people yelling and clapping as each new float went past. Anne picked up the pace, passing the Quilters float and the float from the Mini-Mart. She kept to the edge of the street, overtaking the Ladies' Auxiliary, the Fishing Club, the firemen.

At Franklin Street, there was still no sign of the movie float. She heard the muffled blare of sirens. The police. Thank God. But how close were they? And how fast would they be able to penetrate the slow-moving, snaking mass.

When she got to Ocean Avenue, she pulled up short, panting for breath. On the left side of the street was the glassy green ocean. On the right, the inns overlooking the beach. Sandwiched in between was a line of antique cars, driving two abreast. There must have been close to a hundred of them, stretched out over eight or so blocks.

At the far end of Ocean Avenue, ahead of the cars, she saw the *Dark Horizon* float. She'd miscalculated, big time. The movie people had been in the lead, given the place of honor at the head of the parade. Between Anne and the float were the vintage cars, inching along at about five miles an hour. She plunged into the sea of cars, weaving and bobbing. The ones closest to her were turn-of-the-century models, two-seaters with patent leather dashboards and mudguards arching over tall, sausage-thin tires. They had headlamps and flaring fenders and glistening brass toolboxes on the running boards. The drivers all looked to be over sixty-five, and wore goggles, scarves, and leather gloves. As they toodled by, the crowd waved and cheered. Anne didn't recognize any of the men behind the wheel. Maybe they were from other parts of Jersey, other states.

The road was so congested she couldn't go any faster than a dog trot. Sweat stung her eyes. Her shin ached where Jill had kicked her. She glanced at the float, which was about four blocks south, and thought she saw signs of a commotion on board, people pantomiming alarm. She heard sirens again, but couldn't tell where they were coming from.

The cars were bigger and lower now, with long, rakish silhouettes. DeSotos, Oldsmobiles, Chryslers, Studebakers. A hot pink Cadillac with chrome tail fins swerved to avoid a pothole and nearly ran over her left foot. As the driver shook his fist, she darted out in front of the Caddy, narrowly missing being hit by an enamel blue Ford. Only two blocks to go.

Some people had climbed off the *Dark Horizon* float and were pushing their way through the crowd. Anne skirted a lemon yellow Buick dripping with chrome and tossed her sign onto the ground. The crowd was so loud, she couldn't hear herself think.

When she got closer, she saw people clustering over somebody. Mallory was sprawled on her back, her arms flung out. Nick Fabien knelt directly above her. With one hand, he pinched Mallory's nose shut. His lips were pressed to hers.

Anne climbed onto the float. "Stop," she cried out. "Stop him. He's making it worse."

The sirens sounded again. She craned her neck and spotted a police car heading down Stockton Street, toward Ocean Avenue. Leaping onto the flatbed truck, Anne ran at Nick. She tried to pull him off Mallory. But he merely looked up and shoved her away so hard the blow sent her tumbling backward.

"What the hell are you doing?" Howard Koppelman yelled. Caitlin, Dakota, and the others were staring at Anne as if she'd lost her mind.

"He poisoned her," Anne panted. "With a bad allergy pill. We've got to get her to a hospital."

Nick glanced up from his work. His eyes were expressionless, his mouth a tight, hard line. He bent over the body again. As he pinched Mallory's nose, Anne saw his right biceps flex.

"Stop him!" Anne screamed. "He's suffocating her."

Chapter 22

*Beauty is an attitude
adjustment. Accept your
flaws and move on. It's
the only way to get
through life.*

Anne lunged at Nick Fabien again. This time he was expecting it. His fist connected with the left side of her jaw and sent her flying. She lay on her back, her legs crumpled beneath her. The sky was a pale, almost tender shade of blue. Her mouth throbbed. A knot of pain formed on the back of her head and sprinted down her spine. Everyone on the float seemed frozen in place, motionless as statues.

Her mouth struggled to make words. It seemed to take a long time. "It's Mallory," she said finally. "He switched them."

At least that's what she meant to say. It sounded more like, "S'Mowry. He swished 'em."

"What's going on?" Caitlin shrieked. "What's happening?"

Dakota threw a protective arm around her shoulders.

"Nobody's going to hurt you," he crooned. "You're all right."

Anne pushed herself up on one elbow. She felt winded, stunned, like the breath had been knocked out of her. She looked at Nick. He was still bending over the body, his hand covering Mallory's nose.

"S'Mowry. Mowry."

The inside of her mouth tasted coppery and warm. She leaned forward and spat out a tooth.

Howard Koppelman had taken off his sunglasses and was gaping at Nick, a horrified expression on his face.

Anne crawled over to the side of the float where her pocketbook had landed. Reaching inside, she removed Jill's gun. She pointed it straight up, squeezed the trigger. *Ker-bang.* Nick's head bobbed up, away from Mallory's face. People on both sides of Ocean Avenue were cheering wildly, as if the shot were part of the day's entertainment.

Anne lowered the gun and aimed it at Nick. She felt the soft tissue in her jaw swelling up. The pain had become a dull, steady ache. "Ged away fwom her," she yelled.

Ignoring the gun, Nick looked over his shoulder toward the screaming sirens. The cops were now less than two blocks away. They'd pushed through the crowd and were advancing quickly, against the flow of parade traffic. Scrambling to his feet, Nick vaulted over the side of the float. Moving nimbly, Howard Koppelman ran after him. Anne picked herself up gingerly and climbed down off the float. She hit the pavement in time to see both men swallowed by the crowd.

For the first time since Anne had met her, Mallory Loving didn't look pretty. But then neither would any woman who just had her stomach pumped, her blood drawn, her body poked and prodded by an army of doctors who were trying to determine whether she'd sustained any permanent damage from a near-fatal drug.

When the paramedics arrived, Mallory was still unconscious. But her heart had never stopped, and by the time Anne was allowed in to see her, she was doped up on medication, groggily demanding answers.

Mallory lay in bed, drifting in and out of consciousness, hooked up to an intravenous tube and a machine that monitored her breathing. She had on a short-sleeved blue cotton hospital gown with dark stains on the front. Her eyes were bloodshot, her skin the color of old parchment. Tangles nested in her hair. Mascara had clumped beneath her lower eyelids, giving her the appearance of a bewildered raccoon.

"I don't get it," she kept repeating, each time she woke up. "What's going on?"

So Anne told her about Nick's scheme to sell the house, how he'd made the threatening phone call the night of her birthday party, how he'd murdered Sheila and Betty. Mallory took it all in silently, her face registering each emotion in turn: fear, rage, disbelief, and finally a deep abiding sadness.

"Why'd he hurt my sister?" Mallory said. Her voice was a throaty whisper.

"The money, I guess. He wanted it all for himself."

"The will," Mallory said softly. She twisted her head from side to side, like she was in pain. "I told him I was gonna change it. Even showed him a copy. So he'd know how broke I was." Mallory's fingers plucked fretfully at the sheet. Anne saw it was an effort for her to talk, to keep her thoughts from sliding away. "He kept telling me I was a target. Told me if I didn't hide out, a psycho would get me." Her eyes welled up, and she wiped at them with the back of her hand. "Why couldn't he have waited?" she wailed. "I was gonna get lots and lots of money. Right after we wrapped the picture."

"I don't know."

They sat for a while without speaking. Mallory's eyelids fluttered weakly. She appeared disoriented, lost in the confines of the narrow hospital bed. The afternoon sun filtered in through the window, dappling the hospital coverlet. The room was bare, stark white, except for the machines doing their work. No cards. No flowers. But then who would send Sheila Lovitz flowers? As far as the world knew, Mallory Loving was no more than a memory.

"That was you the other morning on the beach, wasn't it?" Anne said.

Mallory nodded. She looked incredibly tired. "Didn't hear you calling me. My birthday." She managed a small, rueful smile. "Nick told me to hide. On my way to Landsdown when the sun came up over the ocean. I was scared, couldn't think straight. Like that other time. I went out on the beach. Life's a beach. A bitch." Her laugh was cheerless. "Know what? I felt better after. Like I was doing the *wight* thing." Her speech was starting to slur. "What would Sheila say 'bout that?"

"I think she would say you never meant to hurt her."

Mallory closed her eyes. "Least I got to see her before . . . before . . ." Her voice trailed off. Lying there, with her eyes screwed shut, Mallory looked just like Sheila. Same face. Same hair. Identical twins. But they weren't exactly alike. It was the eyes, in the end, that gave it away. Sheila's were calmer, a steadier, cooler gaze, while Mallory's were electric blue spark plugs that lit up her entire face. Why hadn't she noticed it that night by the tents? If she'd realized she'd been talking to Mallory, would things have turned out any differently? Or would she have merely ended up like Betty?

"Where did you meet Nick? When did he ask you to marry him?" Anne said.

"Marry?" Mallory's voice was muffled, like she was speaking out of one end of a long, hollow tube. "Getting married next week." she mumbled, sounding lost, confused. "Vegas."

"You want to rest for a while?" Anne asked gently. She was feeling pretty exhausted herself.

Mallory nodded and turned on her side, facing the window.

Anne took that as her cue to leave. The door swung noiselessly shut behind her. Across the hall, Detective Mark Trasker was leaning against the wall, his hands stuffed in the pockets of his crisply tailored suit.

"Got a minute?" he said, straightening.

"All the time in a world."

"You were holding out on me," Trasker said reproachfully. They walked down the corridor to the hospital's antiseptic-looking waiting room, decorated with white bucket chairs, artificial plants, and low end tables, strewn with magazines. "You never told me about your visit to Pitt Street."

"Gee, I can't imagine why. Maybe it had something to do with my being a murder suspect."

"I thought you'd want to know we found a red wig when we searched Jill Bentley's room."

"Is she the sister? The girlfriend? What?"

"Girlfriend, on and off. Mostly off. She was probably getting a cut of the money. Her brother leases used cars down in Maryland."

"Don't tell me. He's short one '68 Mustang. Fire engine red."

Trasker was studying her again. "Give the lady a cigar."

"Did you honestly think I was mixed up in this?"

"Honestly, no. But it's my job to follow every lead, and wherever we turned, seemed you'd gotten there first. We dusted Nick's room for prints, in case they turn up in Betty Flugelhorn's room. We think it happened just like you said. She let him in, and he killed her." Trasker paused a moment. A sigh escaped his lips, so low Anne almost didn't hear it. "Hey, you like cats?"

Anne shook her head. "Not really."

"That's what I was afraid of. Sheila's cat is going to the shelter. Turns out Mallory was allergic. That's why kitty couldn't stay in Sheila's apartment."

"Is he going to Wee Care?" Trasker nodded. "I worked there one summer, in the comptroller's office. Part of my job was to count euthanasia slips. Harry's kind of old. I hope he gets adopted before they do a mercy killing."

She shifted in her chair, trying to get more comfortable. Her mouth felt a little better, thanks to two Percodans from a sympathetic nurse. But her body ached all over.

"How you feeling?" Trasker said, as if sensing her discomfort.

"I've been better. I lost a tooth. But I think my ex-boyfriend can make me a bridge."

"Ex, huh?" he said, smiling.

Was it her imagination, or did Trasker evince a flicker of interest? "Yeah, you know dentists. They're always bugging you to floss more and take better care of your gums. What's the story with Fabien?"

"Real name's Nick Fabrese," Trasker said, switching back into detective mode. "Ex-weight-lifter. Con man. A regular at the tables in Atlantic City. Likes the ponies, craps, cards, you name it. A poster boy for Gamblers Anonymous. Seems he borrowed a lot of money from a loan shark, and the guy wants it back, with interest. Sent a couple of goons to rough Nick up, and the boys broke his finger. Promised next time it'd be a lot worse, if he didn't pay. Fabrese was desperate to get his hands on some cash."

"Did you catch him?"

"Not yet. But we will. We've got the airports covered. The trains, major roads. It's only a question of time."

"And Jill?"

"Singing like Tweety Bird. Got herself a two-bit lawyer who's angling to plea-bargain her way out of jail. Fabrese's toast."

"Would you do me a favor?" Anne said.

"If I can."

She glanced at the magazines on the table, pulled a subscription card out of *Family Circle*, and wrote Phil Smedley's number on the back of it. "Call this number and tell the guy who answers the phone I can't get him what he needs for a couple of days." She handed Trasker the card. "Tell him I had a medical emergency."

It was close to seven o'clock when Trasker dropped her off. The red Mustang was parked in the driveway where she'd left it. Her note was still taped to the front door. It was only when she drew closer that she realized Helen had left a message on the back of what she'd written earlier:

Annie—

I heard what happened today at the parade. Life is stranger than fiction every time. Hope you're feeling okay. Call me when you get home.

H.

P.S. I left the cookies on top of the refrigerator.

Anne turned her key in the lock and went inside. The Percodans were wearing off, and her mouth was starting to throb again, a deep, steady pain lodged above her jawbone. She wondered exactly what Helen had heard. The shot, probably. And sirens. She might have caught a glimpse of the medical technicians who had rushed Mallory to the hospital or the cops who'd cordoned off the area. But Helen hadn't known it was Mallory. No one knew. Yet.

Throwing her handbag on the coffee table, Anne sprawled out on the sofa, not bothering to remove her shoes. Trasker had taken Jill's gun, as evidence. There was no safety on it. Turned out most handguns didn't have them. You learn something new every day. She was glad it was over. The whole bloody business. There was only the book to write, and in two weeks' time, the movie people would be gone for good, and life would return to normal. Her thoughts drifted to Sheila. Was she already dead when he put her in the car? How had he managed it? Maybe by telling her Mallory needed to see her. A sisterly emergency of sorts. She pictured Sheila driving away from the Landsdown Arms in her beat-up Chevy. There would have been a rendezvous. A dark, deserted street. Perhaps at one of Landsdown's no-tell motels. And then . . . She tried to shut her mind down, to erase the image of Sheila's face, the Lexus tumbling over the embankment. She closed her eyes, feeling a wave of exhaustion tumble over her.

When she opened them again, it was dark outside, and the phone was ringing. She let the machine pick it up and wandered into her office just in time to hear Trasker say they had a line on Nick Fabrese. He'd been spotted an hour ago, driving north on the New Jersey Turnpike. The cops had run a check on his credit cards, and found out he'd bought two one-way American Airline tickets to Buenos Aires last week. His flight left from Newark Airport in an hour and a half.

When Trasker rang off, Anne went into the kitchen and got the cookies down from the top of the refrigerator. She poured herself a tall glass of milk, and chewed slowly on the good side of her mouth, taking her time, savoring the rich, sugary flavor. They were delicious, filling her sore mouth with savory sweetness. Comfort food. Buenos Aires, huh? If he managed to board the plane, Nick would be making the trip by himself. Jill wouldn't be going to South America, or anywhere else, for a long, long time.

She stared out the kitchen window and reached for another cookie. The moon appeared to hang directly outside her window, its pale face vacant and flat. It reminded her of the moon outside the Lovitz house, the first night she'd driven there. Was it only last Tuesday? It seemed like weeks ago. Amazing that that crummy little shack was worth $1.8 million. The real estate

agents were right. *Location, location, location.* Telco
needed the property for the highway extension. Only
how did Nick and Jill pull everything off so fast? The
thing about real estate transactions was that they took
time. Time to go to contract, time to close the deal. How
did Nick cash in a multimillion-dollar prize, pay off the
loan shark (presumably with cash), and plan a trip to
Buenos Aires, if they'd only started the paperwork a few
days ago? Anne paused in mid-bite. She blinked, weighing the possibilities. Taking a swallow of milk, she
reached for the phone.

When she got through to the hospital, an officious-
sounding nurse informed her that Miss Lovitz was sleeping and could not be disturbed for any reason. Anne
washed down two extra-strength Tylenols with the last
of the milk. Then she grabbed her handbag and her car
keys and left the house.

The Wee Care Animal Shelter was a gray, nondescript
building sandwiched between Sir Speedy copy shop and
Fran's Fried Chicken Shack, in a seedy-looking strip
mall on the outskirts of Landsdown Park. Anne had
worked there twenty years ago, a minimum-wage summer job between high school and college. The place
looked like it hadn't changed. Same dirty windows,
same faded sign, same tacky sculpture of a Doberman
on its hind legs next to the entrance. When Anne pulled
up in front of the shelter, the parking lot was empty. The
street lamp was broken; the only illumination was provided by a weak light above the door of the shelter. It
was a quarter to nine, fifteen minutes before closing
time.

Inside a heavyset woman was reading a magazine behind the long metal counter in the lobby, her face bathed
in harsh fluorescent brightness. She looked to be in her
early fifties, with graying frizzy hair and square tortoiseshell glasses. Under her white lab coat, she wore a red
peasant blouse and a red and black Indian print skirt.

Anne glanced at her name tag. *Tammy*, it said, above a picture of a smiling beagle.

Anne approached the counter. "I'm here to get a cat," she said.

The woman looked up from her book. Her eyes were the color of spoiled plums. "You'll have to come back tomorrow morning. We open at nine."

"This can't wait. My name's Anne Hardaway, with the Neptune Township Sheriff's Office." Anne took out her wallet and flashed her Monmouth University identification card, which she'd received two years ago when she was taking an adult education class called "Freelancing for Women's Magazines." "Detective Mark Trasker brought in a black and white one-eyed cat a few hours ago. We need it back."

Again, Anne reached into her wallet. She removed Detective Trasker's card and slid it across the counter.

Tammy examined the card without touching it. "A black man?" she said. "Kinda tall?"

"That's the one."

"I'd like to help you out, but it's late," Tammy said. Her gaze wandered to the clock on the wall. "Can't this wait till morning?"

Anne drew herself up to her full height. "We're conducting a murder investigation here," she said, trying to achieve the right note of self-importance. "Time is of the essence."

She heard dogs barking nearby, a raucous canine chorus. When she'd worked there, she'd gotten so used to the sound she barely noticed it.

Tammy scratched her nose. "Um . . . I'm really not sure I'm . . . uh, authorized to help you out."

"Why don't you give the detective a call?" Anne said briskly. "He'll explain why forensics needs the cat back and why it has to be tonight."

There was a black rotary phone on the desk. Anne picked it up and held out the receiver.

Tammy considered her alternatives. She glanced at the

wall clock again. Ten of nine. Anne could almost hear her pondering which choice would be quickest. Then she got up off her stool and said, "Be right back."

When she returned a minute later, she held a small cat carrier. Harry was curled up in a ball, looking miserable. Tammy put the carrier on the counter, and thrust some papers and a pen in Anne's direction. Anne signed her name in four places and put down the pen.

"That'll be $35 for the carrier," Tammy said, "Unless you have your own."

Anne took out her wallet and handed Tammy a credit card and her driver's license. Great, she thought. Thirty-five bucks for a carrier she was going to use a grand total of once. She heard Harry scratching at the walls of his new digs. Not a happy camper.

"Thanks," she said, picking up the carrier when Tammy had finished processing the sale. "Have a good night."

"Hey," Tammy called after her. "You forgot to fill a lot of this out."

"No problem," Anne said, walking away. "The detective will be by first thing in the morning."

Outside, she shifted the carrier to her other hand and walked toward her car. Was cat-napping a felony? She sincerely hoped not. But she'd probably done Harry a tremendous favor. The shelter was dirty and over-crowded. Harry appeared to have hated his brief stay. He was mewling pitifully, like a newborn crying itself to sleep. The sound almost muffled the footsteps Anne heard when she was a few feet away from the Mustang.

"I'll take him," said a voice to Anne's left.

Anne whirled around and stopped. For the second time that day, a woman was pointing a gun at her chest.

"Thanks for getting him back," Sheila Lovitz said. Her voice was quiet, controlled.

A couple of hours ago, Anne would have been shocked to see Sheila, alive and well. Now it merely saddened her. Harry was the bait and Sheila had taken it. "You can thank me by putting the gun away."

Over Sheila's shoulder, Anne saw the beat-up blue Chevy, parked beneath a tree. "Just give me the cat, and I'll be on my way."

Anne gripped the carrier more tightly. At the sound of Sheila's voice, the cat had stirred. "Was this like hitting the trifecta?" Anne said. "Get the guy. Get the money. And have him bump off your sister, too."

"You don't understand," Sheila said. In the dark, Anne couldn't see her eyes. But her voice sounded tight, her body coiled as if ready to spring.

"Oh, but I do. I finally do. You met Nick where, Atlantic City, right? He was good-looking, a real hunk. And you were going to come into all this money, weren't you? Nearly $2 million. For most people, that would have been enough."

"You weren't there," Sheila said, shouting now, a petulant child with an ax to grind and enough emotional baggage to fill a dozen steamer trunks. "She got everything. *Everything.* Fame, money, Gerald. I stayed behind. Do you think it was easy, taking care of my mother?" Her voice was shrill. "Scraping and saving every dime? Do you think I was having *fun*?"

"Where have you been hiding, Sheila? Where've you been for three days?"

Sheila tightened her grip on the gun. "At school. There's a little room, off the gym. No one uses it."

"Then why did Nick have the cat in his room?"

"It was just for today, until I could take care of things."

"Like collecting your big fat check, I suppose." Anne felt a surge of anger. "Who was in the Lexus? The Pogue woman, the one who's been missing?"

Sheila looked away. "We worked together once. Lynette and me. At Kmart. She had ovarian cancer. A death sentence. Why can't you see?"

Twisted logic, Anne thought. But then, Sheila had been the twisted sister all along. It must have been easy for Jill to switch Mallory's dental records with Lynette's. Everyone in Landsdown and the Heights went to Dr. Chilton, Sr. Isn't that what David had said? "Where was Lynette for four days before Nick put her in Mallory's car?"

"Dead. Nick took care of it. His cousin's in the meat business in South Philly. They have a really big freezer."

She didn't sound sorry, not in the least.

A dry breeze rustled the leaves on the trees. Now and then a car whizzed by. But they were too far away, and the parking lot was cloaked in darkness. Anne could hear Sheila's heavy, uneven breathing. She could almost smell Sheila's fear, palpable and thick, like hot tar. The handle of the carrier dug into her palm, but she couldn't put it down, couldn't stop working the puzzle.

"You had to die, too, right? No more Sheila Lovitz. May she rest in peace."

Sheila didn't answer. Her brown hair hung lankly, framing her cheeks. What had Trasker said? Some people walk out of their lives as easily as snakes shed their skins. It hadn't been easy. But she'd almost pulled it off. Terrifying her sister. A fresh start with a new man and lots of money, in beautiful Buenos Aires. Only problem was, three people had to die before she boarded the plane.

Anne said, "Why'd you bother talking to me that night, after bingo?"

"The book." In the dark, the whites of Sheila's eyes appeared to gleam. "I want you to get everything down, every bad thing Mallory did. For the book."

"We can still do that," Anne said. "But I'll need your help." Harry whimpered mournfully and Sheila lowered her gaze, as if she'd forgotten the cat was there. "Why don't you put the gun down and we can go somewhere and talk."

Sheila shook her head defiantly. "Don't make me hurt you," she whispered, raising the gun.

Just then, the door of the animal shelter swung open, casting a sliver of light on the scene. Tammy the clerk stepped outside, looked at the two women, and froze in her tracks, as if transfixed. When she saw the gun, she let out a single high-pitched scream. The sound jolted Sheila into action. She turned and fled, dashing frantically across the parking lot, as if chased by the devil. When she got to the Chevy, she flung the door open and got in. The motor sputtered, turned over. The Chevy peeled out of the lot, its tires screeching. Anne put down the carrier and hurried to the Mustang.

The car's headlights swept over Tammy and the cat as Anne swung the Mustang around. At the entrance to the shopping center, she made a sharp left, momentarily blinded by the lights from an oncoming car. A jeep with its brights on. Up ahead, the Chevy swerved. Anne slammed on her brakes. Out of the corner of her eye she saw the jeep smash into the smaller car and ricochet away, like a pinball. Spinning at an angle, the Chevy whirled around and around, an electric blue top colliding with the night. Anne heard the shriek of metal, an explosion of shattered glass. The Chevy flipped on its side, skidding to a stop. For one brief moment, before Anne got out of the car and ran over to the wreckage, before she smelled the sulfurous odor of fuel and felt the hot night wind against her face, there was silence.

"Now let me see if I've got this straight," Helen said the next morning, as they sat on Anne's front porch, eating a late breakfast of coconut donuts and iced tea. "Mallory was pretending to be Sheila, while Sheila was hiding out and plotting to kill Mallory with the help of this Nick person."

"Right."

"How did Jill Bentley fit into the equation?"

Anne took a sip of iced tea, running her tongue over the place where her tooth used to be. "Nick was basically using Jill as an errand girl, to help him keep an eye on Mallory. Jill had no idea he was planning to run off with Sheila.''

"How did you know? About Sheila, I mean?"

"It was something Mallory said in the hospital. She told me she and Nick were getting married next week, in Las Vegas. But the license said they were already married. It took me a little while to put things together. I think I was groggy from the Percodans. And Mallory was pretty out of it, too. Otherwise I'd have realized sooner.''

Helen leaned back against the white wicker swing and rested the heels of her feet against the seat cushion. "Is Sheila going to be all right?"

"She has some serious injuries. A broken leg. A collapsed lung. Cracked ribs. But she'll live. The police caught Nick last night at Newark Airport, trying to sneak onto the plane. They're both going to be tried for murder.''

A black and white cat with one eye sauntered up the front porch steps. The cat leaped onto the white wicker chair and curled up in Anne's lap.

"Harry, I presume?" Helen said.

"One and the same."

Anne stroked the soft fur between Harry's ears. "I couldn't let the shelter keep him. He's kind of old. They might have put him to sleep." She paused, gazing down at the puffy fur ball. "You think I could ever become a cat person?"

"Stranger things have been known to happen."

Still stroking Harry, Anne looked out at the ocean. It was choppy today. The wind was blowing hard from the east, and the humidity had dropped. It felt like a September morning, clear, but brisk.

"Sheila had it all planned out," she said. "The whole revenge thing. It wasn't enough to kill Mallory, she wanted Mallory to fall in love with Nick. So she could have the satisfaction of taking Nick away from her sister. Tit for tat.''

"Payback time." Helen said, helping herself to another donut. "What about the book? You've got enough material here for a TV movie of the week."

"Oh, the book," Anne said, smiling. "Fact is, I got a little extension."

Helen grinned. "How little?"

"An extra month. Phil decided I had writer's block. He thought a change of scenery would help. So I'm flying to Venice tomorrow morning for two weeks. Could you possibly look after Harry for me?"

"Sure, you lucky stiff. Jack's going to be thrilled."

The silver movie trucks swung into view, lumbering noisily down the street, one after another. From a distance, they looked like a gigantic, slithering worm.

"How will you ever manage to tear yourself away from *Dark Horizon*?" Helen said sarcastically. "Aren't you going to miss the excitement?"

The trucks rounded the corner, a silvery cavalcade. "You know what I learned about movies?" Anne said. "They're like taxicabs. Or books, for that matter. There's always another right around the corner."